CHASING A RUGBY DREAM

BOOK TWO

IMPACT

JAMES HOOK

with **DAVID BRAYLEY**

POLARIS
PUBLISHING

This edition first published in 2021 by

POLARIS PUBLISHING LTD
c/o Aberdein Considine
2nd Floor, Elder House
Multrees Walk
Edinburgh
EH1 3DX

Distributed by
Birlinn Limited

www.polarispublishing.com

ISBN: 9781913538255
eBook ISBN: 9781913538262

British Library Cataloguing-in-Publication Data
A catalogue record for this book is available on request from the British Library.

Designed and typeset by Polaris Publishing, Edinburgh
Printed in Great Britain by MBM Print SCS Limited, East Kilbride

PROLOGUE

Eagles' Elite Young Players' Summer Academy Camp,
Underhill Complex.
Day Three.

Mike Green looked up from his plate of scrambled eggs and toast. Jimmy Joseph was sitting across the table, his bowl of fruit and yoghurt barely touched, a faraway look in his eyes.

'I heard you had a tough day yesterday, mate,' said Mike.

'You could say that,' said Jimmy, flatly. 'I just don't know what happened. The more I thought about tackling, the worse I got. I just wanted the day to end. My technique was awful.'

Jimmy didn't feel that the time was yet right to share that there had been moments, plenty of them, when he'd felt scared. This was a completely new sensation to Jimmy, one of complete failure on a rugby field, and he had no idea how to deal with it.

'I heard Mr Kane telling Mr Withey that he only asked you to make five tackles all day.'

'Five!' exclaimed Jimmy. 'I did five in the first two minutes!'

'Yeah, I know. I heard that big prop in your group saying that Kane gave you a bit of a beasting.'

'It was brutal,' replied Jimmy. 'Do you know, I was the only player in our squad who didn't get to carry and run with the ball *at all* yesterday? It was one-on-one tackling all morning and tackle bags all afternoon. And Kane didn't even give me any coaching – he just shouted at me for being rubbish! If I'd known the camp was going to be like this, I'd never have come. I'd have much preferred to have gone to the one being run at the Wolves with Kitty, Matt and Manu. They all texted me last night to say how much fun they're having – it sounds like it's all games and fun skill sessions and stuff. Nothing like what Kane's putting me through.'

Jimmy glanced down at his blood-stained (courtesy of his nose) and grass-stained (courtesy of his all-day tackling session) Eagles shirt, no longer as pristine as the day he'd received it.

'I'd really been looking forward to this after the way our season finished,' he continued. 'Especially when my dad was able to find the money to help buy all the proper kit and it all started arriving. But it's now turning into a bit of a nightmare.'

'I know,' nodded Mike, 'but you've just got to hang in there, mate. It'll be worth it. Playing for the Eagles is your dream, isn't it? Well we're here, this is the start. We're on the ladder. You can't let Kane ruin it.'

Jimmy nodded, but was quiet for a moment.

'Yeah, but you know what,' he said, at last, his shoulders slumping a little further. 'Maybe I *am* too young to be here. If today's anything like yesterday, I might just knock it on the head and call it quits.'

2

'No, don't do that!' exclaimed Mike. 'It'll get better. Just give it a day or two and you'll start getting used to everything and Kane will just get bored of picking on you. You'll see.'

Jimmy appreciated Mike's optimism and support, but it would prove sadly misplaced. The third day of the camp was Jimmy's worst by a long way. The first hour was fitness, which Jimmy didn't mind at all. But on every exercise or drill they were shown, Mr Kane would find fault in Jimmy's efforts and send him down for five press ups.

When it came to kicking practice, which was one of Jimmy's strengths, Mr Kane instructed Jimmy to stand behind the posts with the props and second rows, acting as a ball boy and running the balls back to the kickers. Jimmy couldn't have been more dispirited.

Until the tackle bags came out to play again.

Kane immediately threw one to Jimmy as the afternoon session began, and he was lined up as cannon fodder again and again as the other boys – who were all a year or two older – ran at him at full tilt. For the next half an hour, he was bashed and knocked and pummelled. Not once was Jimmy allowed to relinquish the tackle bag, and again he became the only player of the squad not picked to run with the ball. But much worse, as player after player thumped into Jimmy and his tackle bag, so he began to resent each huge impact. That resentment quickly turned to dread, and that dread eventually turned to fear.

At the end of the session, when Mr Kane's whistle blew for the final time, Jimmy threw down his tackle bag and just stared at it. His forearms were aching from the constant battering and the strength he'd needed to keep a grip of the tackle bag each time somebody smashed into him. Surely an elite rugby academy was supposed to be more enjoyable than this? Or actually involve him playing some actual rugby? But then all the other kids in his group were getting to do that. It was just him that was the odd one out. He felt very alone.

'Well, we've found your weakness,' said Mr Kane, sauntering past. He wasn't even looking at Jimmy, but it was clear who he was talking to. 'Can't tackle . . . won't tackle. Never mind, much more of the same tomorrow.'

Jimmy decided there and then, as he watched Mr Kane swagger off towards the doors to the changing rooms near the entrance to the Eagles' training complex, his shoulders rocking as he went, that there wasn't going to be a tomorrow. Forget this relentless slog. He was going home and he wasn't coming back.

GREAT EXPECTATIONS

Four weeks earlier.

'Hey Jimmy!' shouted Kitty across the waste ground behind the row of terraced houses where they'd both lived since they were born.

Jimmy spun around at the sound of her voice and drilled a thirty metre kick towards her. Kitty crabbed sideways a couple of steps and then plucked the ball out of the air. She jogged towards him and then backheeled the ball over her head and into Jimmy's hands.

'Nobody likes a show-off,' he said, grinning.

'And you'd know all about that, wouldn't you?!' laughed Kitty as he started to do keepie-uppies.

'Fair point,' he laughed, just as he lost control.

Since their incredible victory in the Cluster Cup final at the end of the previous rugby season in May, Jimmy had become very much a local sporting celebrity. All the dark days of the bullying by Mike Green and the awful treatment at the hands of Mark Kane were nothing more than distant memories. It was exactly as his beloved grandfather, Will, had promised him at the height of Jimmy's troubles . . . 'Mark my words, Jimmy, once all this bullying is sorted – which it will be – it will all just become a memory that will fade to nothing in time. It's dealing with it now that's the problem; but once sorted, it'll be gone from your life forever.'

Will's wise words were proved correct. The way that Jimmy had handled himself in the final, as an on-field leader, and the way he had encouraged Mike to take that all-important last-second conversion, had transformed the way people viewed Jimmy, and in many ways, the way Jimmy viewed himself. From the headteacher, Mr Davies, to stand-in coach and local rugby legend, Peter Clement, to his former enemy himself, Mike Green, all had been fulsome in their praise of Jimmy. And it had to be said, it all had an effect on Jimmy. He would never have admitted it to anyone, but he'd always felt that he'd lived a little bit in the shadow of his brother, Jonny. Jimmy hero-worshipped his brother, but there had been times in the past when all Jonny's rugby achievements – captaining Central Primary, captaining both the Year 7 and 8 first XVs at Bishopswood, attending all the age group Eagles camps – had seemed to heap an added pressure on Jimmy. And at the height of his bullying by Mike and treatment by Kane, Jimmy privately wondered if he'd ever get the chance to potentially match Jonny's achievements. But now, Jimmy felt that he was very much on his way to equalling his brother's accomplishments and was now clearly up and running in his fledgling rugby career. And, consequently, his confidence levels had shot through the roof.

'You don't really think I'm a show-off do you, Kit?' asked Jimmy, flicking the ball to her. Kitty was the most honest, straight-talking person he knew and always said what she meant, even if her honesty sometimes hurt a little.

She laughed. 'Nah, not really, Jim . . . it's nice to see you being a bit more confident – and not just in rugby either, I've noticed in class and around school too.'

'Not in a bad way, though?' he asked, suddenly feeling anxious about her reply.

'Nah,' she said again. 'I don't think so. My dad's always told me that it's important to be confident in life. "Just don't get too big for your boots,"' she added, in a great imitation of her dad's voice.

'Let's have a pact to make sure neither of us lets the other one ever get too cocky,' said Jimmy.

'Cool,' she said, spinning the ball on her finger. 'Just make sure you don't confuse me using my outrageous skills with being cocky.'

'You're the definition of humility, Kit,' said Jimmy dryly. But he knew they understood each other and that her dad had a point. His grandfather had always echoed a similar viewpoint, especially when he told Jimmy stories of his time in the Marines and the importance of team work and doing the right thing whenever you could.

'And don't worry, I'll keep you grounded, cup final superstar,' she added, starting to bounce on her toes. She shuffled her feet like a boxer and then tucked the ball under her arm and charged at him. Taken totally by surprise, Jimmy was brushed aside as she clattered into him and before he knew it, he was sitting in a heap on the dusty ground.

'There you go superstar, as promised, I'll always keep you grounded. But if you want to make it, I think you're going to have to work on your tackle technique.'

They both roared with laughter, but little did either Kitty or Jimmy know just how prophetic her words would soon become.

FUN IN THE SUN

Kitty and Jimmy made their way from the waste ground beneath a cloudless summer sky. It was getting towards late morning and, on a Sunday, that would usually mean that lots of other kids would be roaming around down at The Rec so there was always a chance to strike up an impromptu game of rugby which could sometimes last for hours.

As they stepped through the wrought iron gates to The Rec, they were greeted by a loud cry of 'Kitty! Jimmy booooooooooy!'

They looked to their right and saw Manu loping towards them.

'Not in church today?' called Jimmy.

'Nah, Mum and Dad let me off this morning,' replied Manu.

'Mate, have you grown since Friday?' enquired Kitty, 'I swear you have!'

Manu did a little swerving sidestep just before he reached them, then flexed his bicep.

'Growth spurts my mother says,' he said with a grin before

exchanging fist bumps. 'She's going crazy, I'm growing out of everything.'

Kitty laughed but Jimmy simply shook his head in wonder. He could barely believe the rapid changes in Manu's body shape over the summer term. He was getting massive, just like his older brothers, his dad and his famous uncle. He looked at Manu's increasingly defined biceps and increased shoulder width and glanced down at his own, relatively skinny, snow-white arms which seemed to hang like two threads of cotton from his red and black hooped rugby shirt.

How on earth am I supposed to compete with him on a rugby field when I look like this and he looks like that? thought Jimmy, 'How are you getting so big?' he asked, tossing his ball to Manu. 'I've never once seen you lift a weight!'

'My mother's cooking, KFC and faith in the good Lord above,' laughed Manu, making a sign of the cross with the ball and gazing skywards. 'You can't go wrong following that path.'

Jimmy laughed. 'Perhaps I'd better stop eating salad cream on toast, then. Doesn't seem to be making much of a difference to me!'

'That would definitely be a good start!' replied Manu. 'Watching you eat that stuff makes me feel sick!'

'Me too!' agreed Kitty.

'Well, I'm not quite ready to give it up just yet,' said Jimmy, 'and in any case, if I got as big as you, I wouldn't be able to do this.'

And with that, Jimmy snatched the ball out of Manu's grip, chipped it over his head, regathered it and then ran away with the ball held out at arm's length, taunting his huge friend to come and get it. Manu sprang after Jimmy and just when it looked as if he was about to devour him, Jimmy slammed on the brakes for the briefest of moments, threw his body to the left, wrong-footing Manu, who jerked to grab him – only for Jimmy to swerve in the other direction to leave Manu grasping fresh air. Manu gave a shrill cry of both frustration and delight at his friend's silky elusiveness, which turned into a roar of laughter as Jimmy dinked a little grubber that nutmegged Manu and bounced up perfectly into Kitty's hands.

'Speed beats brawn every day of the week,' he said with a little swagger to his walk.

'As I was saying, it's so good that you're not a show-off,' said Kitty with a mischievous grin.

'It's not my fault,' laughed Jimmy, 'class will always out!'

Then, just as Manu was about to instigate the first pile-on of the day, another familiar voice called out. It was Matt.

'Hey, you lot, come quick, the groundsman has just opened the gates to the Memorial Ground round the corner, he said we could come and take a look at the pitch if we're sharp!'

Sharp was something all four of the friends were and they set off for the black, ornate gates of the Memorial Ground, as fast as their legs could carry them.

THRILLS AND SKILLS

What an hour the three friends experienced at the home of the Wolves. John the groundskeeper was much younger than Ralph who he had replaced at the start of the summer. Nobody knew how old Ralph actually was, but it seemed that he'd been groundsman at the Memorial Ground since it was built. In fact, Jimmy once told his grandfather that he had it on good authority that was the case. 'Well,' replied Will, 'as the ground was built in 1913, I'm guessing Ralph actually looks a bit young for his age then!'

Ralph was a brilliant groundskeeper, but wasn't exactly great with the kids. Even when Jimmy had started becoming a ball-boy for the Wolves, thanks to Malcolm, his dad, Ralph would always find some reason or other to bark at Jimmy for standing on the wrong part of the touchline – 'How's the blinking grass ever going to grow back there with you standing on it?' Ralph would shout with exasperation at Jimmy. 'Stand on the red-gravel until the ball comes your way, you're plenty close enough to the pitch there.'

But John was completely different. He was only in his twenties and used all the skills he'd learned working on his uncle's farm since he was a teenager to become an expert groundskeeper. Also, as he was a lifelong fan of the Wolves himself, he knew exactly what the club meant to people, especially the younger ones. As a result, and because of his friendship with Matt's dad, he'd often tip Matt the wink when he felt he could allow the youngsters to spend some time on the hallowed ground. And today was one of those times.

'Why is the grass so long, John?' asked Matt when the three arrived, running straight up to the edge of the pitch, just in front of the large terraced bank under the scoreboard at the far end of the ground.

'I seeded it about two weeks ago to get grass growing on the bare patches that appear after a long season. Can't cut it for a while yet, so make sure you don't set those big clumsy feet of yours on there!' laughed John.

Matt blushed, quite proud that John always seemed to have a joke around with him.

'But you're in luck, I cut the training paddock over there yesterday,' said John, pointing to a perfect grassy area that lay beyond the terracing at the west corner of the ground. 'You can have a run around on that if you like. Only for a little while mind, I'm only gonna be here for the next hour or so. I think there might be some training gear lying around too. A couple of the first-team boys came down last night, and knowing them, they wouldn't have put all the kit back in the training cabin.'

The four friends didn't need a second invitation, and bolted to the far side of the pitch. When they arrived, as John had suspected, they saw some kit had been left out on the perfect shamrock-green paddock. The paddock itself was, in area, about the size of half a rugby pitch, but was more of a long, oblong shape with curved corners. It was used by the club to carry out smaller drills and practice sessions, if they didn't need the large expanse of the pitch. But for four ten-year-old aspiring rugby players, it was plenty big enough.

Jimmy's eye caught an odd, orange ball-type object nestling in the grass towards the edge of the paddock, not far from the high, whitewashed exterior wall that surrounded the whole ground.

'What's this?' asked Jimmy, picking it up. It looked like a tennis ball, only slightly bigger, was made of hard rubber and had odd circular bumps all around it.

'Give us a look, Jim,' called Matt.

Jimmy tossed it to Matt, who looked equally confused as he rotated it in his hands, examining it carefully.

'Chuck it against the wall!' bellowed a voice from the other side of the pitch. It was John.

'Chuck it against the wall,' he repeated. 'Bet you won't be able to catch it!'

Matt turned towards the towering white wall above him. He looked down at the ball, then gently tossed it towards the wall, expecting it to bounce straight back at him. Instead, when the ball made contact with the wall, one of the six bumps made the ball spit back to his right. Matt lunged to catch it but missed by a mile.

'Told you!' cried John, his cackling laughter booming around the empty ground. 'The players use it to hone their reflexes – it'll be good for you all to try!'

'Game time!' shouted Kitty. 'Come on. Let's see who's best . . . bet it's me!'

'You're far too competitive for your own good,' .
with a resigned smile as Kitty ran over to the ball, look.
closely before tossing it at the wall. Despite it coming back a.
at a very odd angle to her left, she shot out her left hand and ju.
managed to pluck it from the air.

'Easy! Told you, I'll beat all of you at this!'

'No way!' shouted Manu. 'Come on, let's have a go. In fact,
let's make up some rules.'

So, over the next few minutes, as each of the friends got to
grips with the amazing bouncing reaction ball, they came up
with a game. Standing side by side and starting with Kitty on
the left-hand side, each had three throws at the wall. A one-
handed catch got you twenty points. Two-handed was ten. Then
you got five if you managed to get a hand to it without catching
it. Anything else was zero. They played for twenty minutes,
diving left and right, forward and back, their reflexes seeming to
improve all the time and they quickly forgot the initial rule of
just three throws each. But once Kitty had reached 160 points,
the boys decided to wave the white flag.

'You're completely ridiculous!' said Jimmy with an exasperated
tone to his voice, slumping down onto the edge of the paddock
turf. 'You hardly dropped one!'

'And I only caught one!' grumbled Manu. 'What a stupid game!'

'Rugby's about more than muscle power, Manu,' laughed
Kitty, tossing Manu the ball. 'You need to practise your reflexes!'

'Yeah, clearly . . .' replied Manu forlornly.

'Hey, look at this!' shouted Matt from the far corner of the
paddock, lifting above his head what could only be described as
a large fishing net.

'Oh, I know what that is!' exclaimed Manu, more than happy to leave the reflex ball behind. 'My dad showed me once when we went to watch my uncle training at Bristol Bears. It's a net to hold up as a target for a hooker to practise their line out throws. Hold it up high, Matt.'

Matt did his best, but he wasn't strong enough to hold the pole steady above him. Jimmy trotted over to help.

'Weakling,' said Jimmy as he arrived.

'Pipe cleaner arms,' replied Matt. They laughed and then hoisted the pole as high as they could.

'Cool,' said Kitty. 'But only if you're a hooker – which none of us are.'

'I've got an idea,' said Manu, and instructed the boys to lower the pole to the horizontal, then to move up to the top of the pole, almost to the net, holding it just a metre or so above the ground.

'Passing drill!' he shouted. 'Ten points for getting it in the net, five for hitting the rim, nothing for a miss. First to 200 is the winner!'

'You're on!' shouted Kitty. 'Me first.'

She scooped up the ball, turned sideways to the net, which was being held about five metres away, planted her left foot and delivered a neat spin pass straight into the heart of the net. The boys all groaned. Manu was next and probably not really understanding his own strength, heaved a pass that flew like a bullet, but a good metre over the net, sailing over the paddock grass before crashing into the wall.

'Whoa, steady big boy!' laughed Jimmy. 'You don't have to try to break the sound barrier! Remember what Peter Clement said to us in training before the cup final?'

'Accuracy before power when passing!' shouted Kitty over her shoulder as she jogged off to retrieve the ball.

When she returned, they all continued taking turns, and again, soon lost themselves in the enjoyment of the game.

Kitty was again triumphant, reaching 200 points after twenty-four attempts, missing the net just four times. At that point, Matt was on 140, Jimmy 175 and Manu 120.

'I hate rugby and I hate girls!' Manu exclaimed in mock disgust.

'That's no way to deal with defeat,' scolded Kitty, in jest. 'Like Jimmy said earlier, brains and speed always beats brawn!'

The friends all laughed.

'I wish I'd just gone to church now,' sighed Manu as he sank to the grass. 'At least I get respect there.'

The friends laughed even more.

PREPARING FOR CAMP

The next four weeks flew by for everyone. Miss Ayres, still acting as temporary teacher to the Year 5s, combined interesting learning with fun so well that the final weeks of term went by in the blink of an eye. Then, in the last week of July, everything in Jimmy's life turned to the thoughts of his upcoming rugby camp. Two weeks of heaven, playing rugby with the best players and best coaches of the region. Jimmy's grandfather had made a point of emphasising just how privileged he was to be selected, especially as the Eagles had bent their rules to allow Jimmy to attend the summer camp a year early. 'They never even did that for Jonny; that's how much they think of you. So make sure you give it your best shot . . . show them all that Jimmy Joseph magic, and knock them all out!'

Sadly for Jimmy, it would turn out that he was the one in most danger of being knocked out.

*

18

The whole process of Jimmy joining the camp had started so well. Because he'd received a personal invite from the head of the Academy, Stuart Withey, following that stunning performance in the end-of-season Cluster Cup victory, Mr Withey had been in constant touch with Jimmy's mum over the summer, reassuring her that Jimmy would be well looked after.

Watching in the stands that day, Mr Withey had been hugely impressed by Jimmy's efforts in the cup final, but he had been completely unaware of all the off-field troubles Jimmy had faced, such as being alienated by his teacher and rugby coach, Mr Mark Kane, who was now a member of the Eagles Academy staff. Nor had he been aware of the bullying issues Jimmy had faced with Mike Green. Instead, Stuart Withey had just watched a spectacular individual performance that had convinced him to break one of the Academy's rules so that Jimmy could be invited to their summer camp. Usually, the camp was only open to players from the area who were in Year 6 and above. Jimmy would be Year 6 in the first week of September, but as the camp took place during the first two weeks of August, and Jimmy was still only ten, technically, he was still Year 5, making him a full year younger than anyone else attending.

'Mrs Joseph,' Mr Withey wrote in one of his many emails to her, 'I just wanted to take this opportunity to let you know that because of Jimmy's undoubted potential, we have made special dispensation for him to attend the Summer Camp at The Eagles' Underhill Training Facility Complex. I would like to reassure you that I will be supervising Jimmy's welfare personally, and whilst the camp will be organised by our new Regional Youth Rugby Co-ordinator, Mark Kane, I have spoken with him and discussed that Jimmy's progression and rugby development will be handled with care and with the utmost attention to his young age compared to the other players. He has agreed with this.'

Jimmy laughed humourlessly when his mum had read that part of the email to him.

'Yeah, right,' he said, with a shake of his head. 'He'll probably have me doing twenty laps of the field backwards whilst the others are doing all the fun drills!'

Jimmy's mum was concerned that Mark Kane's involvement was going to have a negative impact on her son, but the repeated emails, calls and texts she'd received from Mr Withey had helped to settle her worries.

As for Jimmy, so had the kit.

It seemed like every week he was getting new gear.

Despite initially saying to his mum that the Eagles would provide all kit, that had quickly changed. In one of Mr Withey's early emails, he apologised for a change in the policy of the region. Instead of free kit, all parents would now have to pay for 50% of the cost which he blamed on funding cutbacks. Initially, Catherine was annoyed by the change, and Jimmy heard her on the phone to his dad complaining about the extra expense. But Malcolm had apparently said that he would make sure that his son would have everything he needed and told Catherine that he was in a position, following a recent promotion at work, to cover the extra cost of the kit.

Jimmy was so pleased to hear this news, not just because he'd be getting a heap of new kit, but also because the tone of the conversation seemed to mark another step forward in the improving relationship between his mum and dad. Some years earlier, something bad had happened in their marriage that had ended it overnight. For the next few years, the split and subsequent divorce had been very bitter with both his mum and dad blaming each other for the break-up. But in recent times things had begun to improve and Jimmy was thrilled to hear them talking so constructively about the dilemma around his kit. And what fantastic kit it was!

The first things to arrive in the post were the tracksuit and training tops. All made by Under Armour, personally fitted to measurements that Jimmy's dad had provided and all with a hand-stitched logo of the club's white eagle emblem. He gently traced the embroidered eagle with the tips of his fingers, imagining he was wearing it in a first-team match in the European Cup.

The tops also carried a squad number on the other side of the chest. In Jimmy's case it was '10'. He was so proud that he put all the training kit on and walked round to his grandparents' house to show it all off. As ever, Will and Betty made a huge fuss of him and made him pose for photographs in the garden.

The week after the training kit arrived, the Eagles backpack turned up which contained a water bottle, a notepad and pen, four pairs of pale blue Eagles socks and two pairs of pristine white Eagles shorts.

But there was still a missing link to all this wonderful kit. Boots. His dad had said that he wasn't able to get Jimmy new boots in time for the start of camp, but that he'd definitely be able to get them by the start of the season. Jimmy understood, but he couldn't help feeling a little disappointed. Seeing the look on his face, Catherine stepped in and offered to get a cheap pair to be going on with – but Jimmy refused. He didn't want to appear ungrateful to his mum and dad, but the right boots were so important to Jimmy as he knew that everyone at the camp would no doubt have a pair that would make his scruffy, almost worn out old ones look ridiculous.

A couple of days later, Jimmy was moping around at home when his grandfather popped in to say hello.

'What's up, Jim?' he asked, seeing the distracted look in Jimmy's eyes.

Jimmy explained the situation, but was at pains to point out that he understood the pressure on his parents money-wise, and that he was grateful for all the kit, but that the boots were really key.

'So what boots would you get if you could?'

Jimmy grabbed his mum's iPad and flicked to an open tab on Safari which had his ideal pair.

Will whistled. 'Very smart,' he said. 'But they're pretty expensive, aren't they?'

'I know,' said Jimmy, quickly tapping the home button on the iPad which instantly removed the boots from the screen. 'It's no problem really, I can wait.'

Less than a week later, there was a knock at the front door. Jimmy was on his mum's iPad, again, watching a documentary about the All Blacks that was on Amazon Prime. He was so completely engrossed by what he was seeing and hearing about the greatest rugby team on the planet, that he missed the knock.

Anyone who knew anything about rugby knew that the All Blacks were the best rugby team in the world, probably of all time, and the documentary was giving Jimmy a behind-the-scenes view of what made them so good. Even players who had sixty or seventy caps didn't take their places in the team for granted and tried their absolute best at all times. But one thing that their coach, Steve Hansen, said really stood out for Jimmy.

While he was speaking to the All Blacks squad, the coach asked them, 'Do you want to be an All Black or a great All Black? That's up to you, guys.'

That one simple question made a huge impact on Jimmy and he knew exactly what the coach meant. It was one thing being an All Black, a pretty amazing thing actually, but you shouldn't settle for being 'just' an All Black. No, instead you should give everything to be a brilliant one, one that will be remembered forever – that should be every All Black's aim. Jimmy had loved that. It was exactly what he wanted to do. He was so proud of being picked to be an Eagle at the camp, but that wasn't enough. Jimmy wanted to be the best one there. That was his aim. He was determined to be a great junior Eagle, not just a good one.

So engrossed was Jimmy in the documentary, that he was startled when the delivery driver, fed up knocking on the front door, tapped on his window and shouted through the double glazing, 'Parcel for Jimmy Joseph.'

Jimmy was confused. His mother hadn't told him to expect a parcel and Jimmy himself definitely hadn't ordered one. He opened the front door and signed on the delivery man's electronic device.

He took the parcel inside and read the label carefully. There, clear as day, on the pre-printed label was 'Jimmy Joseph' followed by his address.

He ripped open the parcel and his jaw dropped. He couldn't believe his eyes. Jimmy whipped his glasses off to take a closer look. In the box contained within the parcel were a pair of Adidas Predator boots, exactly the same as the ones he'd been fantasising about on the website.

He picked up one of the boots and held it up to the light from the front window. He was transfixed. Then he replaced one carefully in the box and ran his hands over the instep of the other. All along the inner area of the surface of the boot were small rubber bumps that were designed to grip the rugby ball when it was being kicked.

There were lots of different styles and versions of football and rugby boots on the market, but there were three types designed specifically for rugby: a forward's boot, an outside back's boot and a kicker's boot. These were undoubtedly kicker's boots. And he loved them.

He tried to work out who'd ordered them for him. Then the penny dropped. It must've been his mum. She'd made a point a few days earlier about what size his feet were and said it was because there was an offer on at Asda for 'Back to School' shoes, but she must have been secretly referring to these incredible boots all along!

Jimmy's excitement levels were higher than the howling Wolves that sat atop the posts on the Memorial Ground and he desperately wanted to show them off, but he was home alone. Then he thought of his grandparents. Bolting through his front door and heading for theirs, he nearly knocked over his grandmother when he burst in, just as she was taking a mug of tea into the front room for his grandfather.

'Oh, sorry, Grams!' cried Jimmy, 'but I've got something I have to show you both.' Betty smiled as she glanced down at the boots. 'Oooh, they look nice, son, take them in and show your grandfather, he was hoping they'd come in time.'

'Wait. What? You knew, Grams?'

Her smile turned into a grin. 'We couldn't let you go to your first camp wearing worn out boots, could we? Think of them as an early Christmas present.'

'Oh Grams,' said Jimmy, wrapping his grandmother in the tightest of hugs. 'I don't know what to say.'

'I do,' called Will from his chair in the front room, 'put your grandmother down and come out to the back garden with me. There's some flower beds that need weeding and you can help me in lieu of payment!'

'Of course I will, Gramp,' said Jimmy. 'I'll weed them for you forever for getting me these!'

'Careful now, I might just take you up on that!'

Jimmy spent the rest of the afternoon helping his grandfather tidy up every corner of the garden while listening to Will's old army stories. And every few minutes he glanced over at his new boots sitting proudly on the garden wall. Jimmy didn't know if a person could actually love an inanimate object, but he reckoned he might well have fallen in love with those boots.

At tea time, Jimmy went home and was pleased to find his mum in the kitchen. He was so excited to show her the boots, he could hardly get his words out. She burst out laughing.

'Oh, calm down, Jimmy, they're only a pair of boots! Honestly, I've never understood why you and Jonny get so obsessed by stuff like that!'

Jimmy ignored her, and just gazed at the boots for about the millionth time that day.

'Oh, I nearly forgot. I saw your dad in town earlier, he had something for you. The Eagles sent it to him by mistake rather than here. It's in the front room on the settee.'

Jimmy rushed to the front room and his jaw gaped open for the second time that day. If he thought the boots were good, they were nothing compared to the jersey that was sitting proudly on the arm of the settee. It was a replica Eagles first-team jersey, made in Jimmy's size. He lifted it silently and held it up in front of him. He was familiar now with the wonderful Eagle badge, but with the sponsors' logos on the arms and shoulders that gave the shirt such an authentic feel, Jimmy thought it was a thing of beauty. Even better than the boots – and that was saying something.

Jimmy quickly turned the jersey around.

10.

That's all he could focus on. After about twenty seconds, Jimmy had to remind himself to breathe. That all-important white number on the back of a genuine pale blue Eagles rugby shirt. He had never been prouder. He brought the shirt close to his face and breathed in its wonderful smell, then held it up to look at again.

'I'm going to be a great Eagle, not just an Eagle,' Jimmy whispered as he turned the shirt around in his hands again, before whipping his t-shirt off to try it on.

FIRST BLOOD

Jimmy looked down at the grass stain on his white shorts and the dirty marks all over the front and side of his, now, no longer new, Eagles shirt, which had been transferred there from the filthy tackle bags. The tackle bags. Man, he hated those tackle bags. It felt like he'd spent just about every second at the camp hitting tackle bags. The only exception had been on the first morning when Mr Withey had spent an hour with the new members of the Academy, making introductions and doing some fun team-building drills. After that first session, Mr Withey had come up to Jimmy and explained that he'd be keeping an eye out for him, but as there were five different age groups in the camp, and because he had responsibility for the Under 16s, he would only get to see Jimmy at break times and meal times.

To be fair to Mr Withey, he did as much as he could in terms of looking after Jimmy, but that was all off the training field. On it, well, he was under the control of another person. Mr Mark Kane.

Jimmy had known all along that it was going to be difficult with Mr Kane after what had happened back at Central Primary during the previous rugby season. In fact, he thought it was going to be so difficult, that his first reaction was that he wasn't even going to go to the summer camp.

It was only his brother, Jonny, who had been to several Eagles' camps and would have been at this one too, if not for an ankle injury that required a summer's rest, who made Jimmy see sense.

'Look Jim, I know what it's like when you're there. It's so different to school where Kane was your only coach. At camp, they have loads, and have different coaches for each age group. They even have specialist coaches like skills coaches, attack coaches and defence coaches. Sometimes they even have strength and conditioning coaches to come and give some advice. So, okay, Kane may well be one of your coaches, but he'll probably be looking after three or four age groups. I doubt very much he'll have anything directly to do with you.'

But Jonny would be proved wrong.

On arrival, Mark Kane greeted every child off the coach that had brought them there. Jimmy had been in one of the seats near the front. Mr Kane said, 'Hello, welcome,' to the three boys who got off first. Then, when it was Jimmy's turn, he blanked him completely. Jimmy was a bit embarrassed, but realised that nobody else even noticed that he'd been ignored. Apart from one person. Mike Green.

Mike was at the camp for the Year 6 boys, who would be returning to school as Year 7s at the end of the summer. Jimmy had seen much more of Mike than he normally would have since the day of the cup final. Mike had started to hang out with Jimmy and his friends at school and down at The Rec, although there were still plenty at Central Primary wary of him and convinced that the old Mike Green would revert to his bullying ways again. But Jimmy was sure that Mike was a different boy to the one he'd been and he gave Mike an enormous amount of credit for turning his life around. It was great to see that a bully could change their behaviour . . . if they really wanted to.

When Mike saw Kane ignoring Jimmy, he walked straight across to his friend and tapped him on the shoulder.

'Don't worry about it, Jim. I doubt if he's going to do you any favours while we're here, but he won't be that bad to you either. There are just too many coaches around for that to happen.'

Jimmy was grateful for Mike's reassurances, but like his own brother's words, Jimmy didn't really believe them. And he was proved right in the very first session he had with Kane.

Whilst the other boys were set up to play a quick game of touch rugby, Mr Kane asked for three volunteers. Four boys put their hands straight up. Jimmy wasn't one of them.

Mr Kane picked two of the volunteers, then said, 'And you,' pointing at Jimmy. 'Come with me, some jobs to do.'

For the next ten minutes, Jimmy and the two volunteers were at the beck and call of Mr Kane, carrying cones, bibs, water bottles, bags of balls and the worst of all, the dirty tackle bags over to the furthest of the six Academy pitches, which would be the home of the Under 11 squad for the next two weeks. Throughout all the instructions and fetching and carrying, Kane didn't speak directly to Jimmy once. He either shouted at them as a group, or told one of the other lads to tell

Jimmy something. They all thought it was a bit strange, but Mr Kane was so fearsome that they didn't dare question him.

Through it all, Jimmy just kept repeating his mantra in his mind: 'Do you want to be an Eagle or a great Eagle?' He wasn't going to be side-tracked from that goal by Kane's pettiness.

Then came the first drill. Tackling and ball presentation.

Before Kane spoke, Jimmy knew what was coming.

He picked out ten boys. Jimmy was one of them.

'Okay, we're going to do tackler-plus-one. So, pair up and get ready to tackle then jackal!'

Jimmy had no idea what Kane was talking about, and judging by the bemused looks, neither did many of the others.

Kane set up two cones about five metres apart and another two opposite, but at an angle. He then told two defenders to stand in front of one set of cones, so that they were about five metres apart and then stood two attackers by the opposite cones. Kane made Jimmy one of the two tacklers. He wasn't surprised.

'Right, *you*,' he said pointing at Jimmy, 'will tackle *him*,' he said pointing across at one of the attackers. 'Then, you'll release him and your partner will battle over the ball with the other attacker to "jackal" it away, gaining possession.'

Then, looking at Jimmy again, he added, 'But this drill will fail if you mess up the tackle . . . so don't.'

And with that, Kane blew his whistle to begin the drill. Because Kane had rushed through the instructions, Jimmy still wasn't overly sure what the drill was all about, but he tried to focus on what he had to do. Tackle.

It wouldn't be fair to say that Jimmy hated tackling, it's just that his joy of rugby was all about everything else that the game offered. He understood the importance of tackling, of course, but he'd never practised it and, in fact, he'd never really been coached or shown how to do it so had never developed a particularly good technique. The one thing about Jimmy, though, was that he was determined. He would rather not bother with tackling, but it was part of the game, so he'd do his best.

As the attackers approached Jimmy, Kane barked, 'Okay, attackers, three-quarter pace please, no sprinting, but good energy at the point of contact.'

Jimmy's attacker came straight at him. He was a forward, a strapping lad who was keen to impress, so as Jimmy went into the tackle, the big forward saw his opportunity and really used his legs to drive his body up and into Jimmy's weak, chest-high tackle and bounced him away.

Jimmy wasn't really expecting such force and was no match for the energy generated by the impact of the forward. The ball the forward was carrying was driven up, straight into Jimmy's face, with his forearm accidentally catching Jimmy across the nose. The force knocked Jimmy off his feet, and as he landed, blood began seeping from his nostrils.

The forward went straight over to Jimmy, horrified at the sight that greeted him, 'I'm really sorry, mate, really sorry. I didn't mean to catch you like that – but you ducked into it a bit.'

Jimmy knew that he'd got all his angles wrong and his head was completely in the wrong place when the impact occurred. He knew he should've gone lower. Oddly, despite the blood, Jimmy wasn't in pain, but the red fluid running from his nose was obviously an issue!

Kane didn't leave his spot on the edge of the pitch. He'd seen what had happened of course, but just shouted across to one of the physios to take a look. He couldn't be bothered getting involved.

As the session was stopped for Jimmy to be looked at, he could hear Kane saying to the other players, 'And that's what you get if you're not committed at tackle time. If you don't fancy it, like he didn't – the blood will undoubtedly flow.' Kane gave a menacing laugh and a few of the players joined in. They were worried about what he might do if they didn't.

Jimmy felt anger. He hadn't lacked commitment at all, and for Kane to suggest he'd somehow been frightened, was infuriating.

Before he could say anything, Mr Withey appeared and began talking to Kane. Jimmy couldn't hear exactly what was being said because the physio was busy trying to stop the flow of blood and was assuring Jimmy that his nose wasn't broken, but it sounded like Kane was saying, 'Let him sit it out.'

Once the physio applied some pressure to Jimmy's nose with some clumps of cotton wool, the blood quickly stopped and while the physio deliberated if he needed to stick two thick sticks of cotton wool up Jimmy's tender nostrils, Mr Withey came over to check on him.

'Let's have a look at you, Jimmy. What a start this is for you! How are you feeling?'

'I'm fine, Sir, thank you. No pain and the blood has stopped now, so no problem.'

Be a great Eagle, Jimmy thought to himself.

'Well that's good. Now, I've spoken to Mark and he says you've had a bit of a bang so it might be an idea that you sit out the rest of the day – and I'm inclined to agree with him. We can't be too careful.'

'No, Mr Withey, honestly, I'm fine.' Jimmy was horrified at the prospect. He wanted to get straight back in with the group. 'There's nothing broken and I'm ready to go. I'll just keep my head out of the way next time.' He laughed, hoping humour would win Mr Withey over.

Mr Withey stared at Jimmy for a moment, a look of doubt on his face.

'I told Mr Kane about the promise I made your mum,' he said, at last. 'Because of your age, I said we'd take no risks with you. He informs me that you tackled well, but took a big bang. I asked for his recommendation and he said straight away that the correct decision regarding our duty of care is to have you sit out the rest of the day. I have to take Mr Kane's advice on this. He's only thinking of you, Jimmy.'

Jimmy almost barked a scornful laugh, but he managed to hold it in. He didn't want to draw Mr Withey's attention to his past history with Mark Kane and realised this was a battle he wouldn't win.

'Okay sir,' was his defeated response.

'Good lad. Now come with me. We'll go back over to the clubhouse, get you cleaned up and give you a drink, and then do a quick HIA for you. Do you know what that is?'

Jimmy nodded. He'd seen it regularly on TV coverage of the Six Nations in recent times, especially since rugby experts everywhere had started to become concerned about concussion.

'Yes, it's Head Impact Assessment isn't it? To check if a player is concussed. I'm not concussed though, honest.'

'They all say that, Jimmy,' replied Mr Withey, 'that's why we carry out an HIA and its correct definition is actually Head *Injury* Assessment and we need to do it with any knock to the head, just to be safe. I'm sure you'll be fine and then after that, you can be my assistant this afternoon. But the rule we have here is: *if in doubt, sit them out*. So I'm afraid there's no question of you continuing with training today.'

Mr Withey turned away to thank the physio and briefly told Kane what was happening before calling Jimmy to follow him. As Jimmy left, he glanced at Kane, who didn't seem to even notice that he was departing. He was in the middle of shouting instructions to the rest of the squad.

'Okay, for those left to put in a full shift, let's get cracking!'

Jimmy bit his lip. He was gutted.

TOUGH TO TACKLE

Day two was no better than day one.

It was an early start. Jimmy had passed the HIA the previous day and after taking it easy with Mr Withey, who just wanted to be certain that Jimmy was 100% right, Jimmy was raring to get stuck into whatever the day had in store for him. And the first thing for Jimmy to get stuck into was breakfast. It was served in the canteen of the Underhill complex, with a buffet of food the like of which Jimmy had never seen before. There were cereals – oats, shredded wheat and corn flakes; there were yoghurts – about ten different flavours; there were bagels, served with cold meats and cheese, which Jimmy found a bit odd for breakfast; and there were the eggs. Jimmy was used to one style: fried. But here were three different kinds – scrambled, poached, boiled and only served with wholemeal toast, not the white doorsteps that Jimmy usually favoured. And then, alongside everything else, was the star of the show: the fruit. My word, the fruit! Jimmy counted twelve different types, which included a couple he'd never seen or even heard of before – guava and papaya.

Jimmy just stood at the counter, peering through his glasses at this incredible array of food, but not having a single clue where to start. He was interrupted by a friendly tap on the shoulder from Mike.

'Mad isn't it?' he said, smiling at Jimmy. 'It's not exactly the fry up option from Albert's Cafe in town, is it?'

Jimmy laughed at the comparison.

'I had a three-day training camp last season, over Easter,' continued Mike, 'and I didn't have a clue what to do on the first day either, so follow me. It all tastes even better than it looks!'

Over the next few minutes, Mike Green gave Jimmy a masterclass in buffet management and what to eat to get him through an intense morning of rugby training. He started by taking Jimmy to the cereals, and ignored the familiar packet ones that Jimmy would probably have chosen, and poured a small amount of oats into a bowl. Then he told Jimmy to pick a yoghurt, pour it over the oats before selecting some chopped fruit to throw on top. Then it was a big dollop of honey.

Jimmy had never tasted anything like it in his life! As he wolfed it down and tasted the sensation of the sweet and sour mixture of fruit he'd chosen, accompanied by the yoghurt and honey all mixed in with the crunchy texture of the oats, Jimmy turned to Mike and said, 'Wow! This is even better than six Weetabix.'

After their oats extravaganza, Mike then led Jimmy up for a couple of glasses of fruit juice, followed by half a bagel with soft cheese and smoked salmon. He then finished it all with scrambled eggs on a slice of wholemeal toast with no butter.

'Everything we've eaten is designed to give you energy that we'll burn off when we get outside, without making you feel horribly full,' explained Mike. 'And it's all really good for you.'

Jimmy nodded in understanding. He felt great and it had all tasted so delicious.

Half an hour later, they were out on their training pitch. Feeling energised, Jimmy grabbed a ball and punted it high in the sky – his speciality – before charging after it and catching it before it hit the ground.

Jimmy's new teammates were impressed by how high Jimmy could kick, and how quickly he crossed the surface of the lush turf to catch the ball as it fell.

'That's enough of that!' came a booming voice from behind Jimmy. It was Kane.

'We all know what happened the last time you tried that particular stunt.'

And from that point on, Jimmy's day – which had started so well – went rapidly downhill.

It started with yet another tackling drill.

'Right then, you're going to do a little exercise I've invented. Listen carefully, the tacklers will have lots to think about.'

Kane explained that two attackers would run at one defender. One of the attackers had the ball. It was up to the defender to rush up and tackle the attacker with the ball. The attacker then had two options. He could either keep the ball and try to break the tackle, or draw the defender and off-load the ball to his support runner. Either way, the defender had to tackle the attacker to try to disrupt the passage of the ball.

Unsurprisingly, Jimmy was picked as the defender. Once

more, he was gutted. Another chance to show his running flair and elusive sidestep, gone.

As everyone took up their places for the drill, Jimmy began to bounce nervously on his toes. He knew he wasn't a natural at tackling, but had always comforted himself that it was because he'd never really been shown how to do it properly. But yesterday, before he'd had the bang on the nose, he watched some of his new teammates tackle. A few of them were incredible. It was as if he was watching mini Sam Underhills or Justin Tipurics going about their business. They seemed to know exactly where to position their feet, how to angle their bodies, where to put their heads, how to drive into the tackle. Everything was based on timing and power. All Jimmy seemed to do was put his head down, get his body in the way and hope for the best.

As he stood there, a little bit worried for the first ever time on a rugby pitch, Kane blew his whistle. Facing Jimmy at the other end of the channel were a very large and mobile prop with legs that appeared to be bigger than Jimmy's chest and would've put Manu's magic pistons to shame, and a centre who seemed to Jimmy to be a dead ringer for Sonny Bill Williams, and about the same size too! Suddenly Jimmy wished he possessed the bulky frame of his Samoan friend back at home and felt a strange feeling of dread rush through his body.

The drill began and the prop confused Jimmy by passing the ball straight to 'Sonny Bill' which meant Jimmy had to change his direction of running. As the tall centre ran at him, Jimmy had a great idea. He guessed that 'Sonny Bill' would pass to the prop a split second before the tackle, as the giant All Black, who was renowned for his legendary off-loads, had often done in real life – Jimmy had seen him do it hundreds of times on YouTube.

But Jimmy had made the fatal mistake of confusing reality with fantasy.

As he rushed towards the centre, Jimmy bounced to his left at the last moment to intercept the off-load that was surely certain to come. It didn't.

Instead, all the towering centre did was throw a dummy, watch the hapless Jimmy dive into fresh air and jog past him to touch the ball down for an imaginary try.

Knowing that Mr Withey was still in the pavilion having a meeting with some of the Eagles' senior officials, Mark Kane was free to give Jimmy both barrels.

'What the hell was that?' screamed Jimmy's former teacher. 'That was the tackle of a fool! It was an embarrassment! A *non-*tackle!'

Some of the boys giggled, and Kane warmed to his captive audience.

'In all my years of rugby, I've never seen someone so scared of tackling that they dived out of the way! What a joke!'

'I wasn't diving out of the way, sir, I was trying to . . .' but before Jimmy could explain that he was attempting to catch an interception, Kane bellowed at him again.

'Don't you dare talk to me unless I ask you, boy!'

Jimmy fell silent, his cheeks flushing hot. The other members of the training squad were now embarrassed too, and relieved that it was Jimmy getting the hammering from Kane and not them.

'I know what I saw, and what I saw was a scared little boy who is out of his depth here, diving out of the way so he wouldn't get hurt. And just because he got a little bang on the nose yesterday.'

Jimmy's eyes filled with tears, a combination of embarrassment, foolishness and rage.

'Right, let's do it again, and this time . . . tackle like a man, not a frightened little boy! Back to your places.'

Jimmy tried to shake off his fear and the dread that was engulfing his thoughts, but his feelings of anxiety just grew worse. He didn't want to admit it, but he was feeling scared.

Kane took the ball off 'Sonny Bill' and walked to the prop. He pushed the ball firmly into his powerful arms. Looking directly into the young boy's eyes, he said 'Run at him. And smash him.'

The prop nodded.

Jimmy had been sorting out his gumshield and hadn't seen Kane's brief instructions, and by the time he looked up, the prop was running at him. And he was running hard.

Bravely, Jimmy ran straight at him, but at the very last second, he turned his head away from the tackle, and half-heartedly threw his arms out in a vain attempt to stop the charging prop. This lacklustre tackle had no effect on the prop whatsoever, who literally trampled over Jimmy like a rampaging rhinoceros would have.

Lying in a heap on the ground, Jimmy heard the whistle again.

'*What was that?*' screamed Kane, 'That was worse than the first time! Again.'

'Again' became the word that Jimmy became most familiar with over the next half hour as Kane got Jimmy to repeat the tackle drill again and again and again. Each time, Jimmy's tackle efforts became worse and worse. And with it, Jimmy became more and more worried about tackling another player. A thing that Jimmy had never really thought about – or even cared about – before in his rugby life, was becoming a huge problem in his mind. Without knowing or understanding why, Jimmy's attempts – or more accurately, non-attempts – at tackling were developing into a significant mental block for him.

That day became Jimmy's worst ever on a rugby pitch.

And it was the day he began to despise tackling.

HOMEWARD BOUND

Jimmy stood behind the Underhill pavilion complex staring down at the cracked screen of his battered old iPhone 5. The phone had received plenty of use over the previous few evenings. Jimmy's grandfather rang him every night at 8.30 and while Jimmy hadn't told him about Kane putting him on defensive drills all the time, nor explained about the problem he was having with tackling, his grandfather had sensed that all was not well. The same was true when Jonny had called. Both had told Jimmy to stay positive and make the most of the opportunity. He didn't have the heart to tell them that the opportunity had turned into a living nightmare.

Jimmy glanced around for about the fifth time to make sure that nobody could see or hear him. Then he tapped the telephone icon, followed by favourites then stared at the list of names, focusing on one. 'Mum Mobile'.

Jimmy took a deep breath, and tapped the screen. The phone sprang to life and dialled his mother. She answered in seconds.

Over the next few minutes, Jimmy told his mother everything. Well, that's not strictly true. In fact, he told her everything but the truth. The first thing she said was, 'I knew it. It's that Mark Kane again isn't it, bullying you, isn't he?'

Jimmy was at pains to explain to his mother that wasn't the case. The last thing he wanted was his mother charging down to Underhill to have a stand-up row with Kane and Mr Withey. Mr Withey had been nothing but nice to him and Jimmy didn't want his family to fall out with the head of the Academy. Also, there was the bigger picture of the Eagles. Whilst Jimmy had made the painful decision to quit this camp, he didn't want to burn all his bridges with his professional region. Maybe a good start to the Year 6 season back at school would see Jimmy invited back to a shorter, weekend camp. He didn't want to spoil his chances of that happening.

Anyway, despite the fact that Kane had been very tough on him, Jimmy knew there was one real reason why he was struggling so much: he'd become genuinely scared of tackling.

Of course, Kane had literally given Jimmy a crash course in tackling, but something deep inside of him had come to the surface each time he'd had to take another stiff contact in yet another tackling drill. Fear. A fear and loathing of tackling. He'd never experienced such an acute dread on a sports field before.

Maybe it had always been there. Jimmy wasn't certain. But he was certain about one thing: he had to get away.

Again, he didn't mention the tackling to his mother. He was embarrassed that he felt this way and he didn't want to develop a reputation for being a nervous tackler. The last thing he wanted to do was admit that to his mother – or anyone else for that matter – so instead, he ploughed straight down the homesick route.

He told his mother how lonely he felt after training, which was partly true, and he also told her that the food was awful, which was an absolute lie, but it was just about enough to convince his mother his time at camp was over and to come and get him.

And then his mother dropped the final bombshell.

'Well, you'll have to go and tell Mr Withey. I'll drive down and come in with you, but you're going to have to tell him.'

Jimmy should have known that was coming. Both his mum and dad had always been insistent that their children should understand their responsibilities and deal with the consequences of their actions. This was no different, so now he had to deal with Mr Withey.

Jimmy agreed to finish the last hour's training that was scheduled to take place after the short break they were on, which would be mainly circuit training at various stations in the massive sports hall, then he would wait for her to come down before going in to speak with Mr Withey. She said that she would be there by 6.30 after work. All Jimmy had to do now was wait.

After his mother arrived, Jimmy again stuck to the homesick story, mentioning nothing about his tackling issues or the way Kane had been treating him. He took his mum to Mr Withey's office and stood outside the door for about ten seconds before moving forward to knock. Just as he did, the door was jerked open and to Jimmy's horror, Mark Kane was standing there.

'And what do you want?' growled Kane. He hadn't noticed Jimmy's mother, but instantly blushed when he did and changed his attitude straight away.

'Ah, Mrs Joseph, I didn't expect to see you. Can I help at all?'

Jimmy's mum really disliked Mark Kane and nearly said something about the way he'd spoken to her son, but didn't want to embarrass Jimmy, so she dropped it.

'He wants to speak to Mr Withey,' was all she said in reply.

Kane looked at Jimmy and his mother with a mix of puzzlement, curiosity and a hint of anger on his face. But before he could say anything more, Mr Withey called them in.

'Thanks for the update, Mark, that's excellent work and you can leave that with me. Now, Mrs Joseph, Jimmy, come on in, what can I do for you both?'

Kane hovered around the door for a moment, wanting to eavesdrop on the conversation but Mr Withey quickly dismissed him.

Then, for the next five minutes, Jimmy told Mr Withey a mixture of half-truths, which all boiled down to one thing: 'I'm really sorry, sir, but I'm not happy here. I'm homesick and I want to go home.'

Of course, Mr Withey had heard all this before and was very experienced at helping young people overcome their anxieties and was usually able to encourage them. But very quickly, he could tell that Jimmy had made up his mind.

The conversation was amicable and Jimmy felt so at ease with Mr Withey that he nearly relented and was on the verge of telling him all about his fear of tackling and asking for some help. But he knew that the person who would be assigned to help him would be Kane. Jimmy just couldn't face that. He would feel humiliated.

Mr Withey told Jimmy and his mother there were no hard feelings and that this wouldn't count against him in any future selections for the Eagles junior squads in the coming season. Then he started to make the necessary arrangements to cancel Jimmy's place at the camp.

When it was all done, Jimmy felt an incredible sense of relief flood through him. He even allowed himself a little smile at the thought of going home and hanging out with Matt, Kitty and Manu for the rest of the summer.

As Jimmy collected his stuff, he bumped into Mike. He stuck to the homesick line, which Mike was kind enough not to question, although he clearly understood the real reason why Jimmy wasn't enjoying the camp.

'Ah, mate, that's a real shame,' he said. 'But fair enough, I wouldn't want to carry on if Kane was treating me like that too. Wish you were staying another few days, though. We've just heard that three squad members of the Eagles, all internationals, are coming down to do some individual skills sessions tomorrow. And one of them is gonna be with English fly-half, Tommy Woodward, who's gonna work directly with us kickers . . . it's such a shame you're gonna miss that, Jim, he'd have loved you.'

Mike instantly regretted sharing the news when he saw Jimmy's face. Not for the first time in his recent rugby life, Jimmy was absolutely gutted.

BACK ON HOME TURF

The trip home only took about twenty minutes, and during it Jimmy had some more bad news delivered by his mother. Reinforcing her policy of taking personal responsibility for one's actions, she told Jimmy that he wasn't allowed to wear any of the new Eagles kit or his new Predators out and about on the waste ground or The Rec. When Jimmy protested, his mother cut him off with a firm glare.

'Mr Withey said you may be invited back to autumn camp if you continue improving, so I'm going to wash everything and keep it packed away until then. And the boots will stay away until the season starts with the school, too. Your grandparents spent a lot of money getting those for you, Jimmy, I'm not going to let you ruin them down at The Rec.'

Jimmy thought about protesting again, but knew it was pointless. When they arrived home, he handed everything over to his mum, before he made his way, dejectedly, upstairs, carrying his now almost empty Eagles backpack up to his bedroom. When he slumped down on his bed, one of the first things he saw was his battered old boots lying in the corner. They were in a sorry old state: laces on the left boot snapped, a stud missing on the right boot and both with the leather on the toes almost totally scraped off, largely thanks to the habit Jimmy had of dragging his toes when he jogged onto the pitch.

Jimmy instantly regretted his decision to leave camp. But then he remembered those tackle drills and a shiver went through his bones.

Suddenly, Jimmy felt the urge to run. And run fast.

It was the one thing he'd hardly done in his short spell at the Academy. Instead, he'd pretty much spent the time standing still and getting smashed, tackle after tackle.

He jumped up from his bed and picked up his boots and focused on the one with the snapped lace. Jimmy knew what to do, he'd done it loads of times. He quickly pulled the remaining lace out, and started to thread what was left of it, back into the boot. The lace was only long enough to get through the top three eyes in the instep of the boot, but that would be okay.

He reached inside his crumpled backpack and rummaged around for what he needed. He found it quickly and pulled it out. It was his inhaler. Jimmy took two enormous gulps and felt the airways in his chest loosen immediately. He stood in front of his bedroom mirror and sucked in a huge gulp of air until his lungs filled. It made his chest stick out as if he'd been on the weights for a fortnight. *I wish*, thought Jimmy to himself.

Then he opened the door of his wardrobe, reached down for his battered old Rhino rugby ball at the bottom, and squeezed it tight. It wasn't fully pumped up, but only gave slightly as he gripped it. 'That'll do,' he whispered. He didn't want to waste any time having to go to the shed to find his pump, he just wanted to get outside and run.

He swept his boots up off the bed, skipped down the stairs and then into the short hallway to the front door, nearly bumping into his mum as she came out of the front room.

'Where are you going now? I'm just putting some food on for tea, it's shepherd's pie.'

'Oh, don't worry about me, Mum,' replied Jimmy, 'I'm just going down to The Rec for a bit, I'll have it after . . . I had food earlier at the Academy.' Yet another lie. Jimmy wasn't proud of himself.

'Oh, Jimmy, why didn't you tell me? I've got things on the cooker now!'

But Jimmy didn't hear a word. He was off, out of the door, and running the well-trodden path to his favourite place.

The Rec.

KICK CHASE

Jimmy tightened his lace as best he could, but without putting too much pressure on it in case he snapped it. He moved his foot about inside the boot as he stood up, to see if the lace would hold firm. It did.

Then, sliding his right boot under the ball, he flicked it up in front of him, caught it, and remembering everything he'd been taught last season by Peter Clement and Liam Wyatt of the Wolves, he rolled the ball out of his hand, arm outstretched in front of him. He leaned slightly into the kick, before drilling it as high and as far in front of him as he was able, following through with his leg as high as he could manage.

If he was doing his kicking training drills, he would've just stood there, admiring his kick as it swirled through the air like a torpedo. But not today.

From the moment the ball left his boot, Jimmy was off. And what a sight it was. That's if anyone had been on the empty Rec to see it.

The speed Jimmy was able to generate from a standing start was quite remarkable. It was one of his many rugby strengths.

Not even looking at the ball, Jimmy covered the first ten metres in an instant. He'd taken a deep breath the moment he'd made the kick and didn't take another until he was twenty metres into his run. He reached top speed with ease. This was no accident. Jimmy had tinkered with his running style for a long time. For a while, he had tried to copy the style of Wales' George North. Jimmy loved watching North, who was all strength, his arms and legs popping like pistons with every stride, covering the ground with almost unstoppable speed and power. But when he copied the Welshman, Jimmy realised he simply didn't have the strength and physique required to run like him. He always felt that he was putting too much effort in without gaining any extra reward – speed.

So, recently, Jimmy had been watching YouTube clips of someone he felt was the most natural and easy-running of the top stars currently playing: Beauden Barrett of New Zealand. He didn't have the all-action style of somebody like North, but whatever Barrett did, it seemed all his energy went into his speed. And that's what Jimmy had managed to achieve. He just wished he'd had the opportunity to show it at the Eagles camp.

After twenty metres, Jimmy looked up at the ball for the first time. He'd struck it too well. He'd really wanted to jump and challenge for it in the air, the way that Liam Williams did so regularly for Wales and the British and Irish Lions, but he'd just kicked the ball too far. Instead, Jimmy bust an absolute gut to get to it before its second bounce.

In Jimmy's mind, he was no longer on The Rec. Now, he was out in South Africa on a Lions tour, on one of their rock hard pitches that suited fast, flowing rugby so well. Even if he had been at a packed Ellis Park, full to its 62,567 capacity, he wouldn't have heard a sound. His focus was purely and utterly on the ball. Jimmy was flying at full tilt now, imagining that South Africa's Cheslin Kolbe was charging at the ball, having come in off his wing to catch and call for a mark.

If anything, after Jimmy's initial lightning burst over twenty metres, he got quicker over the next twenty. Not taking his eyes off the ball, Jimmy arrived just as it hit the earth with a thud, throwing up some dust from the bone dry Rec pitch. Some players would have hesitated at this point and waited to see the ball bounce skywards, before it dropped down again. Not Jimmy. He gambled.

Arriving at absolute top speed, he guessed that the ball was going to land on its flat side and just bounce straight upwards, not right or left, or forward or back, just straight up. He was right.

His chest smashed into the ball a split second before he wrapped his arms around it, smothering it tight to his body, ensuring there would be no knock on. Straight in the bread basket. Then, in his imaginary world, Jimmy moved to his left before instantly stepping to his right, sitting Kolbe down on his backside. Continuing at top speed, Jimmy headed for the posts and dotted the ball down.

Normally, Jimmy would've allowed himself a smile, done a dab or a stupid dance and basked in the fantasy that he'd just scored the winning try in a Lions Test series. But not today.

Instead, he just turned around, steadied himself under the posts, took another deep breath, and repeated the kick and the chase again. And again. And again.

He did it fifteen times before he collapsed under the far posts, sweating like a steel worker at the blast furnace and breathing as heavily as a steam train travelling at top speed. He was glad he had taken a few slugs of his inhaler before coming out.

It had been great to run. *Really* great. He'd missed it so much. The happy bonus to that was that he hadn't given tackling a single moment's thought.

That felt even better.

TIME TO TALK

Jimmy felt better than he had for days. He'd done what he needed to do, blast away all the negative thoughts around tackling by doing what he did best – running, kicking and catching. It seemed like all his woes from the Academy had been blown away by his intense running and chasing.

After taking off his boots, he began walking back across The Rec towards home and noticed someone else walking in the opposite direction. It was a boy around his own age. As they approached one another, Jimmy looked to see if he recognised him – but he didn't. The boy was walking along looking at his phone and, every now and then, glancing around. As they closed in on each other, the boy looked up and saw Jimmy staring at him. He froze, then quickly changed direction, turning around and going back the way he'd come. *Odd*, thought Jimmy, and he paused for a moment so that the other boy didn't feel like he was walking right behind him.

Over at the far corner of The Rec was the house owned by old Reggie Parry. Parry – as everyone called him – was always mending or repairing something, and true to form, he started up his circular saw to cut through some wood. It wasn't overly loud, but as it fired into life, the boy almost jumped out of his skin. Then he shuffled on the spot for a moment, hands clasped over his ears, then he brought his head down into his chest, as if he was going to curl up in a ball. Parry must've seen the reaction the boy had to his saw, so stopped and called out to the boy to apologise for giving him a fright, but the boy didn't seem to acknowledge Parry and instead ran off, his hands still clamped over his ears. 'That was *really* odd,' whispered Jimmy to himself.

He was nearly home when he heard a familiar voice calling him.

'Oi, oi, superstar, what are you doing here? I thought you'd be at the Academy for another week.'

It was Kitty.

Jimmy beamed for the first time in days. He finally had someone he could talk to.

He threw an underarm, one-handed spin pass to her, which she caught with ease and then spun on one finger.

'Look at the state of you!' she said. 'You been running a marathon or something?'

'Sprints,' he replied, realising for the first time how much he was sweating. 'But I think I've overdone it. I'm cream crackered!'

'Lightweight!' laughed Kitty, before tossing the ball back to Jimmy, who caught it one-handed to avoid dropping his boots.

'Seriously though,' she continued, 'I wasn't expecting you back for another week at least. What happened?'

Jimmy looked a bit sheepish. He thought about telling Kitty the same story he'd told Mr Withey and his mum, but he trusted Kitty more than just about anyone else. He took a deep breath.

'It was hard, Kitty. Way harder than I expected.'

Kitty could sense that there was more he wanted to say, but she didn't want to push him.

Looking down at the scruffy ball in his hands, she said, 'Have you got to go back in now? Why don't we go back on the grass and do some kicking and passing?'

'No way, I'm done,' he replied. 'But why don't we go to the swings for a while?'

'Come on then,' she said with a gentle smile, and they headed to the playground at the edge of The Rec.

Jimmy felt relaxed by the gentle motion of the swing and by the ease with which his conversations with Kitty always flowed. He paused for a moment and then said, 'How do you cope with tackling?'

'Tackling? You mean rugby tackling?'

'Yeah,' he replied, feeling slightly hesitant now that he'd brought the subject up.

'I don't know what you mean by "cope",' she said. 'Do you mean, how do I do it?'

'Well, yeah . . . Erm, no . . . Oh, I don't know,' he said, looking to the ground, his cheeks flushing a little.

'Has this got something to do with the Academy?'

Jimmy nodded.

'Mr Kane?'

Jimmy knew he could explain away his embarrassment by blaming Kane. Kitty disliked him almost as much as Jimmy did, but he decided to come clean.

'Well, he wasn't exactly a help, but no, it's not about him, really. It's about me.'

He looked up at Kitty for a moment before continuing.

'Do you remember the Cluster Cup final?'

'Remember it!' laughed Kitty, 'I'll never forget it! It was the best day of my whole life! Apart from Ryan's burp that is. And his fart in the dressing room too. He blamed Andrew Beasley, but it was definitely him! It was rank!'

Jimmy laughed out loud at the memory. It felt like he hadn't laughed all summer.

'No, that tackle,' he said eventually. 'Your tackle. On big Dale, their captain, in the first half.'

Kitty blushed. 'Oh, that was nothing, I just got in the way.'

'No, it was brilliant,' he said, earnestly. 'We didn't know it then, but if you'd missed that tackle, he'd have scored and the way the game went, I don't think we'd have got back in. Especially with the nightmare that Mike was having.'

Kitty said nothing, just smiled modestly at the memory.

'The thing is, I remember every moment of that tackle – and all the others you pulled off during the season. And when you did them, I know they were always brilliant, but they all looked, well, kind of normal, if you know what I mean?'

The puzzled look on Kitty's face showed that she didn't know what Jimmy meant.

'What I mean, is that if it had been me on the wing at that moment, I'd have tackled big Dale too. It's just what we do as rugby players.'

'Exactly!' replied Kitty, 'and that's why I get embarrassed when people talk about my tackles; they're only tackles, anyone can do it.'

Jimmy paused.

'That's just the thing, Kitty, I don't think I can anymore.'

A NEW KID IN TOWN

It was the most difficult conversation that Jimmy had ever had, and that was saying something. After his parents' divorce, his issues with Mr Kane in school and having to speak to Mr Withey to leave the Eagles Academy, there had been many times Jimmy had needed to explain himself, but this was different. This felt like he was admitting to some sort of defeat. He found it hard.

Kitty, for the most part, just sat and listened to everything. The smack Jimmy had taken on the nose that first morning that saw him have his first ever HIA, how Kane had just used him for tackling and nothing else and how the constant impacts, clashes and bangs Jimmy received had really got into his head. There was only one awkward moment for Jimmy and that was when, trying to emphasise just how much of a mental issue tackling had become for him, he said to Kitty, 'I mean, I know I can do it, I just need to look at you, you're a girl and even you can do it.'

Jimmy wished he could've taken his words back the moment they left his lips.

'That's right,' replied Kitty coolly. 'Even a *girl* can tackle, when really I should be inside, in my pink dress playing My Little Pony with all my Barbie dolls.'

Jimmy apologised at once. He'd made a clumsy comment and regretted it. If there was anyone who believed girls could do anything, it was Jimmy. The respect he had for his mum, the strength he saw in his younger sister, Julie, and how she'd handled their parents' split and also the way she basically ran Jimmy and his brother Jonny's daily lives for them, and of course Kitty. The girl he respected most. He wished he could've taken his words straight back.

'I'm so sorry,' he spluttered. 'What I meant was, what you do isn't normal.' She raised an eyebrow and looked thunderous, so he quickly tried again. 'For you to take the field against boys, some of them twice your size, isn't something that many girls do. In fact, I can't think of another girl who plays competitive rugby in our league. The point I was trying to make is, most people would assume tackling to be the weakest part of your game, and it's clearly not. Apart from your speed, it's your strongest asset. I just wondered how you've managed to cope with that?'

Kitty's shrug told him that she had accepted his apology.

'Honestly? I've never given it a moment's thought,' she said. 'I remember telling your mum this before, but when my dad realised I was serious about rugby, he sat me down and told me not to expect anyone to go easy on me and then told me to really embrace and enjoy tackling as part of the game. Once he realised that I understood that, there was a period when he'd come home from the gym and we'd spend time in the garden, just tackling . . . and I really loved it. I think Dad's support, and the way he really bought into what I wanted to do and gave me practical help, was important.'

Jimmy nodded dolefully. There was a time when he had not given tackling a second thought, but the battering he'd had as Kane's cannon fodder had removed that feeling. And it had now been replaced with fear.

'I honestly think this is a temporary thing, Jimmy,' she continued. 'That bang on the nose you got on the first day would have shaken anyone up. Then Kane trying to make you feel stupid just added to it. By the time the rugby season comes around, all this will be forgotten. Promise.'

Jimmy wanted to believe her, but something deep, deep inside him had changed. Tackling was now a serious issue for Jimmy and he had no idea how he was going to deal with it.

'Ji-mmy!' called a loud voice. It was his mum. Tea. He'd forgotten all about it.

'I'd better go,' he said, leaping off the swing. 'My tea is probably burnt to a crisp!'

Kitty laughed. 'You'll have more to worry about than tackling if that's the case!'

'Man, you know it!' laughed Jimmy.

As they walked, they both saw the boy that Jimmy had seen earlier. He was still looking at his phone before glancing around, and had moved to the opposite side of The Rec, far away from the sounds of Parry and his circular saw.

'Who's that?' asked Jimmy, pointing over at the boy.

'Oh, yeah, new family,' replied Kitty. 'Don't know his name, but they've moved into one of the posh new-builds behind the allotments. He'll be in our class when we go back in September.'

'Oh, right. He seems a bit odd, doesn't he? I saw him earlier get into a right state over by old Parry's. It was only Parry cutting some wood with his saw, you'd have sworn a jet was taking off next to him!' He laughed. 'He needs to man-up, whoever he is!'

'Oh, Jimmy, that's not nice!'

'What?' protested Jimmy. 'I'm only saying. Just seemed like it was a pretty over the top reaction to an old bloke cutting up some wood.'

'He doesn't like loud noises, Jimmy. He's autistic.'

If Jimmy hadn't thought he could feel any worse, he now did.

'Oh, I'm sorry, I didn't know he had autism. Poor kid.'

'First thing, he hasn't got autism, he's autistic – there's a difference,' said Kitty. 'And poor nothing! My mum was telling me all about it. He just has a different take on the world to us, that's all. He reacts to and deals with situations in a different way. No one way is right or wrong. My mum knows all about it from her job at the Education Department and she's met his mum. She told me he doesn't want to be treated differently to anyone or pitied, he just wants to fit in – like we all do. That shouldn't be too hard, should it?'

Jimmy didn't answer, but watched as the boy turned around and retraced his steps away from the playground and back towards The Rec, seemingly walking in a way where he considered every step he made.

'All right,' said Jimmy, 'next time we see him, that's what we'll do. We'll help him fit in. I wonder if he likes rugby?'

'Jimmy Joseph, you're obsessed!'

Jimmy laughed. 'Well, I may not be able to tackle, but I'm still going to play! See you tomorrow, shorty.'

And with a little skip in his step, Jimmy was off, thinking of ways to avoid eating the dry and, no doubt, slightly burnt shepherd's pie that awaited him at home.

THE GHOST STORY

The rest of the summer saw Jimmy getting back to normal.

He spent the bulk of it at The Rec with Kitty, Matt and Manu. The long days were filled with passing, kicking and more running. What they weren't filled with was tackling, tackling and more tackling – much to Jimmy's relief. The main reason for this was that summer rugby at The Rec was always of the touch variety, with no tackling allowed. The focus was on the things that Jimmy adored most about the game: using all his running and handling skills and getting as fit and sharp as possible.

In fact, Jimmy had sort of blocked out the thought of tackling from his mind completely. Once he had settled back into life with his friends, he had quickly forgotten about the events at the Eagles Academy. Every now and again he thought about those glorious Predator boots and the Eagles shirt tucked away in his mother's wardrobe, but secretly hoped that when the rugby season began again, when he got back to school, he'd get another chance with the Academy. Things would be different then, he promised himself.

The great thing about growing up on the edge of a small town was that it felt almost like a village, and in many ways, The Rec was like the village green. It certainly was for the kids. At many points during that warm summer, there must have been at least thirty kids of all ages playing in touch rugby games on that scruffy piece of ground. The youngest was probably the smallest of the two Beasley brothers. Well, smallest was probably the wrong word. Incredibly, he'd grown even more during the summer and actually looked as if he could have been one of the kids from Bishopswood Comprehensive School, even though he wasn't even ten yet. The oldest were Sam and Ibrahim, who were about to enter Year 11 at Bishopswood. They were obviously bigger and stronger than the rest, but as it was always touch rugby, their size and strength never really mattered. The games were all about speed, and one thing was certain – no matter what age they were, nobody could match Jimmy for explosive, off the mark, speed.

In her age group, Kitty was still the quickest overall, but her speed was a classic 100 metre runner's speed. The further Kitty ran, the quicker she seemed to get. It wasn't uncommon to see her streaking up the touchline, getting faster and faster with each stride, burning away from everyone.

But Jimmy's speed was different.

He would still sometimes lose to Kitty if it was a longer distance, but over ten to fifteen metres, he was almost untouchable – by a player of any age.

Fifteen-a-side touch rugby is crowded. There's very little space, and the games – which often lasted for hours, with different people drifting in and out – were usually subject to more 'touch' than 'rugby'. Until Jimmy got the ball that is.

He possessed a wonderful ability to receive the ball and then pick his way through the tightest of gaps, without anyone laying a finger on him. Consequently, Mike started to call Jimmy 'The Ghost'. This was because when people desperately held out a hand to touch him, it was as if Jimmy had never been there. He just ghosted past them.

Jimmy's hero, Peter Clement, had been walking his dog one day towards the end of the school summer holidays, and stopped to chat with Jimmy's grandfather, who was returning from one of his long walks in the hills that overlooked the town. He might have been in his seventies, but Will seemed as fit as any man half his age, walking everywhere, often on errands or delivering some of his prize tomatoes to friends and neighbours.

As they were chatting, they saw Jimmy receive a wild behind-the-back pass from Manu.

The ball had looped high towards Jimmy and he had no option but to pause and wait for it. This allowed three players from the other team, one of them being fifteen-year-old Sam from Bishopswood, the school's openside flanker, to close down all of Jimmy's space.

As the ball continued on its slow journey to Jimmy, Peter turned to Will and said, 'Your boy isn't getting out of this one,' but what happened next astonished even a rugby veteran like Peter, who had seen it and done it all himself.

Jimmy had begun to move just before the ball reached him, creating the effect of having almost left the ball behind in mid-air. This caused Sam to take his eye off Jimmy and he looked behind him to where he thought the ball was falling. But in one beautiful, balanced and sweeping movement, Jimmy took control of the ball above and slightly behind his right shoulder, before sidestepping to his left. Then he immediately swapped his body weight to the opposite side, darting right and straight through the gap that the off-balance Sam had now presented him with. Without seeming to look, Jimmy then accelerated towards the second defender, before stopping on a sixpence and sending the player flying past him like some out-of-control Superman. Jimmy accelerated again from a standing start to top speed in just a few strides, ducked inside the third desperate opponent and arched his back as he did so to avoid his despairing grasp. Then he sprinted ten metres at a blistering pace and sent out the most accurate and perfectly timed pass to Kitty, who ran the remaining thirty metres at breakneck speed to the posts. It was her fourteenth try of the three-and-a-half-hour game.

Peter Clement was open mouthed.

'Will,' he breathed, 'I've said it before and I'll say it again: that boy is special.'

Will was so proud, he didn't really know what to say. So he just reached into his bag and pulled out some of the contents. 'Thanks Peter,' he said. 'Have some tomatoes.'

Out on the field, Mike was losing his mind.

'The Ghost, The Ghost! I told you he was a ghost!' screamed Jimmy's former enemy, jumping up and down and punching the air at having witnessed Jimmy's exceptional brilliance.

Then, doing an impromptu rap that brought the whole group to their knees laughing, at the top of his voice, Mike spat out some bars!

'I'm tellin' ya, he's The Ghost, man. He does things that no one else can.

He stops, he starts, he comes, he goes, nobody can touch him with his magic toes.

To the left, to the right you gotta give up the fight – all right!

Because – and I know it most – that Jimmy boy, man, he's THE Ghost!'

Even though they were laughing, everyone was actually very impressed and Jimmy began the applause, which saw Mike take a theatrical bow. But just as the clapping died down, Ryan, who had somehow managed to play the game while eating his way through an energy bar triple pack said, 'Not bad, Mike, not bad at all . . . but it's hardly Stormzy is it?'

Mike's lunge and mock attack of Ryan had the group falling about in laughter all over again.

BACK TO SCHOOL

The yard at Central Primary had that fantastic first-day-back-at-school buzz all around it.

New shoes, new trainers, new backpacks, new haircuts. It was a day everybody loved. Jimmy, Matt, Kitty and Manu were all in the top yard, chatting ten to the dozen.

Manu quietly reached into his pristine new backpack.

'Look at this little beauty then, you lot!' he shouted. 'This. Is. Mint!'

The friends turned around, and there in Manu's hands was what appeared to be a brand new Gilbert rugby ball. It was magnificent.

'Yeah, and look at this,' said Manu excitedly, spinning the ball around in his fingers before pointing to the logo printed on it. It had a red cross, which sat above a blue and white shield. The shield contained a palm tree at the top, and four white stars, that seemed set out like a cross in the sky. Underneath, it said 'Samoa Rugby Union' in thick red letters.

'Wow!' exclaimed Matt, 'where did you get that?'

'My uncle, Alapati,' said Manu. They all knew who he was – a superstar player for Bristol Bears and the Samoan national team. 'He played for Samoa against Fiji in the summer, and when he came back to the UK last week to start the new season, he gave it to my dad for me to have. It's an actual match ball from a real Test match!'

Jimmy was silent, his mouth hanging open.

Manu grinned and tossed him the ball. 'Go on, Jim, kick us a high one! I'm gonna play with this anyway,' and Manu delved into his bag and pulled out a bright orange reaction ball, exactly like the one they'd played with at the Memorial Ground a few months earlier. 'I've been practising, my reflexes are bang on now . . . I'd even beat you now, Kit.' He laughed and waved the odd-looking ball in her face.

But Jimmy was oblivious to Manu's messing. He was completely captivated as he held the ball gently in his hands, almost too in awe to do anything. Then he sprang to life.

'Stand back then, this is about to go into orbit!'

As Jimmy leaned back to give himself the best possible angle to get height on the ball, he heard the quiet, yet firm words of Mr Davies, the headteacher, who had walked up to join the group.

'Jimmy. Now you wouldn't be thinking of kicking that ball in the yard would you? I seem to recall the last time you did that, things didn't work out that well for you.'

Jimmy stopped dead in his tracks, and quickly passed the ball back to Manu.

'No sir, definitely not, sir. I wasn't going to do that.'

Mr Davies smiled broadly. 'Good boy, I know you're much more sensible than that.' Then he turned to Jimmy's friends, theatrically rolling his eyes, and clapped his hands together.

'Right, Manu, pop that ball and that weird-looking tennis ball thing back in your bag until later. I've got a job for you four before school starts. I want you to come and help move some of the new chairs from the hall into your class. Oh, and while you're all there, I'll be able to introduce you to your new teacher, Mrs John. I think you're all going to like her.'

Then turning to Kitty, Mr Davies said. 'And in particular, you Kitty, I think you're going to be very happy with my new appointment. Very happy indeed.'

READING FOR PLEASURE

Mrs John thanked the quartet for helping and asked them all to take their seats with the rest of the class as they shuffled into the room. She noticed that Jimmy had stacked three books on his desk that he'd brought back from the library.

'Keen reader then, Jimmy?'

'As long as it's about sport, Miss,' he replied. 'And preferably rugby, but yes, I love reading. I try to read something every day.'

'That's great to hear,' she replied. 'I happen to believe that reading is the key to success in life . . . you'll probably get fed up with me telling you all that throughout the year!'

'No, it's okay, Miss. My dad tells me exactly the same. He reads loads of sports autobiographies, you know, life stories of people?'

Mrs John nodded enthusiastically.

'But he won't let me read any of those yet because they've usually got lots of swearing in them – but I have had a peek at a few of them!'

'Yes,' replied Mrs John with a crooked smile, 'your dad's quite right, I don't think those books are right for you just yet, maybe best to stick with those you've got from our library . . . is that a Tom Palmer one?'

'Yes, Miss, it's called *Over the Line*. It's not rugby, it's football – which is okay as I really like that, too – but it's set during the First World War. I'm really looking forward to it.'

'That's excellent! We'll be doing the First World War as a class topic after half term, it will fit in very nicely with our commemorations for Remembrance Day on 11th November.'

Mrs John stopped for a moment and thought.

'In fact, I'm pretty sure I've seen on Twitter that Tom Palmer does school author visits to talk about his books, maybe I'll look into that.'

'That would be fantastic!' exclaimed Jimmy, 'I've read all his Rugby Academy books, they're great, it would be brilliant to meet him and ask him how he gets his ideas for his books!'

'Well, let's see what we can do. I'll have a chat to Mr Davies to see what he thinks.'

All the time that Mrs John had been talking to Jimmy, Kitty hadn't taken her eyes off her new teacher. Or, perhaps more accurately, the badge she wore on her tracksuit top.

It was the badge of the Welsh Women's Rugby team, of which Mrs John had been the most recent captain, until her retirement at the end of the previous season. At least, that's what Mr Davies had told Kitty out in the yard.

Kitty was instantly star-struck by Mr Davies's words. She couldn't believe that she'd finally meet a person who had achieved the very thing that Kitty most wanted to achieve herself: to become an international women's rugby player. Everyone in Central Primary knew that Jimmy was obsessed with rugby, but in Kitty's case, many just thought it was a phase she was going through. Even Kitty's own mother didn't really believe that her daughter's interest in the rough and tumble of rugby was anything more than just a passing fad. But she couldn't have been more wrong. If anything, Kitty was more obsessed than Jimmy, it's just that she downplayed it more than her friend because she knew that some of her family and friends didn't really approve. Her Aunt Annie was probably the worst. Kitty and her aunt couldn't have been more different, Annie favouring all the material things in life like multiple handbags, outrageous jewellery and a seemingly permanent tan. When she first heard that her niece was taking part in rugby sessions, she actually visited her sister, Kitty's mum, and offered to pay for ballet lessons because they were run at the same time as rugby training. Kitty was furious. Initially, Kitty's mother had agreed; she didn't hate the thought of her daughter playing rugby as much as her sister did, but she did hope that something like ballet would help move her away from the aggressive nature of a boys' sport.

'That's just the point, Mum,' said Kitty at the time, struggling to hide her fury, 'it's not just a boys' sport anymore. Have you had your head in the sand? Haven't you heard of Emily Scarratt and Poppy Cleall? Or Portia Woodman and Jaz Joyce?'

Kitty's mum just looked back at her with a completely vacant look on her face.

'You haven't heard of Jaz Joyce?' snorted Kitty in despair. 'She's incredible!'

There was still no reply from her mother.

'She's already been to the Olympics and plays on the wing for Bristol Bears. I watched the try she scored for Wales in the Rugby Sevens against New Zealand over and over, it was brilliant. She is brilliant! I want to be like her, Mum, not some ballerina dancing to a song out of *Beauty and the Beast*.'

Kitty's mum knew there and then that it was pointless to argue and while she would have preferred her daughter to be a prospective ballerina rather than a rugby winger, she couldn't fail to recognise Kitty's passion. Her husband had too and he'd spent as much time as possible helping Kitty master the basics of the game so that she had the solid foundations from which she might flourish. Her Aunt Annie had hardly spoken to Kitty since the ballet lessons snub, but that was okay, Kitty could live with that. If anything, it made her more determined to prove people like her auntie wrong. And to do that, Kitty's single ambition was to play for her country in the Six Nations and now, with the appointment of Mrs John, she might just have found the perfect person to help her.

That morning, when they started to move the chairs from the hall, as soon as Kitty had seen the badge Mrs John was wearing, she asked her new teacher about it.

Mrs John had initially tried to brush it off, as if she didn't want to talk about it. As proud as she was about playing for and captaining her country, she was very modest, almost shy about her achievements and didn't want to be seen to be showing off. She'd only worn the tracksuit because Mr Davies had told her that she would be taking games on her first day, because of his strong belief in the importance of regular, meaningful sporting activity for young people.

However, Mrs John noticed that Kitty could hardly take

her eyes off the badge on her tracksuit, so eventually called her over.

'Well, I've heard all about you, Kitty,' said Mrs John, 'It sounds to me like you're developing into a very serious rugby player.'

Kitty blushed. She didn't really know what to say. Mrs John was impressed by her modesty.

'She's one of our very best players,' Jimmy had said, walking past, carrying two chairs. 'There's nobody faster in our school . . . and she can really tackle too!'

Kitty looked at Jimmy and smiled. She understood the irony of his comment. She also understood her great good fortune to now have a teacher who had trodden exactly the same path that she wanted to follow so much. Kitty knew that she could have nobody better to help her to chase her own, personal rugby dream.

Now, with all the pupils sitting in their chosen seats – Jimmy next to Kitty, Matt next to Manu – and having taken the register, Mrs John addressed the class.

'Good morning everyone, I'm Mrs John, and I'll be your teacher this year.'

She then went on to give a little bit of information about herself, what school she had previously taught at – it was one in the big city about thirty miles up the motorway – and how she and her husband had moved back to the town where he had grown up. She then explained that while it would take a little time to get to know everyone, she had just two basic rules to her teaching, that she believed everything else flowed down from.

'The first one,' she said, 'is to always be polite, kind and helpful to everyone in this class.' All the pupils in Year 6 nodded. 'I won't accept anything less than that. And the second one, is to just try your very best at everything that you do . . . I want you all to "be the best that you can be". Does everyone understand those two rules?'

A chorus of: 'Yes, Miss,' rang out from all the Year 6s. Except for one pupil at the back who remained silent. In fact, when everyone said, 'Yes, Miss,' quite loudly, he quickly shot his hands up over his ears as if the sound had caused him pain.

Mrs John noticed.

'Oh, and one last thing,' she said smiling fondly. 'We have a second new person who, like me, is starting at Central Primary for the first time today. It's Oscar, sitting over there.' She pointed to the back corner of the class. 'Welcome, Oscar.'

The rest of the class looked round to see a handsome, blond-haired boy, the only one in the class sitting alone, who was busy setting out his pens, pencils, rubbers, reading book and workbook in neat order on his desk. He was concentrating so much on lining everything up, that he hadn't paid much attention to Mrs John introducing him to the rest of the class.

'Now I know you'll make Oscar as welcome to your class as you've already made me,' continued Mrs John. 'It's never easy coming to a new school, so I ask that you all be as kind as you can to Oscar and help him settle in quickly.'

Everyone nodded.

Jimmy turned to Kitty instantly and whispered.

'That's the boy from the park, isn't it? The one who has autism who you said wanted to fit in?'

Kitty nodded but said quietly, 'Not has *autism*, Jimmy. Is *autistic*.'

Jimmy was annoyed with himself.

'Yeah, sorry. Forgot.' He looked back at Oscar, sitting on his own, and felt sad. He raised his hand. 'Excuse me, Miss.'

'Yes Jimmy? What can I do for you?'

'Well, I was wondering if I could go and sit by Oscar? You know, just to help him feel at home in class while he gets used to things. I can show him where everything is. Sort of help him fit in?'

'Creep,' whispered Matt jokingly to Manu. Manu smiled.

'What a lovely thought, Jimmy,' replied Mrs John. 'Yes, you can, that would be a really good idea.'

Then, looking at Kitty, Mrs John said. 'But that will leave Kitty on her own.'

Jimmy looked at his friend as he was getting his things together, and replied, 'Oh, that's okay Miss, Kitty will be fine . . . she's as tough as old boots.'

Jimmy just about managed to avoid Kitty's dig in his ribs as he swept up everything from his desk.

AN APP MASTERCLASS

Jimmy spent the bulk of the morning with Oscar. It was a little bit of a struggle at first. Oscar was perfectly polite, but seemed very shy and guarded. Jimmy noticed that every time Mrs John popped over to see if Oscar and Jimmy were getting on with a certain task, Oscar would almost visibly tighten and briefly rub his hands together – almost flapping them – as if it somehow comforted him. Then, when he saw Jimmy glance at his hands, he'd stop. Jimmy sensed that Oscar was a little uptight, so decided not to bombard him with lots of questions. Instead, he tried to treat him exactly as he would if he were working on a task with anyone else in the class.

After break, Mrs John asked Jimmy if he'd show Oscar where everything was: the stationery cupboard, the iPad charging station, the cloakroom, the toilets, and anything else that Jimmy could think of that Oscar might need to know. Jimmy noticed that during break, Oscar had stayed indoors, in the library.

'Why don't you come out and join us at lunchtime, Oscar?' he asked. 'We only mess about playing rugby or tag, that sort of thing.'

'I don't really like crowds,' said Oscar, 'especially when the place is new to me. But thanks for asking.'

'No problem,' said Jimmy as they walked over to the storage area between the Year 5 and 6 classes where the banks of iPads were kept. Jimmy knew it might be impolite, but he just thought it might help to get it out of the way.

'Kitty said that you've got autism.'

Without looking up, Oscar quickly replied: 'No, I haven't got autism, I'm autistic . . . there's a difference.'

Jimmy could've kicked himself. He'd made the same mistake again.

'Sorry, sorry, yes, Kitty said that before, I got confused. I'm stupid.'

Oscar looked up at Jimmy for the first time. 'It's okay, most people make the same mistake, mainly because they don't understand. It's sometimes difficult to get across to people as most think we're . . . kind of ill or something.'

'No. I'm really sorry, I didn't mean it like that, I guess it's just that I've never met a person with autism . . .'

Jimmy stopped immediately when Oscar shot him a glance.

'I mean, I've never met an autistic person before. I'd just like to understand more about it. You know, to help you fit in.'

Oscar paused and didn't say anything for a moment. 'Thank you. We moved here because at my last school, a group of boys were unkind to me . . . very unkind. That's why I find it difficult sometimes to make friends straight away. But I'm glad to meet you, Jimmy. I hope we can be friends.'

'Yes, we definitely will, Oscar. Definitely. Anyway, come on, let me show you the iPad trolleys. There are very strict rules to using them.'

Oscar nodded and he seemed very interested in the iPads.

'Okay,' said Jimmy, 'these are the basic rules. You must always make sure that the iPad you put back is plugged in to charge and that they are put back in their number order. Also, you must never take one out unless you get permission from the teacher, they're very strict about that.'

Jimmy leaned forward to slot twenty-two and pulled out the iPad to show Oscar the sticker with number twenty-two on it. He handed it to him and Oscar asked for the passcode.

As the iPad sprung to life, Oscar quickly scanned the apps. 'Ooh great, *Comic Life*, that's a brilliant one.' Jimmy smiled, he loved that one too, although he wasn't very good at it, he always had trouble getting the fonts to fit his cartoon properly.

'*Explain Everything*, that's another good one, great.'

'That's hard!' exclaimed Jimmy. 'Mr Lloyd tried to show us that one last year, before he retired. I don't think he knew what he was doing to be honest, so what chance would we have?'

'It's tricky,' agreed Oscar, flicking quickly through the apps, eyes not leaving the device, quickly scanning everything the iPad contained. 'I can help you with that, it's fun to use.'

'You seem to know a lot about iPads,' said Jimmy as Oscar continued his almost forensic search through the apps.

'Yes, I've always had one. I particularly like the ones that use images. I'm not great with my writing, especially in books, but I much prefer using pictures to tell stories, it's fun.' Then, showing obvious delight that he'd found the app he'd been looking for, he cried, '*Book Creator*!'

'It's never worked,' said Jimmy, 'at least, Mr Lloyd never got it to.'

Oscar tapped on the icon, nothing happened. The app seemed to freeze. Oscar quickly held the home and power button down together, waited twenty seconds, then pressed the power button. The Apple logo soon appeared. 'This works sometimes,' he said.

Once the iPad came back to life, Oscar tapped in the passcode – he'd remembered it even though he'd only been told it that once – and tapped on the *Book Creator* app. Again nothing. Without saying anything, Oscar quickly tapped on the Settings icon and looked for 'Software Update'. It said 'Updates Available'.

'There, that's why it's not working. The software on the iPad isn't up to date. In fact, it's way out of date. When that happens, and updates have happened to the individual apps, they sometimes stop working. The same thing happened at my last school. There was nobody who knew how to fix it.'

'I think we'd better speak to Mrs John then. Mr Pullen used to sort all the iPad stuff but he left a couple of years ago. Since then, nobody's really looked after the iPads, apart from making sure they're always charged.'

'I can see that. The version of *Book Creator* you're running is well out of date. Well, once they're updated, they can be used properly. We've got to get *Book Creator* working, I wrote a great rugby book once. It had loads and loads of pictures. I was sorry I had to leave the last school before I was able to download it to my own iPad to keep.'

'Oh, you like rugby?' asked Jimmy excitedly.

Still focusing on the iPad in his hands, Oscar responded quickly, 'Yes, love it. My favourite sport. Not to play, though, too rough! But I love to watch it on TV. Have you heard of the All Blacks?'

Jimmy laughed. 'Yes, I have, Oscar. I have.'

At lunch, Oscar went to the library to eat, so Jimmy quickly caught up with Kitty, Matt and Manu in the yard.

'Oh, look out, here he comes, teacher's pet!' shouted Matt as Jimmy approached.

'Haha, very good,' said Jimmy and pretended to lunge for Matt, who swerved out the way.

'What's he like then?' asked Matt. 'He looks like a bit of hard work to me.'

Jimmy frowned. So did Kitty.

'Nah, he's all right,' said Jimmy. 'He's just a bit different, that's all. He's nice – and he loves rugby, too.'

Matt wasn't impressed. 'Well,' he said, 'from the way he walks around looking like he's afraid of his own shadow, I can't imagine he's any good . . . I can't see him bringing down Andrew Beasley, put it that way!' Matt laughed but nobody else did and Kitty walked off, unimpressed.

Matt looked suitably embarrassed.

'Well,' replied Jimmy, trying to brush over the awkwardness, 'he might not be the next Sam Warburton, but he makes you look like a caveman with what he knows about apps on an iPad. I learned more sitting next to Oscar this morning than I did in almost a whole year with old Mr Lloyd.'

'Yeah, but did you see the state of his handwriting when Mrs John asked him to start his story plan?' said Matt. 'He was the one that wrote like a caveman!'

'And how did you get on making a voice note on *Explain Everything* then?'

Matt blushed. He just couldn't get the hang of synchronising the record button with starting his speech. Mrs John had to show him about five times before he got the hang of it.

'Was it just the one you managed to do on your own?'

'How many did your new best mate manage, then?' bit back Matt.

'He did six – and he helped me with three of mine.'

'Well goody for him,' he scoffed. 'And what's with that hand flapping stuff?'

Kitty was leaning against a nearby wall pretending to ignore them, but couldn't help but step in. 'He's different,' she snapped. 'Is that so hard to get your head around? He's got different strengths and weaknesses to us. How many times have we got to tell you?'

Matt turned away, realising he may have to start keeping his thoughts about Oscar to himself. The group fell into an awkward silence.

'Well, I like him,' said Manu, 'and if he loves this game so much,' he said, flicking his prized Samoan rugby ball into the air, 'we'll have to figure out a way to let him join in.' And with that, he passed his new rugby ball straight to Kitty, who passed to Jimmy, who flicked it straight to Matt, who dropped it.

Everybody laughed, except Matt. As he jogged forward to pick the ball up, he felt angry. But the odd thing was, he really didn't know why.

FAMILY TIES

That first week back at school really flew for Jimmy. In fact, as he walked home on the Friday, he turned to Kitty and said, 'You know what, I don't think I've ever had such an enjoyable week at school. It was certainly better than last year when Mr Kane took over from Mr Lloyd!'

Kitty laughed, 'Yeah, you can say that again!'

As Jimmy headed for his front door, Kitty called after him.

'I'm really proud of you, Jim.'

He blushed, 'Why?'

'You've been awesome with Oscar. I really thought you were only going to sit by him that first morning, but it's been brilliant how you've stayed by him all week. You've really helped him, and I've noticed how much more relaxed he is around people as a result.'

Jimmy looked bashfully at the floor. 'Oh, it's nothing,' he mumbled. Then he looked up and broke into a smile. 'I've got to be honest, he helps *me* half the time. The stuff he knows about the functionality of different apps is incredible! I learn so much from him, I'm much more confident in class than I've been before. It's just a shame he struggles so much to write stuff down when we get our tasks to do. He gets frustrated and I know he feels bad about it, especially when people make a joke of how bad his writing is.'

Kitty nodded. 'Yeah, that's a shame, but it's just part of who he is. And, as you say, he has other strengths. What's nice is that Mrs John seems to understand him too, so she just encourages him to work on his strengths. I really like her.'

'She really likes you too!' said Jimmy with a knowing smile. This time it was Kitty's turn to blush. 'She hardly leaves you alone, especially when you both start talking rugby!'

Kitty laughed, hardly able to contain her joy. 'I know, she's so fantastic. She's even played alongside Jaz Joyce! She's given me so much advice already about how Jaz trains and prepares and what I need to do to improve. She said yesterday that she'd never seen a girl so young, so . . . Oh, I can't remember the word she used now.'

'Accomplished,' interrupted Jimmy.

'How did you know?' exclaimed Kitty.

'I heard her!' he said, with a laugh. 'What she actually said was, "Kitty, having watched you in the games lessons we've had, I've never seen a girl so young, so accomplished at rugby, both with skills and attitude."'

Kitty blushed again.

'She's right though, Kit. And she'd know – she's captained her country!'

'I know, isn't it fantastic?' said Kitty. 'It really makes my dreams of playing rugby for my country somehow more realistic. You know, actually knowing someone who's done it and from a similar background to mine. I can't wait until she starts taking us for proper rugby training next week!'

'Me too!' replied Jimmy, moving again towards his house. 'Down The Rec later?'

'Yeah, I'll be there about half five.'

As Jimmy walked into the house, he was ambushed by Jonny, who jumped out from behind the door to the front room, frightening Jimmy with a loud shout. He did it often, yet he managed to get Jimmy to jump out of his skin every single time.

Jimmy screamed. Jonny laughed.

'Will you stop that?! You're going to give me a heart attack one day!'

Jonny continued laughing, 'Every time, ref, every time!'

'Oh, shut up,' replied Jimmy, swinging his backpack at him.

'Oi, stop messing about you two,' shouted their younger sister, Julie, as she came down the stairs. 'Come on, kitchen, now. A meeting.'

The boys followed her in and were presented with a pile of ingredients that she'd laid out on the kitchen top.

'Right. Mum's had a double shift today, so we're going to make her tea. Corned beef hash with roasted veg.'

Jimmy and Jonny looked at the mound of food that had to be peeled, prepared and cooked. They both gave a shrug, but neither of them minded. They knew that they had to help out for their mum, and with Julie in charge, it was easy enough to get things done. She ran it like a military operation . . . she clearly got her organisational skills from their grandfather.

Jimmy walked over to the kitchen radio, turned it on and found Bay FM, the local radio station, and turned the volume up. He loved having music on in the kitchen when they were all in there together. After their parents' divorce, the three of them had become such a tight unit. They would literally do anything for each other.

After about twenty minutes of peeling, chopping and cutting, Jonny gave Jimmy a nudge.

'Oh, Jim. Forgot to tell you. Weekend after next over at Briton Bridge RFC, there's a sevens touch rugby tournament.'

Jimmy's ears pricked up at the news.

'Really? That's great news! I've got to play in that!'

'Unlucky, sonny boy, that ain't happening for you! It's secondary school kids and above, so you'll just have to come and watch me take the opposition apart!'

Jimmy felt a pang of disappointment but wasn't too glum at the news – he loved watching his brother play.

Everything that Jimmy was now doing, Jonny had already done. Jimmy knew he was a good player, but he knew, deep down, that Jonny was even better. He probably wasn't as quick off the mark as Jimmy, but in everything else, Jimmy thought Jonny was way ahead. He could read a game brilliantly, could kick the ball a mile, hardly missed with a penalty or conversion. And tackling? Boy, could Jonny tackle! He hit people like a tank! It was the one thing that Jimmy couldn't talk to Jonny about, his newly developed phobia of tackling. He was worried that Jonny would think less of him. So Jimmy would keep that little secret to himself for a while yet. But the good news was that a sevens touch rugby competition wouldn't involve tackling . . . just running. And Jimmy knew that he could do that as well as anyone. He just had to try and find a way to be able to play in it.

'When did you say the tournament was?'

'Week next Saturday. Get Mum to bring an extra deckchair for you so that you can sit and watch my brilliance.' And with that, laughing to himself, Jonny picked up the last potato to peel.

'Yeah right,' replied Jimmy with a thoughtful look on his face.

Then, lost in his own dreams, he thought to himself, *I'm not going to need any deck chair to sit on . . . I'm going to be playing.*

ANYONE FOR SEVENS?

The excitement was everywhere at Briton Bridge Rugby Club. Players, coaches, friends, families, supporters; it was a truly fantastic community sporting occasion.

The weather also helped. Even though it was late September, it could have been high June. It hadn't rained once since the kids had gone back to school three weeks earlier and, as a result, all six pitches at the club were in absolutely perfect condition for a touch rugby tournament. Firm, fast, no ruts or divots, just the most perfect of surfaces for flowing, running, exciting rugby.

Jimmy was a little bit like a fish out of water at first. He'd spoken to his dad in the week leading up to the tournament, to see if there was any way that he'd be able to get him a spot on the Wolves junior team. His dad was the physio for the Wolves first team and Jimmy had hoped that he might be able to pull a few strings to get Jimmy playing, but sadly for him, the club had turned down his father's request.

'I really tried, Jim, I nagged and nagged, but they just won't have it, son,' his father had told him a few days earlier. 'All their players are twelve and above, they just said that they wouldn't allow a ten-year-old to play. It's the rule of Mr Tompkins, the chairman of Briton Bridge and organiser of the tournament, and he's a real stickler for doing things right. I'm really sorry. I tried my best.'

Jimmy wasn't upset – he understood the reasoning behind their decision – but he was incredibly frustrated. As he sat in the sun and watched some of the junior teams warming up, Jimmy knew that, even at his age, his speed and handling ability would have been good enough to play. Disappointed, he leaned back in his deckchair next to his mum. Jonny had been right, Jimmy was going to have to sit and watch his talented big brother. Despite his own personal frustrations and disappointments, he still managed to enjoy watching. And that was mainly because of the brilliance of his big brother.

Jonny was the captain of his school team, Bishopswood, and he stood head and shoulders above everyone else on the pitch. One of the best moments came from a turnover on his own line. The ball was back-heeled to Jonny and he dummied to give a pass inside. Because the opposition were still reorganising their defence after the turnover, Jonny spotted a gap to the right of the spot where the game was restarted and went for it. He was lucky that the gap he went through was between two players that were normally flankers and not backs, but it didn't really matter. He was gone. It was a length-of-the-field try and Jimmy laughed at both the joy of seeing his brother score such a great try and at his mother next to him, jumping up and down and screaming.

Jonny's team crushed the opposition from that point on, running in try after try. Then, just about a minute before the end of the game, one of Jonny's teammates, a centre by the name of Max, went over on his ankle trying to keep his foot in play. Unbeknown to Max, someone had left a can of Coke on the grass which had been knocked on to the edge of the pitch. As he darted around the opposition winger, Max's foot had come down flush on the can, which ruptured, twisting Max's ankle as it did. The scream Max gave out was awful, and people initially thought he'd broken it, but after he'd been attended to, the doctor announced that it was just a very bad sprain and no broken bones. But that was Max's tournament over.

At the end of the game, rather than wait around, Jimmy moaned to his mother that he was hungry, so she gave him money for a hot dog.

As Jimmy walked back to his mum, hoping she'd forget to ask him for her change, he savoured every bite of the hot dog. It was delicious – and made all the better because Mr Francis, who was running the hot dog stall, had given him an extra sausage. 'It'll help you develop your muscles,' he smiled as he forced a second sausage into the bun. There were no complaints from Jimmy.

As Jimmy arrived back at his deckchair, he could see Jonny sitting in it, looking a bit glum.

'Cheer up,' said Jimmy between the mouthfuls, 'you're through to the next round, you should be smiling.'

'No point smiling if we can't play,' replied Jonny.

'What are you talking about?' said Jimmy, looking puzzled.

'Because Max is injured, they're short of a player,' said their mum. 'Kieron was due to be sub but he hasn't turned up.

Nobody knows why. He might be down with that bug that's been going around.'

'And with just six fit players, we're not allowed to play our second-round game,' said Jonny, his face a picture of abject disappointment.

'Yes you can,' said Jimmy quickly, handing his half-eaten hot dog to his mum. 'I'll play.'

'You can't, Jim,' said Jonny. 'You're too young. I told you last week, it's for secondary age groups only.'

'But this is an emergency, surely they'll bend the rules. Come on, we won't know until we ask.'

By now, Jimmy's grandparents had arrived, annoyed that they had missed the first game because of confusion over the start time. Jimmy's grandfather listened to his grandsons discussing the situation and then turned to them and said, 'Well, I'm not going to stand here and pass up the opportunity of watching my two grandsons play in the same team together, that's for sure. I'm going to speak to Terry Jeffries, he's the secretary of this club. He owes me a favour or two from way back.'

'He's not the organiser though, Gramp,' said Jonny, still with his face in his boots. 'Dad told Jimmy that it's Mr Tompkins – and you know how strict he is about everything. He's already warned us that nobody from the schools tournament is allowed inside the clubhouse today, it's adults only. He's so miserable that he won't change the rules for Jimmy.'

'And that's precisely why I'm going to speak to Terry and not him,' said Will. '"Tomcat" Tompkins will be too busy running the adult tournament anyway, I just saw him on number one pitch when we walked in here. What he doesn't know, won't hurt him. Leave it with me.'

And with that, their grandfather marched off to find Terry Jeffries. After five paces, he stopped and turned.

'Oh, and Jonny. Get your brother a jersey. He's going to need it.'

MAKING UP THE NUMBERS

Will had managed to sort things out, so in the green and gold jersey of Bishopswood for the first time ever, Jimmy lined up on the field. Concerned by Jimmy's age and size, the coach had put him on the wing. Jimmy looked across to the opposition. They looked big.

Jonny jogged across and spoke quickly to his brother.

'Look, just stay out wide and concentrate on not letting their wing get past you. This is going to be much quicker than you're used to. Some of these boys are three years older than you, and whilst it's touch rugby, don't be surprised if one or two give you a bit of a bang. I'm here to sort any of that out for you if it happens. Right?'

Instead of thanking his brother, Jimmy just looked at him and replied, 'Why has he stuck me out here, Jonny? I can't do anything out on the wing, it's pointless.'

'It's not pointless,' snapped Jonny. 'He knows how young you are and wants to protect you.'

'I don't need protecting,' said Jimmy indignantly.

'Yes, you do,' said Jonny with a little bit of anger in his voice. 'Just stay out of trouble, Jim, take things easy and remember – you're just on here to make up the numbers for us, nothing else.'

And with that, Jonny jogged back to his position in the centre of the back line.

'Just here to make up the numbers,' muttered Jimmy to himself. 'We'll see about that.'

Even though sevens matches are competed over two halves of seven minutes, in the schools tournament, the halves were reduced to five minutes each. In the first four minutes of Bishopswood's second-round game, Jimmy literally did just make up the numbers. His team were on top, spending lots of time in the opposition half, but with nothing to show for it. Every time it looked like one of the players would break through, one of the players from Johnstown RFC would manage to touch them. Jonny had been the busiest of Jimmy's teammates, but every time he was in space and seemed to naturally drift towards Jimmy's wing, he'd glance across at his younger brother and then instantly switch direction the other way, even if it meant getting touched. He just didn't want to risk involving Jimmy. Jonny was trying to protect his younger brother, but all he was really doing was frustrating him. With four minutes gone in this game of winner-takes-all touch rugby, Jimmy hadn't touched anything, not a ball or a player, and he was beginning to stew.

Then, just as Jimmy thought that he was going to see out the half without making any contribution whatsoever, Jonny got touched right in the middle of the pitch, around the halfway line. As the Bishopswood scrum-half rushed forward to take the back heel from Jonny, he decided to break towards Jimmy on the right wing. Jimmy got ready, hoping he'd finally get his touch of the ball.

The Johnstown defender rushed up on the scrum-half quickly. The scrum-half knew he couldn't risk getting touched as it would have been the sixth touch of the play and would've resulted in a turnover, so he quickly passed to his teammate, Joe, who had looped around behind him. The pass wasn't great and had allowed another defender to rush straight up on Joe. The spectators watching couldn't be sure if it was panic or brilliance that happened next, but whatever it was, Joe threw a fantastic, long looping pass off his left hand, out to the right wing. To Jimmy.

And Jimmy was ready.

Because the ball was passed in such a loopy fashion, the pace on the pass died on Jimmy as it reached him, and he had to pluck it up from his toes, just an inch or two above the grass. It was a brilliant pick-up. But the other problem of the pace dying on the ball was that it meant Jimmy took it standing still, not moving forward as he'd have liked. Jimmy looked up instantly, assuming his opposite wing would be right up on him. However, for reasons known only to the wing, he had dropped back a few yards and had actually drifted in-field, caught out by the long pass by Joe.

The space ahead of Jimmy down the right wing now opened up in front of him, but instead of sprinting into it, Jimmy veered to his left, towards the winger.

Watching on the touchline, Jimmy's grandfather shouted out, 'The space, Jimmy, run into the space, go down the line!'

But Jimmy ignored him and continued running straight at the winger.

Just as he was about to bundle into the winger and obviously be touched, Jimmy sort of jumped into the air, with a hitch kick that looked as if he was considering hurdling the opposition player. This confused the defender, who went low to touch Jimmy around the legs, but as Jimmy landed on the ground following the little jump, he dummied to the left, before sweeping the opposite way, outside of the reach of the despairing dive of the winger.

It then became apparent why Jimmy had initially run inside. He knew that if he had run straight, he'd have been isolated by the covering full back and touched by him, losing possession, because there would have been nobody in support for Jimmy to pass to. What Jimmy's run in-field had done was give a precious amount of time to allow his teammates to regroup and get closer to him. Jimmy had no intention of going for the try. He was looking to draw the full back and pass inside to a teammate – any teammate – who could get up alongside him.

Following the hitch kick and dummy that had worked so well, Jimmy delivered a burst of speed that drew a gasp from the watching supporters. This time, he did head for the space, back out towards the right touchline. Jonny, realising what was happening, had made a run – unseen by the opposition – directly from where he had been touched just moments before Jimmy got the ball. The angle that Jonny ran at was perfect to receive an inside pass from Jimmy – if Jimmy could see him.

Jimmy had seen him, but so had the opposition defence. In the time that Jimmy had run in-field, a second defender had come across to help his full back out on the wing, so now Jimmy was faced with two defenders before the try line. Sprinting as fast as he could towards the touchline, Jimmy drew the first defender. Just as it looked as if Jimmy would have to be touched or run out of room and into touch, he delivered a repeat of his earlier delicious sidestep. By arching his body away from the grasp of the cover tackler and keeping his foot in play by an inch, he was through. That just left the full back.

The full back rushed up on Jimmy in an effort to deny him the space he needed to attempt a third sidestep. But that didn't bother Jimmy. Waiting until the very last second, Jimmy drew the full back, making no effort whatsoever to avoid him. Just as the full back's hands stretched out to touch Jimmy's green shirt, as calm as you like, Jimmy lobbed an over-arm, overhead pass inside which hung in the air like a half-filled helium balloon. Most people had been watching Jimmy, so had not seen Jonny's lung-bursting sprint to get on his inside, and just as they assumed that the ball from Jimmy's pass would bounce safely away, so Jonny met the dropping ball at full speed. He grabbed it without breaking stride. While looking around him and seeing there were no defenders left, he almost stopped running and jogged in under the posts for the first points of the game.

On the sidelines, Will turned to Jimmy's mother.

'Did you see that, Cath? Did you see that?! Jimmy took out three defenders all on his own! That was *class*.'

As Jimmy ran over to congratulate his brother, all the action had happened so quickly that the three Johnstown players were still lying prone on the ground, shaking their heads in disbelief and not really understanding what had just occurred.

'That was brilliant, Jimmy, brilliant!' said Jonny, giving Jimmy a congratulatory high five. 'Great vision.'

Jimmy smiled at his brother, 'Just making up the numbers, Jonny, that's me!'

CENTRE STAGE

The rest of the match was a procession.

Buoyed by the confidence of his run at the end of the first half, Jimmy came in off his wing in the second period and basically stole the show. He was so good, that people who were watching the senior games on the other pitches walked across to watch.

He involved himself in almost every play. The try in the last minute of the first half had knocked the stuffing out of Johnstown and Jimmy took full advantage of their despondency.

In just five minutes of rugby, Jimmy scored three tries. The first was made by his brother. It saw Jonny making a typical break from the back-heel, sending his younger brother skipping in under the posts. But the other two were exceptional, individual, efforts that saw Jimmy running in from the halfway line on both occasions, leaving the Johnstown tacklers in his wake, grasping nothing but fresh air.

Jimmy's performance had been sensational.

At the end, Mr Stanford, the PE teacher from Bishopswood walked over to Jimmy.

'Well, Jimmy. It might only be September, but I can't wait until next September to see you up at Bishopswood so that you can join the team for real. It's going to be a very exciting time for us all.'

'Thank you, sir,' replied Jimmy, blushing as usual whenever he had to field a compliment from someone.

Then, just as Mr Stanford and Jimmy were beginning to talk about where Jimmy would play in the next match, the semi-final against Newford Academy School, a boy rushed up to Mr Stanford, wearing full Bishopswood kit, shouting, 'Sir, sir!'

It was Kieron, the replacement who hadn't turned up earlier. He wasn't ill after all.

'Sir, sir, I'm really sorry, but my dad was late finishing his shift. My mum's car is in the garage, so she couldn't drop me here, so I had to wait. I tried ringing but I couldn't get an answer from anyone, it kept going to answerphone. Am I too late to play?'

Mr Stanford looked at the boy. He hated when players turned up late for training, let alone a match. And in his eyes, turning up late for a tournament was unforgivable, but in fairness, Kieron did seem very sincere in what he was saying.

Before he could say anything, Mr Stanford was joined by Kieron's dad, who, very apologetically, repeated the story. It was clear that Kieron's delay was unavoidable. As a result, Mr Stanford was going to be lenient.

'Okay, okay, I completely understand, these things can't be helped. Normally, I wouldn't tolerate lateness like this, but it's a genuine situation so Kieron can be involved.'

Then, turning to Kieron, he said, 'Get your boots on lad, you'll be replacement in the next match.'

'What?' exclaimed Kieron's father in surprise. 'Replacement? Why replacement? I know you're one short because of the bug and the injury to young Max Robinson – I just saw him with his dad off to A&E for an X-ray. Why is Kieron a replacement? He should be starting!'

'Because of Jimmy,' replied Mr Stanford, calmly. 'He helped us out when it looked like we'd be withdrawn from the tournament, and frankly, he gave one of the finest sevens rugby performances I've ever seen in that second half. He keeps his place, as simple as that. Kieron will get a run if I feel the team needs him.'

'But, but, he's not even in the school!' shouted Kieron's dad, pointing at Jimmy and struggling to control his temper, 'and he's under age, he shouldn't even be on the field.'

'And he wouldn't have been if you'd got your son here on time,' interrupted Mr Stanford, giving the annoyed parent a withering stare, 'and I'll remind you again, if Jimmy hadn't stepped in, there would be no next match to play. We'd have been out of the tournament.'

Mr Stanford turned away from Kieron's dad and addressed his squad.

'Come on boys,' he called, 'we need to talk about this semi-final.'

Kieron's father just watched him and the squad walk away with a rage in his eyes.

Whatever Mr Stanford said to his players before the semi-final against Newford, it worked. The game turned into a rout. But maybe the wisest decision of all was keeping Jimmy in the team.

Mr Stanford changed things, bringing Jimmy in from the

wing to play in the fly-half role, taking over from Jonny who was moved inside to scrum-half. The scrum-half, who had played well enough himself, was moved to the wing.

The Joseph boys dominated the match from the very first minute. But as impressive as Jonny was, it was Jimmy who again stole the show. If it was possible, he played even better than he had in the second half of the previous match. He ran past players like they weren't there, his running as elusive as ever. And, thanks to some outrageous dummies and electrifying pace, he scored all four tries in Bishopswood's dominating performance: one in the first half when things were tight, three in the second when the space opened up a bit.

The buzz that went around the whole tournament was incredible. Even some of the squad players and replacements from the senior tournament that was taking place at the same time had left their matches to come and watch Jimmy. There was a feeling that something special was taking place.

In the last seconds of the match, Jimmy scored his fourth try, out-sprinting the Newford full back after a perfect chip kick on the sixth touch. There didn't seem to be any room for the kick, let alone for Jimmy to get to it before the full back, but it was so perfectly weighted and Jimmy's run so well-timed, that he got there first and dived over in the corner. The roar of the crowd and the applause that followed had to be heard to be believed.

Jonny ran over to his brother, whooping and shouting as he ran, and dragged him up off the floor and hugged him.

'You can definitely make the numbers up for us again, Jim,' said Jonny with genuine pride in his eyes.

Predictably, Jimmy just blushed.

RULES ARE RULES

The final was to be at 4.30 on the main pitch at Briton Bridge RFC, in front of the members' stand. The senior final was at 5.00, so everyone that attended to see both tournaments would be watching. The crowd would be in the hundreds.

Jonny was pacing around like a lion contained in a cage at a zoo. He didn't know what to do with himself. He wasn't nervous, he was just totally wound up for the challenge that awaited him. His grandfather walked across and tried to calm him down, but it was no use. He was totally focused and ready to go. Jonny had always approached his rugby seriously. Very seriously. While he could be a bit of a joker and very popular with his friendship group, Jonny was driven. He had a steely desire that not everyone possessed and his craving for success on a rugby field was unmatched by most. Some people mistook Jonny's approach for some sort of single-minded arrogance, but they were wrong. He just knew that he was a very talented rugby player and, as such, had promised himself to get every ounce out of his talent.

'You've got to leave it all out there, out on that pitch, Jim,' was his oft repeated quote to his brother. 'If you don't walk off there at the end, exhausted, you've got no right being on there in the first place,' was another.

Jonny's commitment to rugby was total, and the way he practically ignored his grandfather's pre-match words of encouragement simply confirmed this.

Will had seen this all before, of course, so decided it was best to leave Jonny, and with a couple of final words of good luck, he went to find his other grandson, whose approach was ever so slightly different.

Jimmy was relaxing back in a camping chair, sipping a drink and just talking to his mother and grandmother as if he was about to have nothing more intense than a quick runabout on The Rec.

Will smiled at the contrast.

'How are you feeling, Jimmy? Only half an hour to go. You're not tired at all? You've put a lot in this afternoon.'

'No, not really, Gramp. Just a bit hungry to be honest, could do with another hot dog I think!'

Catherine laughed. 'Oh, Jimmy. You're so laid back you're nearly horizontal!'

Everybody laughed.

As they did, Will put his hand in his pocket.

'Well it's not exactly a hot dog, but it will give you some energy.'

'Oh, brilliant, a Mars bar! Thanks, Gramp, that's just the job . . . you never let me down,' and Jimmy hungrily tore off the wrapper and took a huge bite.

'Steady, you'll get indigestion, boy, small bites now!'

Just as Jimmy was polishing off the bar, Mr Stanford came over. He didn't look happy. Following behind was Mr Tompkins, the tournament chairman and organiser, dressed in his usual navy-blue club blazer and tie and carrying his clipboard. Alongside him, looking quite smug, was Mr Irwin, Kieron's father. Jimmy knew instantly what this meant. His heart sank to the floor.

'Excuse me, Mrs Joseph, could I have a quick word?'

'Yes, of course,' replied Catherine with a smile. She had no idea what was about to happen.

Before Mr Stanford could continue, Mr Tompkins spoke.

'I'm afraid a clear breach of tournament rules has occurred and your son has played games while being under age. We have these rules in place for the protection of players – and your son has transgressed them.'

'Now wait a minute,' said Mr Stanford. 'This boy helped us out, and his family readily agreed to support him in that decision. If it wasn't for him, you'd have had one less team in the competition. That's what the rugby family is all about, surely? It's about helping out when people are struggling. That's exactly what the boy did.'

'Yes, he did. But what he did was plainly against the tournament rules. And as I'm sure you know, as a man that teaches sport for a living, in sport, rules are rules. Without them we would have anarchy. And I will not allow that in my tournament.'

'Now wait a minute, Tomcat . . .' interjected Will.

'Please don't call me that, Will. In my role as tournament director, I'm to be addressed as Mr Tompkins.'

'Tournament director? Do me a favour, this isn't the blinkin' World Cup, man, it's a kids' competition.'

'Nevertheless,' replied Mr Tompkins with a swish of the hand which dismissed Will's protests, 'as I've clearly outlined, rules are rules, and I'm just thankful that Mr Irwin here brought the situation to my attention.'

Jimmy watched as Mr Stanford shot a glance at Mr Irwin that was laced with anger. If looks could kill, Jimmy thought, he'd be lying on the floor right now.

Mr Irwin looked at Mr Stanford briefly, before turning away.

'How could you?' said Mr Stanford to the parent, who was now looking firmly at the ground.

'I'd like to remind you, Mr Stanford, that my original decision was for Bishopswood to be withdrawn from the final, disqualified and replaced by Newford Academy, the defeated semi-finalists. It was only through the passionate lobbying of Mr Irwin, stating that his son would be able to step into the gap in your team and his willingness not to take action against this young man that persuaded me to change my decision and allow you to play.'

'Take action!' shouted Will at both Mr Tompkins and the now dreadfully embarrassed Mr Irwin. 'What action? Against a ten-year-old kid doing his best to help out and play rugby? I think I'll take some action against you!'

At this point, Mr Stanford stepped in between the two men.

'Leave it, Will. Jimmy's the only loser here and this will just make it worse for him.'

Will looked at his grandson, who was on the verge of tears and realised that his anger wasn't helping.

'Okay, I'm fine, I understand,' said Will to Mr Stanford. 'This just stinks though.'

'As I've said, Will,' said Mr Tompkins, 'rules . . .'

'Yeah, I know, rules are rules,' said Will before turning away in disgust.

Mr Stanford took Jimmy to one side and knelt down to speak to him.

'Jimmy, you've been brilliant. I nearly didn't play you in that first game because I knew it was a risk with you being so young. But getting you out on that pitch has been the best decision I've made in over twenty years of coaching rugby. You've been sensational.'

Jimmy was looking directly down at his bootlaces, using every single part of his mind to avoid bursting into tears, such was the powerful mix of emotions flowing through him.

'I saw things you did out there that will live with me forever, and as I said to you earlier, I cannot wait to have you on my team next year. You are going to go a long, long way in this game, Jimmy, and as disappointed as you feel at the moment, I promise you, this will be something that you probably won't even remember in years to come. Your future is so bright. You've got it all, Jimmy, and I'm going to make it my job from next year to make sure you achieve it all. So don't be too sad about this, it's just a blip.'

A single tear fell from Jimmy's eye, which he quickly wiped away.

Mr Stanford stood and ruffled his hair. 'Make sure you stay and watch us, okay? You're part of this squad and we'll win or lose together. And I know the boys will try and win for you.'

Jimmy nodded and watched as Mr Stanford walked off to tell the rest of the players what had happened.

Jimmy stood next to his mum and grandparents and watched the final. They all hoped for another exciting contest, but it was quite a let down compared to the previous games. So many people who had heard about Mr Tompkins' decision walked up to Jimmy and told him that it was a disgrace and that he should have been playing. If Jimmy had a pound for everyone who said to him and his family that 'he was the best player by a mile', Jimmy would've been a very rich boy.

The game itself was won by just a single try, Jonny brilliantly scoring in the corner in the last minute to seal the victory with a powerful break and dive for the line. Despite his disappointment, Jimmy was really pleased for his brother. He didn't want his own misfortune to spoil Jonny's moment, so he jumped, shouted and cheered with the rest of them.

Jimmy felt a bit sad again when Mr Tompkins wouldn't even allow him to go and collect his winner's medal, but there was one last surprise remaining in this odd day, that would cheer Jimmy up.

In the adult final, Briton Bridge RFC fittingly won the trophy, and to great cheers it was announced how much money the day had raised for Richie Reynolds, an injured former player. Then, after the trophy and medals were handed out, Mr Tompkins announced that the committee had decided that Ellis Curtis, the twenty-six-year-old openside flanker of Briton Bridge, had been voted 'Player of The Tournament' and was asked to come and collect his medal.

When he was handed it, he reached for the microphone from Mr Tompkins.

'I just want to thank you all for coming today,' said Ellis. 'Richie is one of my best friends, and for you all to turn out today and raise such a huge amount of money for him and his family is fantastic, and I know that it will make a huge impact in helping Richie make the full recovery he is heading towards.'

The hundreds who had stayed behind for the presentations, clapped and cheered.

'Today has shown, once again, what a great sport rugby is. But I saw something else today that really lifted my spirits. I watched a kid play a game, the likes of which I've never seen. He showed skill, pace, and sheer rugby brilliance that is only present in very few people and certainly not usual in one so young.'

Shouts of 'Hear, hear' rang out from the crowd.

Ellis continued speaking.

'Then he was dealt some bad news that he coped with brilliantly. Instead of becoming miserable and negative, he stayed and supported his team to the end. I don't think I'd have coped with such a stupid decision so well.'

Mr Tompkins shuffled his feet in embarrassment at that last remark.

'So, for me, I can't accept this Player of the Tournament medal. Instead, I'm giving it to the player that really set this tournament alight, and I hope he uses his success today as a springboard to future achievements. Oh, and if his parents are here, I don't care how old he is, we'll have him in our team here at Briton Bridge RFC any time! So, ladies and gentlemen, your Player of the Tournament, young Jimmy Joseph.'

The gathered crowd applauded and broke into loud cheers, and for the second time in an hour, Jimmy had to battle furiously not to burst into tears.

AYE, AYE, CAPTAIN JOSEPH

Over the next three weeks, Jimmy's life, on and off the rugby field, couldn't have gone better.

Twice a week after school, on Tuesdays and Thursdays, Mrs John took rugby training for every child in Central Primary who wanted to play. After the first week, Jimmy stopped calling it training, and instead renamed it a 'Rugby Masterclass'.

The reason for that was, that as a coach, Mrs John was off the scale – she was amazing. Her focus, from the very first session, was on skills – not on contact or power or hits or smashes, but always on creative rugby and with an emphasis on avoiding contact through speed, sidesteps and quick hands. If ever you were caught in a tackle situation, Mrs John coached ways of offloading the ball. She didn't mind if the offload didn't work. 'We're learning the skill of offloading at the moment,' she would say. 'Not learning the skill of where or when to do it.'

Jimmy found it so refreshing. Gone was the fear of doing the wrong thing at the wrong time or making a mistake that Mr

Kane would slaughter him for. Instead, that fear was replaced by the joy of playing rugby with fun and creativity. Mrs John's approach was that if something went wrong, fine, don't worry about it. Just work out what happened, practise the skill involved and develop a way to ensure it won't go wrong in the future.

She seemed to find a way to simplify everything so that the basic skill at the heart of each drill was easily understood and learned. One drill that Jimmy particularly loved was a very straightforward passing exercise. Mrs John would set up six cones: four red and two green. Jimmy would start the drill standing with one of the red cones just to his right. To his left would be Jimmy's drill partner, usually Kitty, who stood about two metres away, alongside another red cone. Ahead of them, in line with the two red cones by their feet, were another two red cones, about twenty metres away. These four cones would mark out the short-passing zone. On the whistle, Jimmy would pass to Kitty as they both jogged forward, with Kitty returning the pass. This would continue until they reached the top two red cones, where they'd turn and jog back, passing all the way. When they were back at the start, Mrs John would whistle. This would be the sign for Kitty to move further to her left – away from Jimmy to the first of the green cones. The distance between Jimmy and Kitty was now about five metres. Up ahead from where Kitty stood was the other green cone, again about twenty metres ahead, in line with the other two red cones. This larger area was the long-passing zone. On Mrs John's whistle, Jimmy would start to run and send a long pass out to Kitty and they would repeat the pattern. Mrs John would mix it up between short and long passing and get the kids to swap starting positions. She would also get them to carry out the drill at different speeds. Everybody loved it. They were all having great fun but developing their handling and passing skills all the time. Of all of them, Manu was a revelation. His reactions and passing accuracy had come on leaps and bounds since they'd discovered those practice aids at the Memorial Ground.

'Practice makes perfect, Jimmy booooooooooooooy!' exclaimed Manu after one particularly sharp passing drill. Jimmy nodded his approval.

After every training session, Jimmy felt like a better player, but if one player was benefiting more than even Manu, it was Kitty. It turned out, that despite ending up captaining her country from the centre, Mrs John had played all her school and university rugby on the wing. Therefore, there was no better person to coach Kitty than her.

'You're a lucky girl, Kitty, you can't coach speed,' was one of the first things she said to Kitty when she saw her streaking away from Manu in their first practice game. But since then, she had worked with Kitty on just about everything else. 'Every winger must have more than just pace in their armoury,' she said as she put Kitty through a variety of drills that helped her to develop sidesteps, dummies, hitch kicks, and changes of speeds.

And Kitty responded fantastically. She went down to The Rec almost every evening with Jimmy, Matt and Manu to practise all the new skills Mrs John had shown her. On one occasion, after she skinned Manu on the outside – yet again – he waved his arms in mock surrender and said, 'Honestly, this is ridiculous now, that woman has turned you into a rugby monster!' The laughs at that comment confirmed that everyone agreed. Kitty was certainly on the right track to emulate her favourite player, Jaz Joyce.

Above all else to Jimmy, though, was that not in one single session had Mrs John talked about tackling. Obviously there were occasions, in certain drills, where tackling played a part, but Jimmy always seemed to manage to get himself on the attacking side of those drills. Bizarrely, Jimmy had no issues whatsoever when it came to running into contact. Even if it was into a man-mountain like Andrew Beasley, Jimmy would smash into him and try to drive through the contact as if his life depended on it, but on the odd occasion that he was forced to tackle somebody running at him head-on, it was a completely different matter. A feeling of dread and fear would clamp down on him whenever a tackle situation like that presented itself.

Fortunately, apart from Kitty, nobody noticed. Jimmy became a master of timing and manufactured a slip here or a tumble there, just before the tackle, allowing the player to get past, only for Jimmy to pull off a last-second tap tackle to bring his opponent down. He made the slips look so real that he often got applauded by his teammates for his recovery. 'Great effort, Jim,' or 'Well rescued, mate,' would ring out afterwards as he bashfully made his way back to join them, secretly ashamed of his deception. If only they had known the horror he felt, deep inside, at the thought of tackling someone front on, the last thing they'd have done was tell him it was a great effort.

Another trick was to quietly step back a few yards when the opposition had the ball in a practice game. This meant that either Matt on his inside at scrum-half, or Manu on his outside at centre, would naturally be drawn into the hole he had created, to tackle the ball-carrier. Jimmy's plan worked nine times out of ten – especially where Manu was concerned. He tackled for fun, so never once questioned why Jimmy was often out of position – he simply didn't notice.

Off the field, Jimmy's life was great too. Jimmy was still sitting next to Oscar in class and helping him as best he could with things he found tricky to cope with. Jimmy began to understand more and more about autism and tried to ensure the situations that brought stress to Oscar were either managed or avoided completely.

One of the key issues Oscar found difficulty with was dealing with crowds, which was why he often either played alone down on bottom yard at break time or spent it in the library, devouring book after book on his favourite sport, rugby. He would take countless photographs of the pictures in these books and turn them into books of his own using *Book Creator*, or make incredible cartoon stories by transforming the pictures in his other favourite app, *Comic Life*. But it was always the noise and chaos of crowds that really bothered Oscar and increased his anxiety levels, so at the busiest time, home time at the end of the day, Jimmy took it upon himself to wait with Oscar until the rush was over, then they'd walk home together, just the two of them, always talking rugby.

While most of Jimmy's friends didn't seem to think twice about any of this, Matt found himself growing increasingly irritated by Oscar's intrusion into their group. He didn't dislike Oscar, nobody did, but it bugged Matt that Jimmy and Oscar were spending so much time together.

So, as the first half term at school came towards its end, all was really, really good in Jimmy's world, and it was about to get a whole lot better. On the Monday of the final week before breaking up for half term, Mr Davies made an announcement in the school assembly.

'And finally, children, sport. Mrs John has kept me informed about the great progress our rugby team has been making in training this term . . . especially one young lady,' and he smiled as he looked over at Kitty, 'so she has arranged some extra fixtures. Therefore, the first competitive match of the season will be this Thursday evening at The Rec, and you will be taking on your opponents from last season's Cluster Cup final, Rockwood, so we can be assured of a very tough match . . . let's hope you can repeat the result of the final.'

Sitting together in a row, Jimmy, Matt, Manu and Kitty all punched the air and let out a quiet, 'Yes!' They couldn't wait to get back out onto the field in a proper game, and there was no tougher test than Rockwood.

'I'll be sending a school text out to all parents later today and putting the details on the school's Twitter feed and also via your Class Dojo, but please also make sure you tell your parents or carers as well.'

Mr Davies stopped for a moment, then smiled.

'Oh. And one last thing. Mrs John has an announcement to make about the team. Mrs John.'

Mrs John stood up and walked to the front of the hall.

'Thank you, sir. Yes, just a brief announcement from me. I wanted to announce our captain for the season ahead. I've watched and worked with you all for about six weeks now, and so many of you have impressed me with not just your skills, which is important, but your attitude, which is even more important. However, there is one player who combines both quite brilliantly, and will therefore be Central Primary's rugby captain for this season.'

Mrs John, beaming, paused for effect.

'It's Jimmy Joseph.'

A cheer went up around the hall from both pupils and staff.

Jimmy just sat there, blushing and adjusting his glasses, not knowing what to do or where to look. He was so proud, he thought he might burst. He didn't think he could be any happier.

But what Jimmy didn't know, was that by the end of that very week, his rugby world would come crashing down all around him and his dreams of chasing rugby success would be lying in tatters.

THAT'S GOTTA HURT!

Jimmy proudly led the team out at The Rec. Rockwood were already on the pitch, in a huddle, talking loudly and giving very aggressive and tight squeezes. The intensity of their voices revealed just how motivated they were for the contest. Revenge was in the air.

Matt jogged up to Jimmy as they crossed to the other half of the pitch and said, 'They sound like they're right up for it, Jim. I think you'll have to give them some of the Jimmy Joseph magic from the start to shut them up!'

Jimmy laughed. 'No, you can get amongst them first – soften them up for me!'

'You're on!' shouted Matt and rotated his arms rapidly to warm up his shoulders.

Jimmy was called over to the referee along with the Rockwood captain, a lump of a boy who played in the forwards. His name was Alex. The referee turned to Alex and said, 'Away team calls – heads or tails?' The referee flipped the coin, which caught glints

of the bright sun as it spun in the air. 'Heads!' called Alex, his
brow furrowed intently.

He seems quite wound up, thought Jimmy as he watched the
coin tumble to ground.

'Tails,' said the referee, bending down to pick up the coin.
'Central, your choice, kick-off or choice of ends?'

Jimmy had been out on The Rec before any of the other
players to study its conditions. He had kept his eyes on the flag
that sat on top of the Memorial Ground stand that ran alongside
The Rec. It had been still for ages. No wind. That had made
Jimmy's mind up. No wind meant no advantage from one side
of the pitch or the other. Jimmy wanted control from the start.

'We'll kick off please, sir,' said Jimmy politely.

And before the referee could even ask the question, Alex
declared loudly, 'We'll stay as we are,' before turning and running
off towards his team.

Jimmy jogged over to Kitty who was passing the match ball
back and forth with Matt.

Cupping his hand over his mouth so that the opposition
couldn't hear what he was saying, Jimmy said, 'I'm going to
switch the kick, Kit. I'll set the forwards up on the left, but will
knock it long to you down the right wing. Okay?'

'Got it,' said Kitty with a laser-like focus in her eyes.

Jimmy stepped up to the middle of the halfway line and
looked across to his left and towards his forwards, who were
gathered in a cluster about five yards behind the line, ready to
charge the moment Jimmy chose to kick.

Jimmy stood still, then bounced the ball on the ground in
front of him, twice. He'd seen George Ford do it on TV for

England a few times and thought it looked quite cool. Then, he steadied himself, and held his left arm up to show his forwards that he was about to kick. He took one step forward, then to everyone's surprise – including the rest of his team – he swivelled to his right and drilled a monster kick over towards the right wing, and to Kitty, who was off like a greyhound from a trap, having timed her run to avoid offside perfectly.

The Rockwood team were caught completely off-guard, especially their left wing who had drifted way too high up the pitch and had to turn to try to beat Kitty to the bounce. He probably wouldn't have beaten Kitty even if he hadn't had to turn, but by the time he had, she was already past him.

Jimmy's plan would have worked perfectly, but for the bounce of the ball.

Kitty reached the ball just as it bounced up, but instead of it bouncing into her arms, for what would have been a certain try, it bounced on its end and took a second, horrible bounce to its right, running off into touch.

Jimmy sucked his teeth in disappointment. His kick had almost been perfect, but wasn't quite good enough.

'Line out to Rockwood,' shouted the referee running over to the touchline, arm outstretched.

The forwards ran past Jimmy to take their place in the line out and as everyone sorted their positions out, Jimmy looked across at his opposite number, the Rockwood fly-half. He hadn't seen him before and didn't know what sort of player he was, whether he was going to run if he got possession or maybe put in a long kick behind. Jimmy tried to work it out by the way he was talking to his scrum-half, but couldn't tell.

And then, for the first time in a long time, Jimmy thought about it. Tackling. He tried to put it out of his head, but couldn't. He knew he was going to have to deal with it at some point today, but hoped that it would be later in the match, when he'd got up to speed. He just hoped that if Rockwood won the ball, the fly-half would do the sensible thing and bang it long.

The ball came in arrow straight from the Rockwood hooker and was tapped to the scrum-half by their huge second row who had outjumped Andrew Beasley, which was no mean feat in itself.

The ball flew straight to the hands of the scrum-half, who took a step or two forward before passing.

Jimmy had been paying so much attention to their number 10, hoping he'd somehow be able to shadow him over to Manu for him to take the tackle, that he hadn't noticed that Alex, the Rockwood captain, had stepped out of the line out. As a result, he'd lined up behind the scrum-half, so that when the scrum-half had taken that extra couple of steps, it had allowed Alex the time to build up some real speed and take the pass that his teammate had popped to him.

The pace and line of run that Alex had taken meant only one thing. At top speed, he was heading straight at Jimmy.

Jimmy didn't freeze. But something definitely happened to him. It was as if everything was happening at half speed.

It might have appeared in slow motion to Jimmy, but to the watching fans and Mrs John, it all happened far too quickly.

Jimmy completely messed up the tackle. His head was in the wrong position, his body was in the wrong position and he simply wasn't braced enough to stop the marauding Rockwood captain; instead of his body being tight and filled with energy, it was loose and limp.

At the moment of collision, Alex put all his energy into his right hip, and barged his way through Jimmy's feeble tackle attempt.

Jimmy felt a crack in his collarbone and yelped in agony as he fell to the ground. The pain was so bad that he couldn't move. He just lay there, groaning slightly, astonished at how much pain was pouring out of his shoulder and collarbone area.

Then he passed out.

DOCTOR, DOCTOR

Jimmy lay in his hospital bed.

He wore a gown that didn't do up at the back, but still had his rugby socks and shorts on. Draped over his chair at the side of his bed was his red and black hooped school rugby shirt. It was almost in two pieces from where the paramedic had to cut it to get it over Jimmy's shoulder. When they tried to pull the top over Jimmy's head when he was in the ambulance, he had yelped in agony, hence the butchery of the shirt.

Jimmy's dad sat in an uncomfortable bright orange plastic chair while his mum was perched on the end of the bed, her hand resting on Jimmy's foot.

'Oh, he's awake!' said his father when he noticed Jimmy looking around.

Jimmy smiled.

'Now don't move, love,' said his mother standing up. She brushed his hair back gently. 'You've got to stay as still as possible until they know exactly what's happened.'

Jimmy nodded. He'd been for the X-ray almost as soon as he'd arrived in the ambulance, but as he'd been sleeping, he didn't know how long ago that was. He tried to move to make himself a little more comfortable, but the pain that shot from his collarbone made him gasp.

'Try and stay still, love,' she repeated. 'I know it's tough, but that's what they said.'

'Do as your mum says, Jim,' said his dad. 'She's right.'

Jimmy took a deep breath, but only managed a croaky wheeze. 'Have you got my pump, Mum? My chest is tight.'

Catherine nodded and took his inhaler out of her handbag and passed it to him. He took it in his left hand and put it to his mouth and inhaled. He winced again. Even breathing in from his inhaler was painful. Jimmy closed his eyes and tried to blot it out.

A doctor bustled in and stood at the foot of his bed. He was holding a file.

'My name is Mr Sharma and I'm the consultant who is looking after you, Jimmy,' he said with a ready smile. 'Good afternoon, everyone.'

All three replied. Even Jimmy managed to deliver a half-hearted smile in response.

'Ah, good to see you smiling! That makes my job so much easier.'

He walked around the bed, looked down at the torn rugby shirt and moved it aside before sitting down. 'Ah, the spoils of war. This will make a nice souvenir for you one day, I'm sure!'

Despite the pain, Jimmy smiled again. He liked this man.

Then, before the consultant could say anything more, Jimmy blurted out something that had been on his mind since the moment he'd realised he'd been badly hurt, lying on the pitch.

'Will I be able to play rugby again, doctor?'

Mr Sharma looked at him very seriously.

'No,' came his reply.

Jimmy's eyes widened in disbelief.

Then the doctor burst into a grin. 'Well, not today anyway!'

Jimmy's father burst out laughing.

'I'm sorry, Jimmy, my little joke!' continued Mr Sharma. 'Yes, of course you can play rugby again, just not for a little while.'

He turned to Jimmy's parents.

'Mr and Mrs Joseph. Your son has been quite lucky. Technically, he has a broken collarbone, but we have several grades of breakages. The worst can snap and penetrate the skin, or can cause nerve damage or possibly require operations needing plates and screws to stabilise the bone. Jimmy has none of these. However, the X-rays reveal a fracture. I would not describe it as a hairline fracture, but neither would I describe it as a clean break. It is somewhere between the two.'

Then, turning to Jimmy, he said, 'Young man, whilst you are lucky that it's not a serious break, it's still bad enough that we need to treat it as if it's a serious break. We need to ensure that the bone gets the best chance to heal and that it comes back stronger than before. To do this you must follow certain instructions.'

Jimmy nodded, listening intently. He wanted to understand everything so that he could get back playing rugby as soon as possible.

'First, we will manage your pain. I will give a prescription to your mother of the painkillers you require. You take those as per the instructions, but the intense pain you are feeling will get less over the next twelve to twenty-four hours.'

Jimmy was glad to hear that, because the pain was really quite hard for him to bear.

'We will then fit you with a triangular sling that will keep the collarbone stable, and give it the best chance to heal quickly. I will also refer you to a physiotherapist who will give you exercises to do which will help strengthen the muscles supporting the bone. This is important and it is vital that you follow these exercises.'

Jimmy nodded eagerly. He'd read a section of one of his dad's rugby books – even though he knew he really wasn't supposed to – by the former British and Irish Lions captain, Sam Warburton, and read about how he did all his exercises to get back from injuries as quickly as he possibly could. Jimmy vowed he would do the same.

'I'll do everything I can to get myself ready to play rugby as soon as I can,' he replied with a very serious edge to his tone.

Mr Sharma smiled. 'Well, I'm very glad to hear that, Jimmy. You are clearly dedicated to your sport. If you do everything you are asked to do and the bone heals as we hope, then I can see you playing rugby again in . . . oooh, let me see . . . ten to twelve weeks. Maybe a little longer.'

'Twelve weeks?' Jimmy exclaimed, 'but the rugby season will be nearly over by then!'

'I know you will be disappointed,' replied the doctor, 'and who knows, you may be a quick healer. Just take the physiotherapist's advice, listen to what they say and also listen to your body. But whatever you do, don't rush back to play. Another bump on that same spot before it heals, and maybe we won't be so positive about your chances of playing rugby long into the future. It's very important you understand that . . . don't rush back.'

Jimmy listened to the consultant's wise words. For once, he vowed to do exactly as he was told.

ON THE COMEBACK TRAIL

Jimmy remained in hospital overnight, his mother and father staying with him, but having to sleep in the waiting room. It was a worrying time, but when Jimmy was examined the next morning, he was quickly released and allowed home, where he was ordered to rest as much as possible for a week, only doing slight exercises like moving his fingers and arm, slowly, and only if there was no pain.

At the start of the second week, Jimmy began his physiotherapy as an outpatient at his local hospital clinic. He was nervous going there at first, as he was the only person under the age of about forty who attended, but soon Jimmy became everybody's favourite. He secretly enjoyed all the attention he was getting, despite the obvious discomfort he was feeling.

By week three, Jimmy was pretty much pain-free. He had listened to every word that the physios had given him and followed their instructions to a tee. He had even surprised them with the progress he was making. The one thing they had told him was to avoid contact, as even just an accidental bumping of shoulders with somebody could potentially cause the collarbone to break again.

As a result of this, when Jimmy returned to school, after two and a half weeks off, he told Kitty, Manu and Matt that they wouldn't be seeing much of him out in the yard. Instead, he'd be staying in the classroom, keeping out of harm's way and doing his exercises. Jimmy didn't want to risk his rehabilitation in any way whatsoever. The only thing that mattered to him was getting back playing rugby as soon as possible. His friends understood, and apart from some teasing from Matt about being 'soft', everyone pretty much let Jimmy get on with his recovery himself.

Jimmy did have someone to help him, though – Oscar. As he still preferred to avoid the hustle and bustle of breaktimes, Oscar either stayed in class or the library anyway, so he became Jimmy's own in-school physio.

Oscar had taken particular interest in Jimmy's exercise regime as soon as Jimmy had shown him the exercise sheet, and had knocked up a grid on a new book in his *Book Creator* app. He titled the book, 'Jimmy's Rugby Road to Recovery' and had used a picture of Jimmy grinning with his arm in a sling as his cover picture. Then, under 'Chapter One' he took a picture of Jimmy holding up his exercise sheet, and then, with Jimmy's help reading them all out, he created a grid under the picture with the name of the exercises down the left-hand side. In the next column, titled 'Completed', Oscar would paste in an emoji of a rugby ball, and a final column would be the date that the exercise was completed. Oscar quickly got around to altering the colour background of each page, dropping in lots of rugby-related pics that he had stored on his camera roll, and also amended the font to suit his design. The book quickly became an impressive work of art.

In terms of Jimmy's exercise regime, because he wanted to ensure the book remained completely up to date, Oscar became quite the taskmaster, making sure Jimmy did the correct number of repetitions for each exercise so that he could record them accurately. Before long, Jimmy was able to ask Oscar about any of the exercises and Oscar could tell him how many in total he'd done in a session, or in a day or over a whole week. Jimmy loved this analysis as it really helped him understand how much work he was getting through to make his collarbone strong again. It helped so much with his desire to focus and keep going. With Oscar's information always on hand, Jimmy was able to work with Oscar to set targets on a daily basis to ensure all his exercises were not just being done, but being improved too, with everything being recorded in Oscar's digital book.

'This is just like being a pro player,' he said one day. 'All this analysis. It's fantastic!'

Oscar nodded and smiled, then focused back on the book, forever tinkering with its style and re-sizing images to make the presentation of it as good as he could make it.

'I've always loved putting books together,' said Oscar. 'This is the first time someone outside of my family has let me do one. I want it to be perfect.'

'Well, it *is* perfect,' said Jimmy. 'It's so helpful and gives me great motivation. I can't wait to show the others.'

Oscar stiffened a little at that point, and Jimmy noticed that he started to move his hands together and rocked gently back and forth.

'No, I don't think so, Jimmy,' he replied, visibly trying to calm himself, 'Matt will just laugh and I don't like that.'

Jimmy was a little shocked.

'That's okay, no problem,' he said quickly. 'We'll keep the book as our secret, we won't show anyone.'

Jimmy pondered Oscar's comment about Matt. Had something happened while Jimmy had been away from school? He parked the thought when the buzzer rang for the end of break and settled into the usual routine of trying to distract Oscar while the hustle and bustle of their returning classmates sent the volume rising slightly.

*

Each week saw a huge improvement in Jimmy's recovery and in week five he went back to see Mr Sharma for another X-ray to see how the bone was healing. It was good news.

'Excellent, excellent, Jimmy. I am very pleased with your progress,' said a delighted Mr Sharma. 'I can see that you are blessed with being a quick healer. If you continue healing so well I'll be able to sign you off soon!'

'So does that mean I can start to go back to rugby training?'

'No, no, no!' said Mr Sharma, throwing his arms up in the air. 'It's much too early for that! While your progress has been exceptional, a bump on that spot on your collarbone will still potentially break it again. You're still many weeks away from risking any contact.'

Jimmy looked disappointed, but it was only really what he expected to hear.

'Okay then, sir, can I at least start running? You know, to get some fitness back?'

Mr Sharma looked at Jimmy quizzically and then over to Jimmy's dad, who raised his eyebrows as if to say, 'What did you expect?'

The consultant smiled then looked back at Jimmy. 'Okay, stand up for me please.' Jimmy jumped to his feet quickly.

'Now move your hands to your side and then move them around and around in circles as if they are the pistons on the wheels of a steam train.'

Mr Sharma demonstrated, making the sounds of a steam train that made Jimmy laugh.

'Come on then, join in, but not too fast!' Then, looking over to Jimmy's dad, he said, 'You too, Mr Joseph, come on, join us!'

Malcolm laughed, 'You're okay, Mr Sharma, I'm enjoying it here just watching, thanks!'

Mr Sharma laughed, then Jimmy joined in, pumping his arms around like pistons while this lovely medical man did the same, but still making the sounds of a train.

'Okay, any pain, Jimmy?'

Jimmy shook his head, just about managing not to laugh, 'No, sir, none at all.' He was telling the truth, there was no pain.

'Okay, now copy me.'

Mr Sharma started jogging on the spot, exaggerating the movement so that he jumped from one foot to the other like some sort of slow-motion giant. Jimmy joined in. Malcolm Joseph, who'd seen just about every rugby-related issue it was possible to see in a lifetime around the game, couldn't believe his eyes!

After about a minute, Mr Sharma said, 'Okay, let's speed up a bit,' and he started running faster on the spot. Jimmy matched him.

After another minute, Mr Sharma shouted again, 'Any pain?'

'No sir, none at all!'

'Good, well let's stop then shall we? Before I have a heart attack!'

Mr Sharma walked across and gave Jimmy a quick examination. After he had pressed, prodded and twisted both Jimmy's collarbone and right arm, during which time Jimmy had shown no obvious discomfort – apart from when Mr Sharma pressed right onto the break – Mr Sharma gave Jimmy the good news.

'You can run, Jimmy. But just gentle jogging for the first few days, and on grass if you can, not on hard surfaces.'

'What about kicking and catching, can I do that too?'

'Yes to kicking, but be very careful with the catching, for another week at least. Nothing above the head and no sudden movements, I'm still a little worried about what that impact might do. Have a jog and have a kick and enjoy yourself, but take it easy, Jimmy. Nothing too much, too quickly. Oh, and have you ever tried this?'

Jimmy watched with increasing amusement as Mr Sharma picked up his phone, a stapler and a pocket calculator from his desk and began juggling!

'Try this when you get home, but use fruit or tennis balls, not an iPhone, Mr Joseph will kill me if you drop that.'

Jimmy's dad was open mouthed watching the juggling show.

'This will help with your reflexes too, very good hand-eye coordination for your rugby, Jimmy, with no danger to your shoulder!'

Jimmy burst out laughing again.

'But seriously,' said Mr Sharma, ending his impromptu circus act. 'Whatever you do, avoid contact on that collarbone, that's the most important thing.'

Jimmy nodded. He'd already worked out that, from what Mr Sharma had said, it was likely to be at least three weeks before he could take part in contact training. However, he could run and kick in those three weeks, so Jimmy gave himself a target.

As he walked out to the car with his dad, he said to himself, quietly enough so only he heard, 'In three weeks' time, I'm going to be the best place-kicker that Central Primary has ever seen.'

25

10,000 HOURS

It was Saturday morning, the day after Jimmy had seen Mr Sharma.

It was 8.30 and nobody was about. Just Jimmy, his rugby ball and his kicking tee.

His mum had made an early start because of an extra shift at work, so Jimmy had got up when he heard her leave, while Jonny and Julie were still sleeping. Not wanting to waste any time, he didn't bother with a proper breakfast. Instead, he just took a banana and ate it quickly whilst glugging down some milk. He glanced across at the box of Weetabix that his mother had left out for them and smiled at the thought of when he used to eat six every morning. He still had some now and again, but never six! One thing the Eagles Academy had shown him in his short time there was the importance of eating properly, especially for breakfast. Usually it was oats, yoghurt, honey and fruit for Jimmy these days, but a banana and milk would do today. At least it was healthier than the sugary cereals that Julie still loved!

Despite it being the very end of November, it was a beautiful bright morning. It was a little chilly, but Jimmy soon warmed up as he jogged around The Rec, taking his time and making sure there was no obvious pain from his collarbone. Every now and again he would stretch his arm out and rotate it as he ran. No pain, just stiffness. Good news.

On his second lap, Jimmy began to sweat and warm up. It felt really good to be able to get out and about, even if it was just for a gentle jog. It was the first time in over five weeks that Jimmy had done anything aerobic, and by the end of the second lap, he stopped and took a deep breath as he was starting to feel a tightness in his breathing. The chilly morning air had gone straight to his chest and Jimmy wheezed and was unable to gulp enough air to fill his lungs in that satisfying way that you need to when you get a little out of breath. Jimmy reached into his tracksuit bottoms and pulled out his trusty inhaler. He flipped off the cover to the mouthpiece and took two, deep puffs. Instantly the airwaves to his lungs opened and Jimmy was able to take the deep breath he needed. His asthma was a big pain in the backside for him sometimes, there was no doubt about that, but Jimmy had learned to manage it properly and there was no way that it would ever get in the way of achieving his rugby dreams. He just wouldn't let it.

He decided to do one last lap to get really warm and then jogged to the posts at the far end of The Rec, stopping about fifteen metres in front of them. He dropped the ball and the tee and then took a big lunge forward with his right leg, keeping his left leg rooted to the floor. In this position, Jimmy started to stretch his leg muscles, as he'd been shown in the warm-ups during his brief spell back at the Academy. Even though Jimmy was sweating quite nicely after his three laps, he knew that his muscles weren't warm enough yet to cope with the sharp, sudden impact and explosive power experienced when place-kicking. So that meant stretching, and lots of it. Jimmy did exercises to stretch his calf, hamstring and quad muscles in his legs, before stretching the muscles in his lower back and glutes . . . also known as his backside!

Jimmy knew that anyone watching him doing these stretches for the ten minutes or so that he did them would think him a little bit mad, but he didn't care. If he wanted to be the best kicker in his age group, then this level of commitment was the right way of going about it.

Once his stretching was complete, Jimmy picked up his tee and ball and stood straight in front of the posts. He knelt down on one knee and lined the tee up with the posts in front of him. Then he took the ball and placed it on the tee, pointing it away from him at an angle of about forty-five degrees. Jimmy stood up and looked down over the ball and then up to the posts.

He thought about his kicking competition with Mike last year and the stress he had felt kicking off a tee for the first time. That stress was no longer there as Jimmy had used one many times since, but he would still hardly call himself an expert. Jimmy could kick, but he knew that if he didn't work at it, by practising regularly, then when he had to take a kick under pressure again, his technique might let him down.

He remembered Jonny telling him about an article he'd read when Jimmy was still laid up and resting in bed, not long after the collarbone injury. It was an article about mastering a particular skill in sport like taking a penalty in football or a putt in golf or a conversion in rugby.

'Muscle memory, Jim, it's all about muscle memory,' his

brother had told him. Jimmy looked at him with a completely vacant look on his face. Jonny had a theory for everything and it seemed like this was going to be his latest one.

'What do you mean, "muscle memory"? How can muscles have memories?'

'It's how we learn everything: to walk, to run, to write, to click our fingers, everything. It says here that you can teach your muscles to learn any skill, as long as you are willing to devote the right number of hours to practising it. If you do, you become an expert. Simple.'

'It can't be that simple or everyone would be doing it.'

'And that's the point,' said Jonny with an excited look in his eye, 'most people can't stick to the task and don't put in the hours, and that's why they don't become experts; only the ones that stick to it do. All the repetition you do, time after time, hour after hour means your muscles remember your movements and you become an expert. It really isn't rocket science, Jim. I'm going to do it to practise passing off my left hand. When you're fit, you can come and practise too.'

'I will!' said Jimmy, looking forward to getting out and about with his brother again. 'But how many hours do you need to become an expert then?'

'10,000,' replied Jonny without hesitation. 'That's all.'

'That's *all*?' laughed Jimmy. 'Have you any idea how long that will take?'

'A while, I suppose.'

'A while!? Jonny, if you practise two hours a day on your passing, that's fourteen hours a week. Multiply that by fifty-two weeks and you get . . . um . . .' Jimmy closed his eyes as he worked it out in his head. '728 hours!' Jimmy laughed. 'At that rate it'll be over ten years before you become an expert at passing off your left hand, and by then you'd probably have forgotten how to pass off your right!'

'You can scoff all you like, Jim. It might take me a while, but I'm going to be the best in the world at passing off my left hand . . . by the time I'm, well, maybe twenty-three. But I will be the best!'

Jimmy laughed but he loved Jonny's enthusiasm, and watched him bound out of the bedroom to begin his 10,000 hours of passing. Jonny did have a point though. Maybe 10,000 hours would be too much, but continued practice definitely did make you better. Jimmy had seen how all the work he had put in with Peter Clement and Liam Wyatt last season, when they taught him how to kick out of hand, had worked so well. Jimmy wondered how many hours he'd spent practising, or 'being professional', as Peter Clement told him. It was impossible to know. Jimmy guessed at thirty days at about an hour a day, 'Wow!' he said to himself. 'That's another 9,970 hours to go!'

But the point had been made in Jimmy's mind. He may not get up to 10,000 hours, but as soon as he could get out of his sick bed and was up and about again, he would focus all his attention on place-kicking. It was one of the parts of rugby he truly loved. He'd watched incredible kickers like Handre Pollard of South Africa, Richie Mo'unga of New Zealand, Dan Biggar and Leigh Halfpenny of Wales, Owen Farrell of England, Johnny Sexton of Ireland and Greig Laidlaw of Scotland, and noticed they were all different. He wanted to try to take the best bits from all of them and make himself the best around.

Which was why, five weeks later, he stood over a ball on a tee on the deserted Rec at 8.30 on a cold Saturday morning.

The 10,000 hours would begin here.

AIMING HIGH

Jimmy adopted the Owen Farrell approach first.

He took four steps back from the ball, followed by two to the left. He then looked down at the ball with a sideways tilt of his head, before looking up to the posts, then back to the ball, then up to the posts for a final time, tracing an imaginary line along which the ball would travel.

He took one final look down at the ball, before moving forward smoothly, planting his left foot next to the tee on the ground, pulling his right leg back before swinging it through the ball. The ball flew off Jimmy's foot, straight as an arrow and right between the posts.

'Yes!' shouted Jimmy to himself, as he watched the ball fly over the cross bar, before jogging to collect it so that he could repeat the process again.

Jimmy decided he was going to start with five kicks from in front of the posts, then move five yards to the right to kick five more, then move five yards over to the left of where he had started to kick a final five. Jimmy's personal target was to see how many of the fifteen he would kick. Even if he managed fourteen out of fifteen, that wouldn't be good enough. He would start again until he scored all fifteen in succession.

He kicked the first five like a dream. All five kicks were pretty much spot on and flew over. His next five were pretty good too – all high, all accurate, all over. It was just the last five that caused Jimmy an issue. He didn't know if it was because he was trying to curl the ball in from right to left, which was the natural angle from the left side of the pitch, or that he was somehow lined up wrong, but he began hooking the ball. Not so badly that he was missing, but badly enough that they were all just creeping nearer to the left-hand post. Jimmy tried to correct it by only taking one step to the left after marching back from the ball, but the ball was still moving too much towards the left-hand post. But at least he was still slotting them over.

He jogged behind the posts to collect the ball after successful kick number fourteen. He was really starting to sweat because, as he only had one ball, he had to jog after it each time he kicked it. When he jogged back to kick number fifteen, he was breathing heavily and as he knelt down to place the ball on the tee, his legs felt as though they were beginning to take the strain. Jimmy had forgotten that he'd not really done any exercise for five weeks and the fatigue in his thighs was starting to show.

He finished placing the ball and took his mark. He did his Farrell glancing routine, but when he looked at the ball for the final time, he suddenly felt a little pressure. If he kicked it, he could move on to his next drill or go home or call in at his grandparents' house for a cup of tea. Whatever he wanted to do, it would be up to him, he would have hit his target of fifteen out of fifteen – he could move on. But if he missed it, well, that was a different story as he'd have to start all over again.

Jimmy felt his body visibly stiffening, tightening. He loved kicking the rugby ball, so he didn't really mind having to kick some more, but he knew that taking another fifteen would be tough, and of course, he had started to hook them too. What if he hooked this one as well? His body tightened again. Would he start the next fifteen straight away or would he have a breather? Also, would he kick them in the same order, or would he start from over on the right or back in the middle? Or maybe he would start here on the left again?

'Jimmy! Stop it!' he cried, trying to banish these negative and confusing thoughts. He realised that he was mentally piling the pressure on himself by thinking of all these differing scenarios, all of which were based on an unsuccessful outcome. Okay, not all the previous fourteen kicks had been perfect, but he hadn't really thought about them; now, all of a sudden, this one felt really important, as though a huge amount depended on it. And it did. Suddenly, this kick was crucial. He couldn't take his mind off it. He tightened again.

Jimmy stepped away from the ball and reset. He knelt back down and replaced the ball, and went through his Farrell routine perfectly. He took a huge breath just before the kick to try to relax himself, then stepped forward to strike the ball. And as he did, he hooked it, badly.

The ball flew way to the left, missing the posts by a good five yards. Jimmy screamed, 'Arghhhh,' before sinking to the ground. He was devastated. Not because he'd missed. Not because he would now have to take another fifteen. And not because he'd have to run after the ball again. But because he'd let the pressure get to him. He'd really allowed the importance of this final kick get under his skin and he'd buckled under the pressure. Completely. That's what annoyed Jimmy the most.

Then he heard a voice.

'Owen Farrell wouldn't have been happy with that, but fourteen out of fifteen is pretty good. That's over 93%. A high percentage return.'

Jimmy recognised the voice straight away and turned around smiling. It was Oscar.

'Hey, I thought that was you,' said Jimmy as he got to his feet and walked towards his friend. 'Have you been watching?'

'Yes. I was over on the swings. I could tell that you were doing some sort of competition, so didn't want to interrupt. I did take some pictures for our book, though. It'll illustrate good progress.'

Jimmy smiled. 'It'll look good in the book, nice one.'

'You looked angry at the end, but over 93% success is excellent. Pretty good kicking. You did look exactly like Owen Farrell too.'

Jimmy laughed. 'Yeah, not bad, but I was after 100%, so I'm a little annoyed that the pressure got to me on the last kick.'

'Well, 100% is a tricky target, especially as this is your first time back. You failed, but you should be happy.'

Jimmy smiled again, he loved Oscar's matter of fact way of looking at things. Jimmy wished he could do the same . . . especially when the pressure was on.

'Right, 100% is a tricky target, but, I'm going to try again. Do you want to help?'

'Well, I'm happy to watch, I don't know exactly how I can help.'

'To be honest, Oscar, it'll help you just being here, to have someone to chat to between kicks. It might help me deal with the pressure if I get on a roll again.'

Oscar smiled. When he was around Jimmy, he didn't have to wear the mask that he so often had to put up in front of so many people to protect himself from painful sneers, unkind comments and sometimes much worse. He was able to be more himself, the real Oscar. An autistic child can demonstrate so many behaviours that non-autistic people simply cannot understand and become threatened by, so they often almost try to hide in plain sight and avoid confrontation or awkward situations. Something as simple as putting an arm around an autistic person can lead to very real stress and actual pain for them, something that a non-autistic person simply can't understand and can often get angry about. But on the occasions that Oscar had exposed some of his own unique behaviours to Jimmy, Jimmy had just recognised them and simply asked Oscar about it gently. Then, if necessary, Jimmy would alter his own behaviour to make Oscar more comfortable. Oscar hadn't come across many schoolchildren who would make those allowances so willingly. He loved Jimmy for that.

But now, it was back to rugby, and for the next half an hour or so, Oscar watched Jimmy try his fifteen kicks again. Jimmy completely relaxed with Oscar being there and loosened up while chatting to him in the gap between each kick. After each successful attempt, Oscar would quietly tell Jimmy what number kick it was, his running percentage success and how many he had left. Oscar, like Jimmy and most sports fans, was a sucker for a statistic, and as he was particularly good at mental maths, was able to quickly transfer Jimmy's kicks into an immediate form of sports performance statistics.

Jimmy had moved nicely to ten out of ten, but then missed number eleven. He then missed number twelve too. Quickly followed by thirteen, fourteen and a shocking number fifteen, all hooks. All missed. All from the left side of the pitch. After each miss, he turned to Oscar in exasperation, but Oscar said nothing, he just tapped into his phone Jimmy's attempt/miss ratio. A pattern was developing in Jimmy's kicking and he was confused and frustrated by it.

When the last one had dived left, Oscar quickly shouted over, 'That's ten out of fifteen which works out at just over 66%. You failed again. And even worse this time.'

Jimmy grimaced, but quickly relaxed. With Oscar around, he didn't get as uptight as he had been earlier, and hadn't felt any pressure from any of the kicks. Even though he hadn't hit his target, he did feel like he was making some progress. He'd got every kick over from the middle and right, probably striking the ball better than he had done earlier. It was just when he kicked from the left-hand side that he struggled, but he could live with that. It wasn't as though he was going to give up. The whole point of this was to find out what his weaknesses in place-kicking were, to fix them and then practise. It was clear he had a weakness kicking from the left side of the posts, so he'd just have to try and work it out. Jimmy would be back tomorrow for another session, but for now, he was done. His legs were like jelly.

'No point flogging a dead horse, Oscar,' said Jimmy picking up his tee and ball.

Oscar's blank stare in response to Jimmy's quip made him

smile.

'What I mean is, I think that's enough for one day,' he said. 'Come on, let's walk home.'

BREAD AND BUTTER KICKS

The next morning, Jimmy was out there again. He repeated his jog and his warm-up stretches and then began kicking. He also began hooking. Straight away. He missed four of his first six. He wasn't as good at percentages as Oscar, but he knew it was poor.

'You're leaning too far to your left, I think.'

Jimmy turned around to see a man in a tracksuit walking towards him. Jimmy had never seen him before. Jimmy just nodded, then turned and jogged after his ball behind the posts. When he got back, the man was standing by Jimmy's tee.

He repeated his advice. 'I think you're leaning slightly too much to your left as you plant your foot by the tee, that's why you're hooking them. You need to plant your left foot into the ground strongly. You strike the ball well enough, though.'

Jimmy looked at the man. He was about mid thirties, a little under six foot, very fit looking with a trendy short back and sides haircut, gelled to a wave at the front. There was something very friendly about his face.

'You wouldn't be Jimmy, would you?' asked the man.

'Erm, yes, I am,' replied Jimmy, slightly warily.

The man noticed Jimmy's discomfort.

'Oh, gosh, I'm so sorry, I haven't said who I am. I'm Kevin, Kevin John. My wife teaches you in school. Mrs John?'

'Ahhh, right,' said Jimmy, 'I've heard about you from my grandfather. You used to play with a Mark Kane didn't you?'

Kevin visibly shuddered at the memory.

'Mark Kane. Yes, yes I did. But I don't like to think about him too much. My wife said he taught at her school last year before she joined, did he teach you, then?'

'Yes, he did. But I don't like to think about him too much either.'

Kevin nodded.

'I think I can guess why you feel like that. To be honest, I can't believe he was ever allowed to become a teacher.'

Kevin stopped talking, as if lost in some bad memory, but after a few seconds seemed to snap out of it and remembered he was talking to Jimmy about his kicking.

'Anyway, let's forget about him, let's talk about you. My wife says that you're a seriously talented player and she doesn't say that about many people.'

Jimmy didn't know what to say, so did what he always did when given a compliment, he blushed.

'You're out early this morning, have you got a game today?'

'No, I'm out injured at the moment, I broke my collarbone,' replied Jimmy, moving his right arm in rotation as if to show Kevin where the injury was.

'Ah, yes of course. I remember her telling me now. Mistimed tackle, wasn't it?'

Not wanting to share the truth of it being more of a chickened-out tackle than a mistimed one, Jimmy just nodded in reply.

'Well, don't worry, you'll be as right as rain soon and back at it before you know it. So, you're practising your kicking before you get back to the rough and tumble, are you?'

'Yes,' replied Jimmy, 'I want to make sure that by the time I get back playing, I'm going to be the best place-kicker in the district. I never want to miss a single kick. Especially the pressure ones.'

'That's an excellent attitude,' replied Kevin. 'And pretty impressive to see someone so young with such a professional mindset.'

'Peter Clement taught me that,' said Jimmy proudly.

'Ah, Peter. Yes, a great bloke. I met him for a pint this week. It's been great to catch up with him since I moved back; what a player he was.'

'Yes, I know!' exclaimed Jimmy. 'I've seen his medals. He won the Man of Steel award once, it's huge!'

'No better person to win it, either,' said Kevin. 'I used to practise here when I was a kid like you too. A lot of us did. Well, we did before Mark Kane spoiled things.' Kevin tailed off into silence again.

'Anyway, enough of all that,' he said, springing to life again, 'let's have a look at your kicking.'

Jimmy explained about yesterday and how he got fourteen out of fifteen, but had started to hook the ball and how that had continued this morning. Kevin asked him to kick a couple, just watching and saying nothing, before he spoke.

'Okay. I can see that you're following the Owen Farrell technique.'

Jimmy nodded.

'Yes, I've watched lots of kickers on YouTube and he's the one I like best.'

'Well, that's okay. There's nothing wrong in modelling your style on someone, but just be sure that you try to replicate their kicking 100%. Success is all in the detail.'

Jimmy nodded again.

'The key thing,' Kevin continued, 'is to be able to repeat. If you can repeat – exactly, mind you – every process of every kick, from the lining up of the tee and placing of the ball to the final strike of the ball and follow-through, then you will be getting close to guaranteeing success. There are two things that will always potentially affect that success though, no matter how much you practise. Do you know what they are?'

Jimmy thought back to yesterday when it all started to go wrong on that fifteenth kick.

'Pressure?' asked Jimmy.

'Bang on. Pressure,' replied Kevin. 'Well done. The enemy of nearly every kicker who has played the game. The very, very top players manage to overcome the pressure. Someone like a Jonny Wilkinson. Even though he would still miss a couple, he turned the pressure thing around. He enjoyed it *more* when the kick was crucially important, when there was the most pressure. Having a mindset as strong as that, well, that's a talent in itself.'

Jimmy listened intently. He knew how the pressure had affected him yesterday, he wanted to know how to overcome that.

'What do you think the second thing is?'

Jimmy thought for a minute.

'Concentration?' He offered.

'Well, yes. But I'd link that to pressure. If you can deal with the pressure, it shows you're concentrating anyway, yes?'

Jimmy agreed, 'Yes.'

'I'll tell you. It's fatigue. The more tired you are, especially later in a game, when the kicks usually really count, that's when your body can play tricks on you. You'll think everything is okay, but if your muscles are tired or fatigued, then that can be enough to start you hooking, slicing or just not connecting with the ball perfectly. That's what it sounds like happened to you on your fifteenth kick yesterday, a mixture of pressure and fatigue.'

Jimmy realised Kevin was right, he nodded vigorously in agreement.

'Okay. Kick another for me.'

Jimmy stepped up and kicked another. He went through his Farrell set up which impressed Kevin with its attention to detail, then struck the ball absolutely beautifully. They both watched as the ball flew high off Jimmy's boot, but half way to the posts, the ball started to arch away to the left, just missing the post as it flew by. Jimmy was disappointed, but nevertheless, he sprinted after the ball to collect it and bring it back to see what Kevin had to say.

When he got back, Kevin had another question.

'Do you run like that after every ball you kick?'

'Yes, pretty much,' replied Jimmy. 'I jog sometimes, but usually get it as quickly as I can.'

Kevin nodded, but didn't say anything. He was clearly thinking about something.

'Okay,' said Kevin, 'that was a great strike, it really was. And I can see how much you've copied Farrell. But there's one thing he does that you're not doing.'

Jimmy thought quickly, but couldn't think what it was.

'You're falling away slightly to your left,' continued Kevin. 'Which is where the dreaded hook comes from. If you watch Farrell, on his first step, after his first movement, he makes a big effort to stand his body up as straight and tall as he can. No leaning left or right, just straight up to the sky. Only when he does this, does he move forward with his next stride to the ball. The other really important thing to avoid a hook, is to connect with the centre of the ball when you strike it off the tee, right in the middle of it. Also remember to get your bodyweight through the ball. Watch, I'll show you.'

Kevin then lined up the ball, exactly like Owen Farrell, took his four steps back and two to the left. Then he did his head to the side thing, tracing the flight of the ball, then he made his first movement. Jimmy watched as Kevin almost paused to make sure he was standing up straight, then moved towards the ball, striking it perfectly in the middle, and drilling it as straight as an arrow through the posts.

'Wow!' said Jimmy as the ball flew high over the posts in a dead straight line. 'That was brilliant!' And then Jimmy was off to collect the ball. When he got back, Kevin said,

'Right, your turn.'

Jimmy did everything he usually did, it was like clockwork. The thing he was concentrating on most was the short pause to stand up straight before striking the ball. He pictured the way Kevin had just done it. Jimmy copied it exactly and as he struck the ball, it flew as perfectly as Kevin's, on a dead straight line through the posts. It wasn't as high as Kevin's but it was just as straight, right through the middle of the posts. Not a hint of a hook.

'Excellent!' shouted Kevin and clapped loudly. 'No sign of you falling away to your left with that one.'

Jimmy was chuffed and was beaming as he ran to retrieve the ball.

He didn't miss one of the next five he took under Kevin's watchful eye. Each one as straight as the last. Not a hook in sight.

'That was great, Jimmy, really well done. You're a good listener, you must be a pleasure to coach.'

Jimmy smiled.

'But I can't emphasise enough how important practice is. And don't forget, all we've done here is slot them over from in front of the posts. It'll be different from the wider angles and also when we start to go back in distance. You see, that's when a kicker really gets to understand how good their technique is, when they're at the edge of their range, as that's when it can really start to fall apart! But that's for another day. The important thing is that you learn to convert the bread and butter kicks, the ones bang in front of the post. Kicks from angles and distance can come later in your development. Always remember – bread and butter!'

Jimmy nodded.

'Right,' said Kevin, 'I'm off to watch Laura's . . . sorry, *Mrs John's*, sister play rugby now, so I can't be late.'

'Thanks for the help,' said Jimmy, about to run after the ball again.

'That's okay, my pleasure,' replied Kevin. 'Oh, and Jimmy?'

Jimmy turned to look at him.

'Where do you live?'

Jimmy pointed across The Rec to his street and told Kevin his house number.

'You can't go on chasing after the ball each time you kick it, it adds hours to your kicking sessions and I always found it a right pain when I practised here. A top pro like Farrell would always have a bag of balls. Kicking practice is for practising kicking, not running. I'm guessing that's the only ball you've got?'

'Yes,' said Jimmy, 'my brother Jonny has got one, but he goes mad if I take his!'

'Okay,' replied Kevin, 'well I've got a load back at home that my wife used to use and old ones I've got from the club I work at. What if I drop a bag of them around to you later, about half a dozen or so? That'll help you focus on the kicking and not running off like a robber's dog after each kick.'

'Really?' replied Jimmy, unable to hide the excitement in his voice.

'Yeah, why not?' replied Kevin. 'And then, when you're the best kicker in world rugby, you can tell everyone that it's because Kevin John gave you a bag of old balls!'

'You're on!' said Jimmy, who all of a sudden didn't want to just be the best kicker in his district. He now had a much bigger target than that.

EVEN CHRISTMAS DAY'S
A TRAINING DAY

Over the next three weeks, leading up to Christmas, Jimmy didn't miss a day of taking his bag of scruffy balls over to The Rec to practise. Whatever the weather, rain or shine, he just kicked and kicked and kicked. Often alongside him would be Oscar, helping Jimmy with his stats and becoming his own personal data analyst, always taking photos to continue with the digital book he was making about Jimmy's rugby journey. Oscar had even picked up on Jimmy's continued use of the word 'pressure' and had made Jimmy laugh when he said one day, just as Jimmy was placing the ball on the kicking tee, 'Pressure kicks between the sticks!' That had become Jimmy's new mantra and he loved it. He whispered it to himself before each kick, it really helped him focus.

Jimmy saw much less of his usual gang, Matt, Kitty and Manu. Their time was taken up by rugby practice with Mrs John on Tuesdays and Thursdays and when they did show up at The Rec to play, Jimmy didn't want to risk his shoulder, so apart from the odd occasion when they'd chat over by the swings, Jimmy usually ended up down the bottom of The Rec, place-kicking with Oscar.

His friends, especially Kitty, all understood that Jimmy didn't want to risk a knock to his collarbone and left him to it. Except Matt. He hardly spoke to Jimmy at all, especially when Oscar was around. He never said anything outright to Jimmy, but the fact that he usually just walked away when Oscar turned up with his iPhone or iPad to record Jimmy's kicking stats said a lot.

But Jimmy was too focused on his kicking to notice anything, he just kicked and kicked and kicked. He might have been nowhere near 10,000 hours, but Jimmy's place-kicking had improved out of sight. In fact, the only time he struggled was when he was kicking from the furthest distance. Kevin had said that would be an issue, and when Jimmy reached that point, about thirty metres out from the posts, that's when the dreaded hook would come back. Jimmy knew it was because he was trying to kick it too hard to gain the distance, meaning he was losing control, but thought there must be a way to sort that out. Then he remembered Kevin's words about 'bread and butter kicks'. He'd explained to Jimmy that accuracy from a shorter distance was much more important than trying to get distance – 'That will come,' Kevin had said. So when Jimmy started to hook the longer kicks, he'd stop and go back in front of the posts and kick for accuracy. Bread and butter.

The three weeks of kicking had brought about another milestone in Jimmy's recovery: the all-clear to return to full contact rugby. Jimmy couldn't wait. He'd been to see Mr Sharma again, and he'd given Jimmy all sorts of tests and checks and then announced to Jimmy and to his mum and dad, that all was okay. His collarbone was completely healed. Mr Sharma's words were music to Jimmy's ears.

However, much to his dismay, there was no rugby at school the week after Jimmy's good news from Mr Sharma. It was the final week of term before Christmas, so everything was geared towards the annual Central Primary Christmas Concert.

Jimmy really enjoyed the Christmas week in school. Similar to how he was on the rugby field, Jimmy was a bit of a performer. He loved singing in the school choir and in particular loved 'O Come All Ye Faithful' because along with Kitty and Manu, they all really enjoyed when they were allowed to sing the third, 'O come let us adore him' line as loudly as they could. It was a great time to be around school.

But despite all the fun and joy of Christmas, both in that final week at school and also at home with the family, Jimmy viewed the school break as a distraction. He just couldn't wait to get back on the rugby field and test his shoulder out. And by test it out, Jimmy meant taking it into contact by carrying the ball, not tackling someone running straight at him. Jimmy knew he was going to have to deal with his tackling issue at some point, but that particular treat could wait.

Jimmy pretty much spent the whole of his Christmas break at The Rec, which had been his home, more or less, since Mr Sharma had told him he could do some kicking practice at the end of November. But now it was time to work on something else: fitness. While he still did some kicks at The Rec, Jimmy used the venue as his personal fitness centre. He practised sprints by running from the try line to the twenty-two-metre line.

Then he would extend the sprints by running on to the halfway line. He would work on his endurance by running laps of The Rec pitch – usually jogging along the touchlines and then at a slightly quicker pace when he ran behind the posts. He worked on strengthening his shoulders and collarbone area by using one of the green benches in front of the old, green and white changing pavilion as a press up station. He'd incline his body, so that his collarbone didn't take his full bodyweight and do as many press ups as he could until the lactic acid in his arms built up so much that he could hardly move them. He trained like a demon. Even on Christmas Day he was over at The Rec.

'Nobody else will be training on Christmas Day,' Jimmy whispered to himself, 'that's bound to give me an advantage.'

That was one thing about Jimmy, he was nothing if not single minded.

29

STARTING OVER

Before Jimmy knew it, his prayers were answered. Despite having had a fantastic Christmas and New Year with his family, including some time watching rugby videos over at his dad's that he really enjoyed, it was playing competitive rugby itself that Jimmy really wanted. And that happened on Tuesday 7th January, in Mrs John's first training session of the New Year.

Jimmy ran out of the pavilion like a spring lamb and sprinted up and down the pitch.

'Blinkin' heck, Jimmy,' said Manu, 'slow down or you'll be worn out before we start the session!'

'I know, I know,' said Jimmy, 'it's just that I've missed being out here with you all so much, that I can't wait to get started again.'

The whistle blew. His wait wouldn't go on much longer.

Now Jimmy really wanted to test out his collarbone, that was the one main thing on his mind. And he knew exactly how he was going to do it. He was going to wait until he had his hands on the ball, and wherever he was on the field, he was going to run at big Andrew Beasley and smash him. If his shoulder survived that, he thought, it'll survive anything.

So when Mrs John split the squad into two teams, Jimmy was chuffed to see that Andrew Beasley was on the other side. It wouldn't be long now before he'd get that collarbone tested.

But then Mrs John called him over.

'Nice to have you back, Jimmy,' she said, 'you wouldn't mind kicking off for us, would you?'

This wasn't part of Jimmy's plan. He wanted the ball to be kicked to him so that he could catch it and charge.

'No, it's okay, Miss,' replied Jimmy, 'the other side can kick off.'

'Nonsense, it's a big moment to have our captain back after so long out, we'd be delighted for you to start the New Year for us.' And with that, Mrs John tossed Jimmy the ball.

Jimmy trudged to the centre of the halfway line. He looked across and saw Kitty, who smiled and gave him the thumbs up. Jimmy half smiled in return.

Then Jimmy took a look at where the opposition were standing, and in particular, Andrew Beasley. The last thing Jimmy wanted to do was to kick it at him and deal with him rampaging straight at him like some angry wildebeest.

Jimmy looked over to his right and saw little Aaron Conway, Kitty's deputy on the wing. He was fast and competitive, but he was no Andrew Beasley. And anyway, if Jimmy put the kick in the right place, Aaron would just streak down the wing and Jimmy wouldn't have to worry about tackling.

Jimmy bounced the ball in front of him. He looked across to his left where his forwards were, and then swivelled and drilled the ball to his right, where Aaron was standing. The problem was, Jimmy was leaning back a bit too much when he struck the ball, which meant it went higher than he wanted and nowhere near as far. This meant that Aaron had to come in off his wing to collect it, changing his angle of running.

Aaron was off like a shot when he saw the ball heading towards him, and when he gathered Jimmy's kick he was travelling at full speed. Now, most wingers would've looked for space at this point, looking to sidestep the onrushing defence and get back towards their wing, but for some reason, Aaron took a different approach – and headed straight for Jimmy.

Jimmy glanced quickly to see if Manu was going to rush up and cover, but Manu had been surprised by Jimmy's kick and was caught slightly too deep and out of position.

In what seemed like a split second, Aaron was right in front of Jimmy. And then, exactly as had happened to Jimmy previously, time seemed to stand still. In that split second, everything that Jimmy had experienced in the last three or so months went through his mind: the bang on his nose on the first day at the Academy; all the tackle practice with Mr Kane; the moment he broke his collarbone; running on the spot with Mr Sharma; the hundreds of place kicks; the hours of fitness training. All geared towards this very moment.

Then, as quickly as time seemed to have stopped, so it started up again, and just as it did, just as he was going to have to really test out his shoulder and find out its strength by tackling little Aaron, Jimmy just couldn't face it.

He turned his back.

THE TALKING TO

Jimmy's back-turning moment and complete lack of any defensive contributions in his first training session back was the talk of the dressing room. He had followed his embarrassing incident with Aaron Conway with a succession of missed tackles. Even Jimmy's coordinated slips and tap tackles were now seen for exactly what they were: missed tackles.

Matt was the most unforgiving of all the commenters in the dressing room.

'Rugby is a game of tackling. Simple as that. I know he's my mate, but no matter how good you are, you've got to tackle. Defence is a massive part of the game.'

'Oh, come on Matt,' said Manu. 'He broke his collarbone you know. It's bound to have an impact when you have to make that first tackle back. He must have been terrified it was going to snap again. Cut him some slack.'

'Nah, I think it's deeper than that. All those slips, he was doing that before he got injured,' said Matt, having none of it. 'I think he's lost his bottle.'

'We're supposed to be his friends, Matt,' snapped Kitty. 'And when friends are in trouble, which Jimmy clearly is, we help them. We don't make the matter worse. Manu's right. He's just worried about his injury. Once he's tested it, he'll be fine. He'll be back tackling as he always has.'

Kitty didn't really believe what she was saying, but felt it was important to publicly stick up for her friend.

'Yeah, well, we'll see,' said Matt, shaking his head. 'We've got our next game on Thursday, we'll just have to see what happens then.'

'Yes, we will,' said Mrs John who had been listening to everything just out of sight of the friends. She called everyone together.

'Now listen, you lot. Jimmy's our captain and we support him, whatever the situation is. There's no room in my team for people who aren't willing to support their teammates – whatever issue they may have. Yes, things didn't go his way today, but he's the most determined and committed young rugby player I've ever seen. The only reason we're able to have this conversation is that he's out there now, with a bag of balls and practising his kicking to make sure he's at his best for the team. For *you*.'

She looked across at Matt.

'I haven't seen any of you show that commitment to improving yourselves, by putting in the extra work and time that Jimmy does. Did you know that the very next morning after the doctors had told Jimmy it was alright to start some light training after his injury, he was out on The Rec, doing everything that his shoulder would allow him? He was still on pain killers.'

Mrs John paused to ensure her message was getting through. It had. Everyone sat in total silence.

'I know somebody who had to try to come back to rugby after a very nasty shoulder injury and it wasn't easy. They suffered from people saying they had lost it, too, and because of all the whispers and lack of support, they never really came back from that. I won't let that happen to a player on my team.'

Again, she paused to allow her message to sink in.

'We will all support him until we get to the end of it. Hopefully that will lead to a positive outcome. If not, well, we'll deal with that if it happens. But until then, we will support our friend and teammate no matter what.'

She stopped again and looked around the room. Everyone was looking at her apart from Matt who was picking the mud from the studs on his boots.

'Is that understood?'

'Yes,' came the unified reply. Apart from Matt who just nodded.

'Good.' Then she walked over to Kitty to have a quick chat about her positional play when her team didn't have the ball.

Out on The Rec, Jimmy stood over his fifteenth kick, completely unaware of the conversation inside. He knew he'd had a terrible session and was just trying to shut it all out and concentrate on his kicking. As awful as his tackling had been, his kicking was superb. Fourteen out of fourteen.

'100% so far,' said Oscar. 'Get this one and you can stop. If not, you'll be starting again.'

Normally, Jimmy would laugh at Oscar's accurate, yet blunt, assessment of the situation, but he hardly heard him. He was just focusing on the ball and the posts.

Jimmy did his usual routine – took his first step forward,

standing up straight as he did, before striking the ball perfectly between the posts, high and as straight as an arrow.

'100%!' said Oscar enthusiastically. 'Fifteen out of fifteen. That can go in the book and we can go home now. I took a photo of the last kick. Well done, Jimmy.'

Jimmy smiled.

'Thanks, mate. Let's get these balls back in the bag and get you home. I don't think I want to go back into the dressing room today.'

But Oscar was already off, gathering up all the balls for his friend, seemingly, without a care in the world.

Jimmy wished he didn't have a care in the world either, but at the moment, he had plenty.

THE GOOD, THE BAD
AND THE UGLY

It was fifteen minutes into Jimmy's comeback match against St Peter's Primary School, and he had been absolutely superb.

Everything he had tried had come off. He'd made a try for Manu within just two minutes, after he had gathered his own brilliant chip through, before popping the ball to Manu to streak in down the left wing to score. Jimmy followed that with an outrageous drop-goal. After receiving a scruffy pass from Matt following a scrum, he dummied the onrushing St Peter's second row only to be closed down by their scrum-half. Realising he was going to be tackled, Jimmy somehow managed to find the time and space to lean back and drop a goal from about twenty-five metres, just as he was hit by the scrum-half. The ball had gone very high because Jimmy was leaning back so much, but had just enough legs to drop over the bar.

The parents that were watching on the sidelines gasped. Firstly, because of the brilliance of his drop-goal. It looked to everyone that at the exact moment that Jimmy managed to get his kick away, he had already been tackled by the scrum-half, it was such a brilliant skill to manage to complete the kick with such accuracy. Secondly, because of the power of the tackle. As Jimmy was concentrating on getting his kick away, he hadn't been able to tense his body to deal with the impact. As a result, there was a sickening thud as Jimmy was smashed to the ground. Lots of the parents, including Jimmy's own, feared the worst as he appeared to land on his shoulder/collarbone area. But Jimmy was more concerned about whether his kick had gone through the posts than worryied about his previous injury.

Once everyone realised that the kick had made it, Kitty ran across and checked her friend was okay. Jimmy rotated his arm a couple of times before breaking into a smile for Kitty and saying, 'Good as new!' Everyone was relieved, especially his parents.

Everything seemed to be going Jimmy's way on his return to competitive action.

Until the lineout.

Jimmy was busy organising the back line to defend the lineout when the St Peter's hooker surprised everyone. Rather than throw it in for one of the forwards as usually happened, he threw an enormously long throw over the back of the lineout to his powerful centre, a lad called Elliott Ridge. Elliott caught the ball without breaking stride and sprinted on a straight line towards the nearest player. Jimmy.

Jimmy lined up Elliott, and having just minutes before satisfied himself that his collarbone was fine, prepared to make the tackle. But just as had happened in the training session earlier that week, an instant before the moment of contact, something in Jimmy's brain switched off and made him pull out of the challenge. It looked awful and, standing alongside Jimmy's parents, his grandfather bowed his head to the floor. He didn't want to watch.

And that was the pattern for the rest of the match. Jimmy not tackling and Will not watching.

The St Peter's players had worked out that Jimmy was the defensive weak link and ran at him at every opportunity. It was tough to watch. Jimmy appeared to have completely lost the ability to tackle. He would make some sort of effort but it was never a committed tackle – just a couple of outstretched arms trying to scrag his opponent's shirt as he ran past. If it han't been for Manu, Central would have been hammered, but he was covering for his friend and sweeping up the mess. He tackled himself to a standstill.

In fairness to Manu, he never said a word to Jimmy. Well, that's not strictly true, he said plenty of words, but all were encouraging. He knew what was happening was bad, but stood alongside his friend, shoulder to shoulder.

The opposite was true of Matt. From the moment Jimmy had pulled out of the tackle on Elliott Ridge after the long throw at the lineout, Matt had been huffing and puffing every time Jimmy missed a tackle. Whatever the opposite of supportive was, well, that was Matt. He hardly spoke to Jimmy at half-time, choosing instead to stand with Andrew Beasley and the forwards rather than Manu, Kitty and Jimmy. Then, as the players ran to their positions to start the second half, Matt said loudly, 'Come on, we can win this . . . if we all start to tackle.'

Jimmy heard his friend and felt a stab of hurt, but didn't react.

Then, as if to emphasise the strangeness of the situation, Jimmy had one surprise left.

As awful as he was in defence, he remained brilliant – and oddly brave – in attack.

With St Peter's ahead by the five points of Ridge's last try, and in the last minute of the game, Matt made a break but was hauled down about fifteen metres out. The teammate that was closest to him, having followed his run, was Jimmy. He was in the perfect place to receive an offload from Matt. Any sort of pass to Jimmy would have led to a certain try.

But Matt had stopped passing to Jimmy after the half-time break. Instead, he was making solo runs or miss-passes inside to Manu and ignoring Jimmy. Jimmy understood why, but was getting frustrated by it.

This time, when Matt was tackled, he looked up to make the pass, but saw his only option was Jimmy, so instead of offloading, Matt clung on to the ball and took it into the tackle. On the touchline, Mrs John put her head in her hands, the last chance to snatch victory from St Peter's was surely gone.

Immediately, one of the St Peter's forwards was over Matt, jackalling him, trying to get the ball for the turnover which would have given his team possession and ensured their hard-fought victory over Central.

Jimmy knew what he had to do. He looked at the forward crouched over Matt's body, feet spread wide apart for stability. His upper body was low to prevent himself from being moved away, and he was reaching forward to pluck the ball that Matt was obliged to release. But that powerful position he adopted meant nothing to Jimmy. With all his might, he flew low into the forward, getting underneath him and driving upwards, using all of his strength to move him off Matt and, far more importantly, away from the ball. The forward was surprised by the intensity of Jimmy's hit.

Following Jimmy was Andrew Beasley, who was now able to pluck the unprotected ball up from the floor, skip through the gap in the defence that Jimmy's ruck clearance had created and jog in for the winning try.

Strangely, nobody mobbed the try-scorer as usually happened, instead they mobbed Jimmy. All except Matt, who stood alone muttering to himself, 'He can drive someone off the ball, but he can't tackle anyone. What's that all about?'

Jimmy didn't hear what his friend said, but if he had, he'd have agreed. He had no idea himself why he was so scared of making a head-on tackle, yet was able to relish the contact with an opponent who wasn't moving. He wished he knew the answer. But he had no time to worry about that now. There was a kick to be taken.

Jimmy placed the ball and focused on his routine. As usual, it was immaculate and Jimmy added the extra two points to confirm the victory. The final whistle went and a big cheer went up from the Central players.

Jimmy didn't get involved in the celebrations, just quietly picked up his tee and went to look for the opposing captain to shake his hand. When Jimmy had finished commiserating with the opposition players and leading his team in their 'Three cheers for St Peter's', he walked off alone to the dressing rooms. Despite his excellent offensive contribution to the victory, Jimmy felt very down about his tackling issues. It just seemed to be getting worse and worse.

On his way off the field, he felt a familiar hand on his shoulder, it was his grandfather.

'Hey, are you okay?'

Jimmy just nodded in silence.

His grandfather could tell that Jimmy was upset, so decided to leave things for the moment; he didn't want to be the cause of further embarrassment for his grandson.

'Okay. Well I'm off home now. Your grandma is going shopping with Mrs Buckley from number 37 so I'll be at home on my own. Pop in on your way past for a chat. I'll see what we've got nice in to eat.'

Jimmy just nodded again, too embarrassed to look at him, then broke into a jog towards the dressing room. He couldn't wait to get changed, grab his kitbag and get out of there.

As much as he loved his grandfather, he couldn't face him.

He just wanted to be alone.

GRAMP

Jimmy walked home slowly. He'd decided to walk the long way round to his house, behind the allotments, so that there was less chance of bumping into someone and having to talk to them about the game. His plan worked and he walked silently on his own without seeing another soul.

He eventually reached his home and glanced across to the open front door of his grandfather's house. As much as he loved his grandfather, he wasn't sure if he wanted to see him. He knew if he did, he would have to explain his fear of tackling. Jimmy knew how brave a man his grandfather was and felt that, somehow, he'd be letting him down. Jimmy wasn't sure he could face that.

But something was compelling him to do so. Will had always put Jimmy at the heart of his life and even though Jimmy didn't want to have the conversation with him at that precise moment, he felt that he had a duty to.

So he walked towards the open door of his grandfather's

house. Jimmy didn't know it then, but that change of mind saved his grandfather's life.

Jimmy walked in and called out for his grandfather. There was no reply.

He walked into the front room, but there was nobody there. Then he went into the kitchen and again there was no sign of his grandfather. *Strange*, thought Jimmy.

Then he noticed the back door was slightly open, so Jimmy went out.

There, sitting on his garden bench was his grandfather. It was quite chilly and Jimmy thought it odd that he would be sitting out there without a coat.

'Hi Gramp, what's happening?' he asked, trying to appear upbeat and not show how much the rugby match had affected him.

Will turned around slowly, but seemed a little confused to see his grandson.

'Jimmy,' he said. Then, as if he was struggling to find the right words said, 'How are you son? I haven't seen you for a while.'

Jimmy frowned. They'd spoken less than half an hour ago. And what was wrong with his grandfather's voice? It sounded different, as if he was pausing over every word.

'Gramp, what's wrong? You don't look so good.'

His grandfather's reply was quite slurred, as if he'd been drinking, which Jimmy knew he hadn't been. 'Oh, nothingsh wrong, Jimmy . . . I just feelsh a bit short've cold . . .'

Jimmy went to his grandfather's side quickly.

'Gramp! Gramp! What's wrong?' he cried, starting to panic.

172

His grandfather looked at him, but didn't seem able to answer. His eyes were wide, staring at Jimmy.

Jimmy was scared. He didn't know what to do.

Then he realised that there was only one thing for him to do. Run.

Jimmy ran like the wind, back into the kitchen, down the hall and out onto the road in about two seconds flat.

He burst into his own house, screaming, 'Mum! Mum! It's Gramp, there's something wrong with Gramp!'

Jimmy's mum was in the kitchen at the sink, she spun around and saw the terror in her son's face.

'What's wrong, Jimmy, what's wrong?'

'It's Gramp. He's not right. I think there's something really wrong with him. He's just sitting there, not able to speak.' His eyes were filling with tears.

With that, Jonny appeared, having heard all the commotion while he'd been watching TV in the front room. 'No, no, no, not Gramp,' said Jonny, stricken with fear. 'What's wrong with him, Mum?'

Their mother rushed past both her sons heading for the front door. She hurried but was extremely calm.

'Jimmy, come with me,' she called while passing her mobile phone to Jonny, not breaking a stride as she went.

'Ring 999, Jonny, call for an ambulance and just say "suspected stroke". Do it quickly. Then come to Gramp's.'

Jimmy and his mother then rushed straight out of the front door and in to see to his grandfather.

33

SAVED BY THE BELL

Jimmy and all his family sat in the waiting room of the hospital.

Hardly anyone spoke. It had been twenty-four hours since Will had been rushed in and it had been confirmed that he had had a stroke. Only Jimmy's mum and grandma had been allowed to see him, but all the grandchildren had insisted on coming to the hospital straight after school, even if they were only allowed to stay in the waiting room.

By the time they'd all arrived, Jimmy's mum had said that the consultant was in seeing him and finding out how serious Will's condition was.

They all sat in silence, the adults looking out of the window and Jimmy and his brother and sister glued to their mobile phones, playing Minecraft.

After about half an hour, the door to the waiting room opened and in walked the consultant.

He sat next to Jimmy's mum and grandma and told them the news. It was good.

Apparently, with a stroke, the first hour is critical. If the patient can be assessed and treated in that first hour, there's every chance that they can make a full recovery. If they are left alone and not treated, then the stroke can be 'catastrophic', in the words of the doctor, or even result in death. Will had been very lucky apparently.

The doctor described Will's recovery as like watching a flower opening, and said that every hour saw an improvement in his speech, his movement and his coordination. He was very happy with his progress. Jimmy could see the relief in the face of his mother and grandma.

The doctor got up to leave and as he reached the door, he stopped and turned to Jonny.

'Oh, I forgot. Are you Jimmy?'

'No, I'm Jonny,' replied his brother. 'That's Jimmy.' He pointed across the room.

'Ah, Jimmy, hello.'

Jimmy replied with a quiet, 'Hello.'

'I've just been chatting to your grandfather for twenty minutes and he has been telling me all he can remember about his episode. He told me that you are the one that found him and raised the alarm?'

Jimmy replied softly, 'Yes.'

'Well, I need to tell you, young man, your quick actions have probably saved his life. We understand from your grandmother that she wasn't due back home for a few hours and that might have been too late for Will. Your decision to call to see him and your speed in alerting your mother saved him. Well done.'

Jimmy didn't know what to say.

He felt a mixture of happiness and relief but also guilt. Happiness that he'd done the right thing in getting his mother so quickly when he realised that something was wrong, but guilt at how close he had come to not going to see his grandfather at all, just because he was so down about his bad game of rugby. Jimmy realised how selfish that had been, possibly not going in to speak to his grandfather, basically because he had been feeling sorry for himself. That one decision could have cost his grandfather his life.

Jimmy knew that he had an issue to sort out with his rugby, but he would never again let it affect him so much as to even consider ignoring his family or anyone else that was willing to help him. Whatever it took, Jimmy would get it sorted, but he would never, ever feel sorry for himself about it again.

THE LADDER TO SUCCESS

Over the next two weeks, everyone rallied around Jimmy's grandparents. Will's recovery continued at a positive rate. He had spent the first week in hospital working with speech and language therapists and physiotherapists. After five days, all of them had said they could do no more for him and were very pleased with his recovery and the speed of it. He had regained his speech perfectly. He was monitored for the rest of the week as he began taking Warfarin tablets to thin his blood and make sure he had no more blood clots in his system. Once they were satisfied with that, they let him go home.

By the end of the second week, Will's recovery had been so rapid that Jimmy's family had to stop him from doing too much.

It was such a relief to them all, especially Jimmy. Every night after school, Jimmy would head straight to his grandfather's house and watch *The Chase* on TV with him. Jimmy loved it. Strangely, in that first week back home, the one thing that Jimmy and Will didn't discuss was rugby. But then, at the start of the third week of Will's recovery, after one very enjoyable episode of *The Chase*, when 'The Beast' had been caught and three contestants shared £63,000, Will said to Jimmy, 'Turn the TV off, son.'

Jimmy did as he was asked. Then Will said, 'Right then. What's this issue with you and your tackling? Are you worried about your collarbone?'

Jimmy looked at his grandfather and said, 'Oh, don't worry about me, Gramp, it's more important that you stay well rather than think about anything else.'

'Nonsense!' replied Will. 'I'm absolutely fine and I've had just about enough of all this mollycoddling! I'm not allowed to drive and your grandmother won't even let me go to the allotment for half an hour, just to do some weeding, it's ridiculous!'

Jimmy laughed.

'So, seriously, Jimmy, I just want to get back to normal – and normal for me is making sure everything is okay with you.'

Jimmy understood and nodded.

'So, what's up then, *is* it your collarbone?'

The easy answer for Jimmy to give was 'yes'. He knew it would be completely understandable to be nervous about tackling for that reason and he'd be able to get away from telling his grandfather the real truth if he blamed his injury. But Jimmy realised it was time for honesty.

'No Gramp, my collarbone is fine. I took a big smack on it in my first game back. I didn't want to say anything to anyone as they'd worry, but when that scrum-half tried to block my drop-goal, his elbow caught me right on the very spot that my collarbone broke. I was worried for a second, but it was fine. No, it's got nothing to do with my collarbone at all, that's completely perfect.'

'So what is then?' asked Will, confused. 'Why have you suddenly stopped tackling?'

Jimmy took a deep breath and said the three words that were haunting him:

'Because I'm scared.'

Jimmy then told his grandfather everything, repeating all he'd told Kitty, the only other person he'd shared the full truth with.

He explained all about his time at the Eagles Academy and how, for some reason, the thought of tackling just grew and grew as a massive negative in his mind. He explained how the collarbone injury had dented his confidence further, how badly Matt had reacted to his shortcomings as a tackler and how much of a liability he knew he had become to the team.

He spoke for about five minutes and Will listened in silence to every word.

Jimmy ended by saying, 'But above everything else, Gramp, I just feel ashamed. Ashamed that I'm basically scared to make a tackle and I honestly don't know the reason why.'

Will looked at his grandson, trying to process everything he'd been told. It was tough to listen to and even tougher to see his grandson in such mental distress. Then he spoke.

'Okay. Firstly, it's good that you feel ashamed.'

Jimmy knew his grandfather was a straight talker, but even he was surprised by the bluntness of the statement.

'And what I mean by that,' continued Will, 'is that feeling ashamed like you do shows that you care. It shows that you're deeply affected by this and that it matters to you. That's a good thing, Jimmy. But it's something you have to let go of quickly.'

Jimmy said nothing in reply.

'All this feeling of shame does is make you feel more negative about the situation, son, and eventually that will just make things worse and worse. You've got to try and adopt a positive attitude about the situation. Once you do that, you'll be on the road to finding a solution, and the first stage of that is to stop being ashamed. So, while this shame you feel is good, because it shows you care, it's also bad because it will ultimately bring you down. Understand?'

Jimmy nodded.

'Good. So from this moment on, no more feeling ashamed. Instead, let's find a solution. Okay?'

Again, Jimmy nodded.

'Good. Now then. What if I told you, I was ashamed once because I was scared of doing something when I was in the Marines?'

Jimmy looked up in surprise.

'You? Scared of something, Gramp?' said Jimmy, 'I don't believe it. Mum told me once that you've never been scared of anything in your life.'

'Yes, well that's because she wasn't with me when we did cliff invasion training down in Cornwall when I was just a seventeen-year-old rookie. If she had been, she'd know that there was a time when I've been scared – very scared indeed. The training session was based on something that happened in the Second World War. Have you heard of D-Day?'

'Yes,' replied Jimmy eagerly. After sport, Second World War history was one of his favourite subjects and he quickly told his grandfather all he knew about D-Day – the five Allied landing beaches in Normandy, codenamed Utah, Omaha, Gold, Juno and Sword. He also explained the importance that 6th June 1944 – D-Day – had for the allies defeating Hitler's Nazis.

Will was impressed.

'That's good knowledge, son, very good. Well, if you know so much about D-Day, have you ever heard about the 'Pointe du Hoc' mission?'

Jimmy shook his head. He hadn't.

Will explained.

'Well, it's hugely famous, especially in America. Pointe du Hoc is a very high cliff that juts out into the sea on the coast of France. It's about thirty metres high and is a sheer cliff. On the morning of D-Day it was to be climbed by the US Rangers, who are similar to our Royal Marines. The cliff was located between Utah and Omaha beaches on the Normandy coast. Above it was a German defensive point, filled with German soldiers who protected it.'

Jimmy listened in silence, absolutely spellbound.

'Under heavy fire, about 200 Rangers arrived at the bottom of the cliff in boats. The boats then fired grappling hooks with rope ladders attached to them, high to the top of the cliff. Once the ladders were secure, the Rangers climbed the cliff. From above, the Germans tried to shoot them and cut the ladders, but under the most awful conditions, the Rangers made it all the way to the top. They fought off the Germans and secured the location for two days, despite being surrounded by the enemy, until they were rescued by other troops who had made it across from Omaha beach. It's still regarded as one of the bravest missions of the war.'

Jimmy's eyes were wide with wonder. 'But I don't understand, Gramp, you've told me before, you didn't fight in the war.'

'I didn't,' replied Will. 'I'm old, but I'm not that old!'

Jimmy laughed.

'But for many years after the Second World War, a lot of the training exercises carried out in the British military were based on things that had happened in the conflict. The idea was that if a war ever happened again, we all had to learn the tricks that had been successful during the war, but we had to learn to do them even better. That's why the Marines spent so much time training.'

Jimmy understood and nodded.

'So,' continued Will, 'one of the training exercises the Marines did was to try to replicate what the US Rangers pulled off at Pointe du Hoc. Somebody found a cliff down on the coast at Cornwall that was almost identical to Pointe du Hoc and one day, as a nervous seventeen-year-old, I found myself on a boat, bobbing up and down on a choppy sea, before being ordered to climb the cliff by a rope ladder.'

Will paused.

'And that's where the fear hit me. I was one of the last off the boat and there were five different ladders to climb. I'd never been very good with heights, but I'd managed to somehow deal with it if I had to, but this was different. The cliff above was just straight up, no angle at all. That meant, when you were at the bottom of the ladder, you couldn't see the top at all. In fact, when you looked up, it was so steep, it just felt as if you were falling straight backwards down into the sea. I was terrified. I managed to climb about four rungs of the ladder when I felt it give, as if it was coming loose at the top. I froze. I was certain that the ladder was going to come away from the top of the cliff and I was going to fall back into the sea, bash my head on the rocks and drown.'

Will stopped talking. Lost in his memories.

'So what happened, Gramp?' asked Jimmy at last. 'Did you climb it?'

'No son, I didn't. And this is my turn to be ashamed. I froze completely, neither able to go up nor down. Our sergeant had to climb back down from the top of the cliff to get me moving. He started screaming and shouting at me to move, but I just couldn't. I went into this odd zone of not caring, just not really listening to what he was saying.'

Will paused again.

'Apparently, I was stuck on that ladder for about ten minutes. In war, I'd have been killed, as simple as that and, much worse, others would have died too. Somehow, they finally got me down from the ladder and into a boat. I was the only marine not to make it up the cliff face.'

'So what happened, Gramp? Did you have a row?'

Will laughed, 'Ha, you could say that. When we got back to base, the officers slaughtered me! I was told in no uncertain terms that I had to climb that ladder or I'd fail basic training and be booted out of the Marines. But the worse bit wasn't the rollicking I had from the officers, it was the silence that greeted me when I went back to my barracks from my mates. Everyone ignored me. I was ashamed.'

'That's like what Matt's been doing to me,' said Jimmy. 'Ignoring me.'

Will nodded, then continued.

'But the trouble was, even though I was ashamed, it didn't help the situation. I still knew that the following morning at 7.30, we had to do the whole thing again. I had no option. That night,

I hardly had a wink of sleep, worrying about the next morning and just realising that I wasn't going to be able to overcome my fear and probably be booted out of the Marines.'

'But you weren't booted out, Gramp, I know that,' said Jimmy, 'so what happened?'

'Well, basically, I had some help, Jimmy. That morning, in the Mess room queuing for breakfast, this quiet lad called Tom came up to me. I hadn't really had much to do with him at that point, but he just started to talk to me about the climb. I tried to ignore him at first, but then he told me how this was his second time in basic training and how he'd been thrown out the first time because he'd been unable to climb the ladder. Over breakfast he just explained how he'd got over his fear by breaking down every part of the ladder climb into separate pieces, until his brain treated the climb as lots of small things, rather than one huge task. And then a great thing happened.'

'You climbed the ladder!' said Jimmy triumphantly.

'No. The weather changed,' laughed Will.

Jimmy looked confused.

'In the time it took for us to complete breakfast, a storm came in, a bad one. I was terrified. It was bad enough to be scared about climbing the cliff in good weather, let alone in pouring rain and driving wind. Luckily for me, the officers must have agreed and they called the exercise off, postponing it for a day. They then told us that we had a day of physical training in the gym instead. I'd never been so relieved to have to train myself to a standstill as I was at that moment.'

Will laughed again, as did Jimmy; he loved his grandfather's stories of the military, he just came so alive when he spoke of them.

'Anyway, we had two forty-five-minute breaks, plus lunch, during the training day, and in that time when everyone else went back to barracks to rest, Tom took me to the corner of the gym where the rope ladders were and explained, step by step, how to climb one. I was still very scared at first, but as Tom explained the physics of it all – how to stop the ladder swirling around by climbing it sideways, how to shift your weight to gain the best angle to climb and how to use arms and legs together for stability – I became better. Then, the better I became, the less fearful I was of it. That day, in the end, I must have climbed that ladder forty times with Tom, and just understanding how to do it, removed all of the fear for me.'

'So did you finally climb the ladder up the cliff, Gramp?'

'No,' laughed Will, 'the bad weather continued for the rest of the week and time basically ran out, so we never went back. However, every day, I went into the gym with Tom before breakfast and climbed that ladder five times. I got so good, that I nearly ran up it in the end. My fear of heights and my fear of that ladder had gone. And there was one simple reason why.'

Jimmy looked, waiting for the answer.

'Somebody showed me how to do it. And once you learn how to do something, no matter how much you dread it or are worried about it, the fear will leave you. You gain confidence from knowing exactly how to do something. And that's what you're going to have to do, Jimmy. You're going to have to find someone to show you exactly how to tackle.'

THE LOWEST POINT

The month of February wasn't very kind to Jimmy. Despite understanding everything his grandfather had told him, the tackling issue just got worse for him. There were three school games in the month and the pattern was repeated in each.

Jimmy would start the game well . . . no, that wouldn't be correct. Jimmy would start the game *brilliantly*, before, inevitably, he would be called upon to make a tackle. Then everything would go wrong. Horribly wrong. It got to the stage that Jimmy's brilliance on the field in an attacking sense was being cancelled out by his defensive limitations. It wasn't pretty to watch.

Mrs John had now become aware that tackling was a huge issue for Jimmy, and while she was sympathetic, there was not much she could do. During training she had so much to concentrate on with all the other players, that apart from the odd bit of encouragement, she was unable to give him any one-on-one coaching, especially in the tackling department.

She was as bemused as anyone because, even in training sessions, Jimmy was head and shoulders above anyone else when he had ball in hand, it was just defensively he struggled so much. She'd never really seen anything like it before.

Soon, Mrs John started to move Jimmy around in his position. She tried to work out where best to place him to reduce the amount of tackling he'd face while still using him as an attacking force. She first moved Jimmy away from fly-half to inside centre, swapping him with Manu, then, in the following game, she moved him again, this time to outside centre. In the third game, towards the end of the month, she even moved him onto the wing in the second half of the match, so bad had his tackling – or more appropriately, non-tackling – become.

The only person that really understood was Kitty. She became Jimmy's closest confidant, the only one Jimmy would really open up to.

'I just don't know what to do, Kitty,' he said the morning after the game he'd been moved out to the wing. 'The whole thing just seems to be getting worse.'

Kitty listened as Jimmy explained what his grandfather had said about finding someone to teach him how to tackle properly and how he hoped that would help him.

'The trouble is, Kit, I'm just too embarrassed to ask anyone. I don't want to go and see Peter Clement because I've not seen much of him since last season and would just hate to have to admit to him this fear I've developed. I've tried to watch Manu, who's our best tackler, to try to work out how to tackle properly by seeing what he does, but he doesn't seem to have a technique, he just smashes anyone who goes near him. I'll never be able to do that.'

Kitty nodded. She knew Manu was something special as a tackler, but even she winced when she saw some of the tackles he made. There didn't seem to be any plan with his tackling, apart from absolutely munching the opponent.

'What about Mrs John? Why don't you go and explain to her? I'm sure she'll help,' said Kitty. 'She's been brilliant with me, sorting out my positional play and game awareness.'

Jimmy paused for a moment before replying.

'I've thought about it, but I still feel a bit shy around her. I really like her, but I still feel like I don't know her well enough to ask her for help. Also, the way she's moved me away from fly-half in the recent games, I'm worried that if I admit everything to her, she'll drop me from the team for good, and it's the quarter finals of the Cluster Cup next week.'

Kitty interrupted.

'She'll never do that, Jimmy, she's too nice to do something that drastic.'

'I wouldn't blame her if she did, to be honest,' said Jimmy looking down at the floor.

'Don't talk like that,' snapped Kitty. 'I know it's tough, but we'll find a solution to this. Why don't you let me talk to Mrs John and tell her all about it? I really think she'll help you if she knows what the problem is.'

Jimmy thought for a second, and said, 'Well maybe that is the best thing. Would you do that for me? I know it might be a bit awkward for you.'

'Of course I'll do it,' she said. 'And it won't be awkward at all, I know Mrs John will think of something.'

She did. She dropped Jimmy for the next game.

36

FINDING THE ANSWER

In fairness to Mrs John, she had already made the decision to drop Jimmy before Kitty had a chance to speak to her.

She had been away on a two-day training course on the Monday and Tuesday, and when she got back in to school on the Wednesday, she announced the team for Thursday afternoon's game before doing anything else.

Everyone swung around and looked at Jimmy for his reaction when it was announced that he was one of the replacements, but Mrs John had broken the news to him personally before registration that morning, so the public announcement wasn't a shock for him.

Surprisingly, he wasn't as upset as he thought he would be. In fact, a small part of him was almost relieved – maybe it was best for him to have a break.

Mrs John had explained that the team they had been drawn against in the quarter-final of the Cluster Cup, Woodview Primary, were a particularly tough team and she felt that Jimmy would benefit from not being exposed by them. Jimmy knew all about Woodview, and tough was the perfect word to describe their team. They loved their rugby there and took no prisoners when they played. Maybe it was a good one for Jimmy to miss.

Mrs John made everyone understand that she was giving everybody from the squad an opportunity to have a game and confirmed that Jimmy would remain her captain when he played, but still, his omission was the talk of the playground at break time. At the end of the day, Mrs John asked Jimmy to stay behind and when everyone had left the class, she spoke.

'I'm really sorry about the timing of the announcement today,' she said, sitting down on the edge of her desk. 'Kitty saw me at lunchtime and explained everything. You must have thought me incredibly heartless this morning when I told you my decision, but I hadn't spoken to Kitty at that point.'

'It's okay,' replied Jimmy slightly awkwardly. 'I understand.'

'Well, I'm not sure that you do, Jimmy,' replied Mrs John with a smile. 'You see, there is another reason why I wanted to leave you out of the team this week, and luckily, Kitty's explanation earlier was the perfect timing.'

Jimmy looked at her, confused.

'You know my husband, Kevin, don't you?'

'Yes,' he exclaimed. 'He helped me with my place kicking when I was injured, he's great!'

Mrs John smiled. 'Yes, he's not bad, but I'm not going to tell him what you said, he'll get big headed!'

Jimmy laughed.

'Well, did you know that Kevin is one of the strength and conditioning coaches at the Reds in the National League?'

'No, but I knew he had something to do with them, I just wasn't sure what exactly.'

'Well, he was originally involved with them as a player, years ago, long before I met him, but he had a really nasty injury in one of his very first senior games for them and he never really recovered. He struggled to come to terms with tackling when he came back, and his career just fizzled out before it really began.'

Jimmy nodded, he felt like saying, 'I know how he feels,' but he remained silent.

'Anyway,' continued Mrs John, 'the Reds felt a bit to blame about how his career ended so early, with the injury happening while he was playing for them, so they looked after him. Once it was clear that the injury wouldn't fully recover, which meant he'd never regain his confidence to tackle, they offered him a job on the back-room staff. Part of the job meant that they would sponsor him to go to university – and he chose to study strength and conditioning, where he learned all about the way the body works in sport and, in particular, rugby, and how best to prepare people for it. I was actually at the same university doing my teacher training, which is how we met.'

Jimmy nodded, wondering where this was heading.

'Now,' she continued, 'I've been telling Kev all about you and we've come up with a bit of a plan. He thinks that players who have issues around tackling, the fear often lies in the fact that they don't really know what to do in terms of technique.'

'Yes!' replied Jimmy quickly. 'That's exactly it! It's what my grandfather told me weeks ago, but I didn't know who to tell.'

'That's what Kitty explained to me at lunchtime. And Kev wants to help. He wants to try and teach you how to tackle properly. How does that sound to you?'

Jimmy almost jumped with excitement. 'It sounds great! Really great! When can we start?'

'How about tonight?' came a voice from behind Jimmy. It was Kevin. 'There's no time like the present!'

THE GARDEN OF EDEN

Jimmy looked around the huge garden that stretched from the rear of Mrs John's house. It was massive. It was almost the size of half a rugby field with long, high hedges either side of the perfect grass. At the end nearest the house, there was a small patio and barbecue area, but from there down to the far end, which was easily fifty metres, was lush, green grass, all surrounded by mature trees. At the bottom was a small fence that led out onto some farm fields which gave the impression of the garden being even bigger.

When Kevin came out, Jimmy turned to him and said, 'This is the biggest garden I've ever seen!'

Kevin laughed.

'Yes, it's not bad is it? It's one of the reasons we came back here to live. I used to play in this house when I was a kid. It belonged to the grandparents of a mate of mine when we were both at Central Primary, the same as you. His name was Steve and his grandparents had a bit of money and spoilt him rotten.

They actually marked this out as a small rugby pitch, complete with posts.'

'Wow!' exclaimed Jimmy. 'Real posts? Are you serious? That's so cool!'

'Yes, cool it most certainly was. Come here, I'll show you.'

Kevin walked off the patio and onto the grass, just about two yards on from a flower border.

'Here, look at this,' said Kevin, kneeling down and pressing his hand into the grass.

Jimmy looked and saw what appeared to be a lump of rotten wood. He knew instantly what it was from the shape.

'Is that a post?'

'Yep,' smiled Kevin. 'There's another one just over there, and two more, way down the bottom of the garden.' He got up and pointed to the end, near the fence.

'Steve and I played here all the time. I loved it. I learned to kick conversions here, before we outgrew it and moved down to The Rec. I have such happy memories of this garden. When we found out that the house was for sale last summer, we set in place all the details for the move back here from the big city. It helped that Laura . . . sorry, Mrs John! . . . had a job to go to at Central and I always wanted to live here, so everything fitted perfectly.'

Kevin smiled to himself as he looked around his wonderful garden.

'When we viewed it, the first thing I did was come out to see if the posts were still here. I knew they'd have probably been taken down, but was chuffed to see that the base of them was still here. As soon as Laura . . . sorry, Mrs John!' said Kevin laughing again. 'As soon as we have our first child, I'll be getting new posts put in. I want my son or daughter to have as much fun learning about rugby here as I did.'

'It will be brilliant,' marvelled Jimmy, taking in as much of the surroundings as he could.

'But, until then,' said Kevin, 'this is where you'll be learning your rugby. Or more specifically, learning how to tackle!'

'And it was all going so well,' said Jimmy with a half-smile.

Kevin laughed, 'You'll be fine.'

'But before we do anything, you need to tell me your story and then I'll tell you mine. I think you'll find we have quite a bit in common.'

TACKLING THE PAST

Jimmy told Kevin everything about his tackling fears and how they had grown out of all proportion over the preceding months, and when Jimmy finished talking, silence fell between the two of them.

Eventually Kevin spoke.

'I smashed my collarbone tackling someone I needn't have tackled. I was trying to prove to people that I was something that I wasn't. It sounds like I was a bit like you. I was also a fly-half and I was like lightning off the mark. I just loved running with the ball.'

Jimmy nodded, it was clearly familiar to him.

'I made all the age group teams, made the national schools team and the Under 18 national team when I was still in Bishopswood Year 11. Everything was going brilliantly. It was just my bad luck that I lived in the same street as a certain Mark Kane.'

Jimmy winced at the mention of Mr Kane.

'As you know by now, Jimmy, Mark Kane is a bully. And

from the age of about ten until I was seventeen, he bullied me. Incredibly, I really think that the bullying began because of this garden. Steve's grandparents knew the Kane family and didn't like them, so when Mark came here with Steve and me one day, well, Steve's grandparents told him that he wasn't welcome.'

Kevin paused for a moment as he looked around the garden, clearly remembering his childhood days.

'I remember feeling that they were being a bit harsh on Mark and actually felt sorry for him, because we were all friends at the time. But that stopped soon enough.'

'But why did he bully you and not Steve? It wasn't your fault that they stopped him playing; they were Steve's grandparents, not yours.'

'You're right. But the problem was, Mark soon found out that I was coming back on my own to play with Steve without telling him and he hated me for that. It was from then on that he always picked on me.'

'That's so unfair,' said Jimmy.

'The main problem was, Mark was a year older than me and I was much smaller then, a really skinny boy actually. I don't suppose you remember a Welsh fly-half called Arwel Thomas? A bit before your time, maybe.'

Jimmy shook his head, he hadn't heard of him.

'Well I was his sort of build, quite small, but very quick and tricky. But being so small, I was an easy target for Mark. He was almost the size he is now when he was thirteen! Everyone was scared of him. Because I was quite talented at rugby, when we got to secondary school, I played up a year in terms of age rugby. That meant I played in Mark's team. He was captain. I remember one match we played and I missed a tackle. He went absolutely nuts with me after the game, threatened me, everything. Then he decided to make it his job to mock me. His mocking about my poor tackling never really stopped from that day on.'

Kevin stopped for a second, lost in his memories.

'I have to admit, though, I wasn't much of a tackler,' he continued. 'I never really learned how to do it properly. But to be honest, I never actually thought it was that important. Rugby has changed a lot since I was a kid. These days, fly-halves like Owen Farrell see big hits as part of their game, a really important part of their approach, but it wasn't always that way. Have you heard of Jonny Wilkinson?'

Jimmy answered enthusiastically.

'Yes. Yes, I have! He was brilliant. I've watched loads of him on YouTube. He tackled like a demon!'

'Exactly!' replied Kevin. 'Jonny really changed the way a fly-half plays the game. Before him, it was understood that fly-halves weren't really expected to tackle. In fact, some coaches didn't want them getting involved at all. They were so critical to the team's success in terms of creating tries that some coaches didn't want them risking injury by getting too involved in tackling. But Jonny Wilkinson changed all that.'

Kevin looked at Jimmy who was taking all this information in. He could see that his young friend was hanging on his every word.

'So, things carried on as they were for a while. I was still playing great attacking rugby, but still missing the odd tackle. When I did, Mark would jump on me and humiliate me on and off the field. It was horrible. Some people said it was because he was jealous of the way I played the game. Maybe that was true. I'd really like to say that he wasn't very good, but he was. The problem was, his game was so different to mine. Mine was all about flair and creation, playing the game fast and loose, his was all about destruction. I've never seen anyone so ferocious in the tackle and he took real pleasure in hurting people. It's a fact of life that rugby needs super-competitive people like that, but his nastiness took it to another level. And because of the way he bullied me, I hated him.'

'It doesn't sound like he's changed much then.'

'No, it doesn't, and that's really sad to hear. I'm not sure he's the right person to be coaching kids at the Eagles, but that's their problem, not mine.'

'So what happened? How did you get injured?'

'Well, I think it was a lot of things coming together that eventually saw me getting the injury. While still at school, I put up with about four seasons of Mark's bullying, but still managed to progress my career. I tried to improve my tackling bit by bit, and I did get better eventually, but I still relied on my attacking skills. Luckily for me, that's all that my coaches were interested in. I eventually got picked for the district sides, county sides and in the end, as I said, I played for my country at youth and Under 18 level. Then I got picked up by the Reds Academy system and really flourished. They had a fantastic attack coach who really developed my offensive game and who wasn't that interested in my defensive qualities. His view was pretty simple: to develop your strengths to the best they could possibly be and not worry too much about your weaknesses. Initially, I thought that was great, but working with elite players day to day, I could see how hard they worked on tackling and defence and realised I had to get better at it. Nobody taught me how to tackle as such, I just started to copy them and lay my body on the line a little bit more. That became my first problem.'

'How so?'

'Have you heard of concussion?'

'Yes, I have,' said Jimmy. 'It's become quite a big thing hasn't it? I was watching the highlights of an old Six Nations game and I think it was Leigh Halfpenny of Wales, he made such a brave tackle to save a try but he was completely knocked out. Then, when he came around, he didn't really seem to know where he was, but he wanted to continue playing. But they didn't let him, they took him off.'

'I remember it well,' said Kevin, 'I was actually at the match and he took a heck of a bang to the head. The medical team were straight on and looked after him instantly. There was no way they were going to let him play on . . . even if he wanted to. But it wasn't the same in my day, sadly.'

'What?' asked Jimmy, 'you mean in your day they would have let him play on?'

'Absolutely!' replied Kevin. 'In fact, it was encouraged, it was expected of you. It makes me angry just thinking about it.'

Kevin went quiet for a moment.

'I remember my first concussion. It was terrible. It was around about the time when I started to realise that I needed to have more of a presence on the field in terms of my defence. It was in a full squad practice session with the Reds, one of the first times that I was in a full practice match situation with the whole squad, including our internationals, and I really wanted to make an impression. Anyway, and I don't remember all the details because my memory of it is quite blurred, but all I really recall is Peter Robinson, an England B flanker, picking up a short pass from his scrum-half and him running straight at me. I have no memory of the tackle itself, or what happened next, but all I remember is waking up, with the physio squeezing a sponge over my head saying, 'You're all right son, shake it off, you'll be fine.' Apparently, I'd tried to tackle Peter from completely the wrong angle and his hips just collided with my head. The bizarre thing is that I played on and even scored a try, but I have no memory of it whatsoever!'

'Wow, that's so brave,' said Jimmy.

'But it's not, Jimmy, that's the point. The last thing it was, was brave, because I have no recollection of it and no memory of making any sort of decision. The decision was made for me by the physio. It was reckless and extremely dangerous. If I'd had another bang on the same part of my head, who knows what might have happened?'

Jimmy looked a little confused.

'But the thing is, Kevin, I thought that the whole point of rugby is playing on through the pain. That's what I meant about you being brave. I remember last season, Peter Clement told me of a time he broke his finger in training with the Wolves and he played on. That's why I don't understand why you thought it was a bad idea to play on when you came back to your senses.'

'That's the issue, though, Jimmy. I never did come back to my senses. I didn't know where I was and had to be told the next day that I'd scored a try . . . I had no idea.'

Kevin looked intently at Jimmy.

'Do you actually know what a concussion really is, Jimmy?'

'Well, yes, I think so. As I said earlier, it's a bang to the head.'

'It's actually much more than that,' interrupted Kevin. 'It's a form of brain injury, and unless a doctor diagnoses a concussion quickly, rather than just letting him or her carry on playing after a squirt of water on the back of the neck, the player's future health is being put at risk. That's why we have HIA's in rugby now.'

'Head Injury Assessment,' it was Jimmy's turn to interrupt.

Kevin looked impressed.

'Very good, Jimmy. Do you know what they are though?'

'Yes,' said Jimmy with some pride, 'I've had one!'

Kevin looked surprised.

'You've had one? Really? When?'

Jimmy told him all about the bang in the face he'd had that first morning at the Eagles Academy.

'So how did they assess you?' asked Kevin, clearly interested.

'Well, they took me back in the changing room, asked me to sit down, then someone asked me if I felt okay, which I did, then they asked me to look to my right and left, which I could, then I had to follow his finger in front of my eye and that was it, really. They said I was fine, then Mr Withey came in and said that he didn't want to take any chances so wouldn't let me play again that day.'

'Good for Mr Withey, but that's awful by the Eagles, especially to a young kid. Really awful.'

'But I was fine!'

'Yes, that's what they all say.'

Kevin looked away for a moment, as if trying to remember something.

'Boomerang, Venus and waterfall.'

'What?' exclaimed Jimmy, surprised.

'Did you hear those words, Jimmy?'

'Yes . . . you said, "Boo . . ."'

'Don't tell me!' said Kevin quickly, 'let's move on.'

'Move on to what?'

'If in doubt, sit them out.'

'What's that mean?' asked Jimmy, he was getting confused.

'It's a phrase that anyone in rugby who has responsibility to a player from six years of age to a British and Irish Lion should memorise by heart. You didn't have an HIA with the Eagles, Jimmy; at best, you had a quick check up. Thank goodness Mr Withey acted on, "If in doubt, sit them out". Good for him!

'You see, Jimmy,' continued Kevin, 'an HIA is an important examination that must be carried out strictly to the guidelines. The type of thing they should do if they suspect a concussion is to ask you some questions like, "What venue are you playing at today?", "What's the current score?", "Which team scored last in this game?" Then they should ask you to do something like count backwards from fifteen to ten or say a few months of the year backwards in order, or give you three random numbers like six, eight, and five to memorise then ask you to repeat them backwards, again in order. Then they should do a balance test on you, standing on one foot for thirty seconds to see how many times you put your other foot down. Another one is outstretching your index finger away from your face and then bringing it back to touch the tip of your nose ten times. The Eagles should have done all of that to you, Jimmy. They should never have just assumed you were okay because you said you were and it looked as if you were, that's awful by them . . . I'm just glad that Mr Withey appeared to have such good sense.'

'If in doubt, sit them out,' whispered Jimmy.

'Exactly,' replied Kevin. 'What were those three random words I said earlier?'

'What? You mean, boomerang, Venus and waterfall?'

Kevin laughed and clapped, 'Very good, Jimmy, very good . . . you clearly haven't got concussion!'

'Ahhhh,' said Jimmy realising what Kevin had done. 'Is that another concussion test? Three random words to see if you can remember them a little later?'

'It is. But all of these tests go to help the doctor make a picture of what level of concussion – if any – a player has. If the doctor has any doubt whatsoever . . .'

'Then he should sit you out!' finished Jimmy.

'Exactly, Jimmy, exactly.'

39

A TOUGH BREAK

Kevin carried on telling Jimmy about his experience with concussions that weren't treated properly by the Reds. He'd had a further two – one in a second XV game and another in a training incident. He'd also started to tell Jimmy about another one, but half way through stopped talking and put his hand up to his right collarbone and felt along it. He could feel the bumps and scars that still remained from the fateful evening that his rugby career effectively ended. He told Jimmy the sad tale.

'I'd been at the Academy for about a year and had really impressed with my game management and had been on a weights programme that had really started to fill me out. The Reds had an evening game against the Eagles. It was a regional cup game and a few of the first teamers were away on international duty and we had some injuries, so I was called up to the bench. It was the first time I'd been involved with the first team.'

'Wow, it must have been fantastic!' exclaimed Jimmy.

'It was. I was so excited. All my family were there and my friends from school, it was a special evening. I was looking forward to it so much and just desperate to get on.'

'Hey, you two!' A voice from the house interrupted Kevin. It was Mrs John. 'Do you want a drink or something?'

'No thanks, love,' said Kevin, 'we'll get one a bit later.'

Jimmy waved to his teacher who smiled, waved back and went back inside.

'Now, where was I?' asked Kevin, turning back to Jimmy.

'You were saying you were desperate to get on.'

'Ah yes, I was. Well, I got my chance. Our centre got injured, he pulled a hamstring chasing a kick and had to come off. So the coach moved our wing to centre and I came on to play right wing.'

'That must have been difficult, having to play out of position.'

'Yes,' replied Kevin, 'it wasn't ideal, but I didn't care really, I just wanted to get on, that was the most important thing and I was pretty quick back then, so I wasn't worried.'

'It must have been a great feeling.'

'It was, but sadly short-lived. I hadn't touched the ball for about five minutes. We were on top, but were mainly keeping the ball tight and driving up through the middle of them, ruck after ruck. If the ball ever came out, our scrum-half usually just popped it to the nearest supporting forward who took it back in. I just tried to stay sharp and alert in case someone decided to take a cross kick to me. I didn't want to mess up. But then we lost the ball.'

Jimmy noticed a sadness in Kevin's face at that last statement.

'I often wonder what would have happened if we'd retained

possession. But it's too late to turn the clock back now. What happened, happened.'

'So what did happen?'

'Well, one of the Eagles' props counter-rucked and secured a turnover. They quickly moved the ball and attacked. I think everyone thought they would kick as they were so deep in their twenty-two, but they surprised everyone and ran it. Before I knew it, the action was heading my way. I didn't have time to think or be nervous about making a tackle, because their huge flanker had the ball and was heading at me, at pace. Then, before I even had a chance to get ready, Tom Slattery, our beast of a centre, had decided to save me the trouble and take him out. It all happened so fast. I didn't actually need to get involved because Tom had the situation covered and to this day, I don't really know what came over me and why I decided to get involved when I didn't have to. I think it might have been because our coaches had been on to us to make double tackles – one high, one low – but to be honest, Tom had already made the tackle before I decided to get involved. I was just trying to make a point, I guess.'

Jimmy sat motionless, watching Kevin tell his story. It was clear that after all this time, it was still difficult for him to talk about.

'I've tried to work it out for years about why I did what I then did. I've just put it down to all the frustration of not being able to tackle effectively and all the mocking and bullying I'd had for all those years from Mark Kane, maybe that's what it was. But here I was, in my first ever game at the top level and I had the chance to make a point to everyone. That I could tackle and mix it up with the big boys. So I did.'

'But I thought you said that Tom Slattery made the tackle?'

'He did,' replied Kevin quickly, 'he made a great, low tackle, pretty much stopping the flanker in his tracks, but instead of not getting involved and waiting for the ruck, I thought I'd go in high, smash the bloke and try to dislodge the ball at the same time, pulling off a double tackle. I just wanted to show everyone I could tackle and do it on rugby's highest stage. I also wanted to do it to show the Eagles player who was carrying the ball that I wasn't scared.'

Kevin stopped and looked at Jimmy.

'You see, that player was Mark Kane.'

40

A BIGGER PICTURE

Jimmy's hand shot to his mouth in startled surprise. He couldn't believe what he'd just heard.

'Oh my God!' exclaimed Jimmy. 'It was Mark Kane that injured you!'

Kevin laughed.

'This *is* the funny thing, Jimmy. It wasn't Kane that injured me. It was Tom Slattery. I've tried to work it out to this day how it happened, but it's crazy, neither of us know exactly what occurred. Basically, the tackle that Tom put in on Kane was immense, really powerful. As I said, it didn't need me to get involved at all. But when I saw it was Kane, I just thought it was a perfect opportunity to make a joint hit and show him once and for all that I wasn't scared of tackling and I certainly wasn't scared of him. The problem was that the force of my tackle actually smashed Kane backwards and because the impact of Tom's tackle was still working on Kane's body, it altered the forward momentum of Tom's body. The result was that Tom flipped over onto me, and his left knee smashed into my collarbone. The force was such that not only did my collarbone shatter, but Tom also broke his knee cap. Two for the price of one.'

Kevin laughed again, shaking his head.

'How can you laugh, Kevin, that's terrible bad luck. It ended your career.'

'I know, it did and the big bang on the side of the head as I hit the ground – my third undiagnosed concussion – didn't help either. But one thing about the passing of time, Jimmy, is that it shows you there's always a bigger picture. As awful as it was at the time, if I'd not had that injury, the Reds would never have put me through university once they'd realised I'd never play again. And if I'd never gone to university, I never would have met . . .'

Kevin put his index finger in the air to show Jimmy he'd remembered not to use her first name in front of one of her pupils.

'. . . Mrs John. Then I'd never have got married, never have been able to buy this fantastic dream house and not be in a position to help a fantastic young player like you! So, in the end, Jimmy, things happen for a reason and you've always just got to make the best of certain situations and focus on the good stuff. One door closes, another one opens.'

Jimmy nodded. He understood the point Kevin was making.

'But it must have been tough knowing that Kane was the cause of it all?'

'For a few years it was, Jimmy, I won't lie. But then I realised that nobody forced me to make that tackle. I should have been professional and realised that it wasn't a tackle I needed to attempt. Tom had made the tackle, a double hit wasn't needed on that occasion. I can't blame Kane for that. I should've treated him like any player and done the right thing: let Tom complete the tackle and wait to see if I could've taken the ball off Kane in the resultant ruck. That would've been the smart rugby thing to do in that particular situation.'

Kevin looked at Jimmy for a moment.

'Mind you, there was another bonus to the tackle.'

'What was that?'

'Well, a split second after Tom's knee broke itself by shattering my collarbone, Tom's other knee somehow managed to swing round and catch Kane in the nose. Absolutely splattered it all over his face. But I shouldn't laugh.'

Kevin and Jimmy looked at each other for about three seconds.

Then both screeched laughing.

After a couple of minutes giggling about the thought of Mr Kane having some of his own medicine, Jimmy turned to Kevin.

'Obviously, the collarbone was a bad injury, but what about the concussion, what was that like?'

'Well that was quite scary, to be honest. Again, most of what I've told you I can't actually remember, it's just what I was told by Tom Slattery when he came to visit me in hospital from his bed in the next ward. The collarbone mended itself in time, even though it was a bad one, but I suffered headaches and sickness for days afterwards. I would also feel dizzy and vomit if I moved around and bright lights, like just watching the TV, gave me an instant headache for hours. That's when I realised how dangerous concussions can be. There was a definite build up in the seriousness of my concussions, having had three in a relatively short space of time. Then when I went to university and started learning so much about the human body, and realised how dangerous it is to ignore them, that's when I became passionate about protecting players with head injuries – especially young ones like you – and getting them off the field and not encouraging them to play on if it's clear they aren't 100%; that's just gone on for far too long.'

'If in doubt . . . sit them out.'

Kevin nodded.

VISUALISING THE FUTURE

Once Jimmy and Kevin had bared their souls to each other, Jimmy felt a lot better. Knowing that he had so much in common with Kevin meant that he was able to be himself around him and be open and honest about his feelings. That was hugely important to Jimmy. He really trusted Kevin, especially as he had told Jimmy so much about his nervousness as a tackler and his later issues with injuries and concussion.

Following their deep discussions about tackling, the one thing that they didn't do much of that Wednesday evening was actually tackle. Instead, Kevin decided to talk to Jimmy about the *importance* of tackling and why his game would move to another level if he could find a way to embrace it.

Kevin threw a pass to Jimmy out on that lush, perfect lawn, then started to jog down to the far end of the garden. All the way, Jimmy and Kevin just passed the ball gently back and forth to each other while Kevin talked to Jimmy about the art of tackling and also told Jimmy about the players who he felt were the very best and would be worth watching in order to pick up some tips.

'Brian O'Driscoll,' said Kevin. 'Have you seen him when you've been looking at YouTube?'

'Yes, I have,' replied Jimmy, 'he was an amazing player!'

'He was,' agreed Kevin, 'brave as a lion, O'Driscoll, an incredible tackler. He brought an extra dimension to his game with his tackling. A bit like Owen Farrell does now with England.'

Kevin looked at Jimmy.

'Have you seen George Ford play for England?'

'Yes, I have,' said Jimmy. 'I think he's a great player to watch. In fact, I prefer watching him than Farrell. I mean, Farrell is really good, but Ford seems a more fluid player to me, he attacks the line more and seems to bring more players into the game.'

'Nice evaluation,' replied Kevin. 'But in all internationals, Farrell has started way more Tests. Also, Farrell has played for the Lions and Ford hasn't. I think the reason for the difference between the two is probably tackling. Rightly or wrongly, Farrell is believed to be a better defender than Ford, and at the highest level, that counts for so much.'

Jimmy nodded. He understood.

'So there's no way around this then? If I want to become the best rugby player I can be, I've got to sort out this tackling problem I've got?'

Jimmy looked quite sad as he spoke to his new friend. All his fears of tackling flooded straight back into his mind.

'Yes, you have, Jimmy. But we'll get there, please don't worry about it. And we won't rush it, we'll take it one step at a time.

But first a question. Has anyone ever explained to you how to actually make a tackle?'

'No. Nobody. That's the problem. When I was at the summer camp with the Eagles, when all my worries started, I wasn't scared of tackling, it was just something that I wasn't really confident in doing. But as the sessions went on and my confidence got lower and lower, that was when the fear came in. The more hits I took, the worse it became because I just didn't really know what to do. I was too embarrassed to ask anyone, especially Mr Kane, so everything just went downhill really quickly.'

'Yes, I understand that,' replied Kevin. 'It's obvious to me that you developed a mental block in those few days at the Academy. Any decent coach worth his salt, especially one working with kids, should have seen that. What Kane did, in beasting you the way that he chose to, was turn a worry into a mental block and ultimately a type of trauma. That's what's led to this fear you have and that's why we're not going to rush things. Is that okay with you, Jimmy?'

'Yes,' replied Jimmy, 'I just want to get it sorted, so will do whatever you say.'

'Good lad,' replied Kevin. 'So let's get started.'

Kevin walked up to the patio area of the garden, pulled out two chairs from under the wooden table and ushered Jimmy to sit down. Then he began.

'Okay. The first thing about tackling is to be prepared for it, long before it happens. There are relatively few times in rugby when a tackle comes as a complete surprise. Usually, a defender will have an amount of time to plan for a tackle, unless it comes off the back of late runners or decoys, but we'll talk about those again. Let's simplify things first. I want you to think about a scrum for a moment. Close your eyes if you want to, it'll help you visualise it better.'

Jimmy closed his eyes, and thought of the last game he'd played in, when a scrum had been awarded at the very start.

'Right,' continued Kevin, 'imagine you're positioned at fly-half and the opposition have won the ball, and the scrum-half has just picked it up and is about to pass it. I want you to focus on the person who you are most likely to have to tackle.'

Jimmy was deep into his imaginary rugby world, visualising the play developing in front of him. He was looking at the scrum-half, but realising that if the scrum-half ran, it would most likely be Jimmy's own scrum-half, Matt, or one of the forwards, who would tackle him. He didn't need to focus on the scrum-half. *But if the scrum-half passes,* thought Jimmy, *then it's going to the fly-half, and he's the one who's going to run at me.*

'Who are you focussing on, Jimmy?' asked Kevin.

'The fly-half. If he gets the ball, he's the one I'm going to have to tackle.'

'Good boy, that's correct, excellent. Now, imagine that the scrum-half passes the ball to the fly-half and he's running straight at you.'

Jimmy visualised it. It was not a comfortable thought and he gave a little shiver.

'Now I want you to look at his feet as he's running at you,' said Kevin, 'you'll notice that every stride he's taking toward you is about a metre in distance.'

In his imaginary world, Jimmy looked at his opponent's feet and could see his strides eating up the ground.

'Okay. I want you to imagine that on the ground, as the player runs towards you, is a circle, which is a metre in circumference, and that circle moves forward, as the player moves towards you, as if it was highlighted in a computer game or in some rugby analysis on TV.'

Jimmy nodded. He knew exactly what Kevin meant by the bright circle on the ground and he could see it.

'Good. Well your first job is to get into that circle. You must carry out your tackle from within that circle, not before it, but as soon as you are in it. Do you understand what I mean?'

'Yes,' replied Jimmy. 'I've got to get really close to him.'

'Exactly!' said Kevin. 'Now we are going to make the tackle. The area of your body that you are going to use to make contact with the other player's body is your shoulder. Whatever leg you step into the player's circle with, that's the shoulder you use to hit them. So if you step in with your left leg, then go in with your left shoulder. If it's your right leg, then it's your right shoulder. You don't have to use the same shoulder all the time, your feet position should determine which shoulder you use. Also, be aware of the angle the player is coming at you from. If he's coming from your right, then it's right foot and shoulder. If from your left, then left foot and shoulder.'

Jimmy concentrated hard on visualising what he had to do. When he got it clear in his mind, he re-ran it over and over again.

'Right then,' said Kevin, 'now the important bit. We are going to focus on where you should hit him and what you should do with your head.'

Jimmy nodded again, eyes still tightly shut, still clearly visualising the scene.

'The simplest form of tackling is to aim for the top of the opponent's thighs or waist area. That way, your body and arms will naturally envelope their legs which will stop them from running. We call that, "the ring of steel". Now, we can do tackles that are higher or lower, but in Under 11 rugby you can't tackle above the waist, so we'll focus on these mid-body tackles first. Understand?'

Jimmy nodded again, 'Yes,' he replied.

'Good. Now, which leg are you stepping into the player's circle with?' asked Kevin.

'My right one,' replied Jimmy.

'So which shoulder are you going to use?'

'My right one,' came Jimmy's instant reply.

'That's good. Now because you're tackling with your right shoulder, you need to move your head the opposite way, to your left. You're looking for the right side of your face – your ear and your cheek – to actually brush alongside the right butt cheek of your opponent, just below his hip. You don't want your head to make contact with his body at all, especially his hip, you want to get it out of the way. The closest you want to get it is to almost slide it below his right hip as you make the tackle. This is called, "cheek to cheek".'

'Cheek to cheek?' questioned Jimmy.

'Yes. Now don't be tempted to dip and drop your body too early, but at the exact moment that your right shoulder hits his waist and your arms wrap around him forming the ring of steel, the right cheek of your face, should be alongside his right butt cheek. That way, your head is completely out of the way. Get your feet in close at this point and drive your legs.'

Jimmy opened his eyes for the first time. He blinked in the sunlight.

'That's where I think I've been going wrong. When I've been tackling, I've been sort of ducking my head into the tackle which hurts. To avoid that happening, I've also been twisting my head, to the right or left, so that it doesn't come into contact, but it often does and it hurts. Getting hurt has been my biggest fear.'

'Exactly!' said Kevin. 'And that's why you've developed the fear. It's all about a safe head position. Always move it the opposite way to the shoulder you're using to tackle, and always aim to get it alongside the opponent's butt cheek. Remember, it's hugely important to avoid his hip, that's a tough bone! Focus on getting a little lower and alongside that butt cheek. That way, there's nothing at all that can come into contact with your head, it will be in a completely safe position.'

Jimmy let the instruction sink in for a moment, to again visualise what Kevin was saying.

'Cheek to cheek tackling, keeping my head out of the way, forming a ring of steel.'

Jimmy looked at Kevin's smiling face.

'I get it, Kevin, I get it.'

'That's good. But there's another aspect to all of this too. I've been talking to you about the technique of tackling, how we physically pull a good tackle off. But there's something else you need to understand as well.'

Jimmy didn't take his eyes off Kevin, he was taking in every word, every syllable.

'Tackling and defence in rugby is also a mindset. You can have all the technique in the world, but if you don't go in with the mindset of "I'm really going to make this tackle", then you're still going to struggle. You've got far more chance of pulling it off if you're positive.'

Jimmy understood. But he also understood that being positive about any of this was going to be his biggest challenge.

ENJOYING SUCCESS

Almost every evening after school for the next week, Jimmy met Kevin at his house and went into the back garden to continue Kevin's tackling masterclasses. It would be a stretch to say that Jimmy loved the sessions, because he didn't. Whatever fears Jimmy had in his mind about tackling were still there, quite deep and unable to be completely shifted. But one thing that had improved, was Jimmy's *understanding* of tackling. Kevin had instructed Jimmy in both the nuts and bolts of physical tackling, especially how it could be done safely, but also in understanding the importance of being a solid defender for your team.

Kevin had been excellent. The way he explained and demonstrated everything had been so clear. The main problem continued to be Jimmy himself. He couldn't understand why he still felt nervous about tackling, especially as he now understood the theory of it and after all the time he'd spent following Kevin's instructions to a tee. Everything in Jimmy's rugby life so far had been based on learning, practising and then improving where it mattered, out on the field. He remembered Jonny's '10,000 hours' idea and while Jimmy hadn't done 10,000 hours of anything, when he'd put his mind to something, he usually improved.

His kicking out of hand had improved during the previous season when he'd been shown how to do it by Liam Wyatt and Peter Clement. When he was coming back from injury, his place-kicking had improved when he put in the hours down at The Rec with Oscar, after the tips he'd got from Kevin. But the tackling was different. He was putting in the same effort and the same time and the same commitment, but he was still extremely nervous when the crucial moment came to make the physical tackle, even when he was tackling Kevin who was using a soft tackle shield.

Another thing had also happened while Jimmy had been putting the hard yards in with Kevin. Central had reached the Cluster Cup semi-final, but without Jimmy.

Jimmy hadn't been able to bring himself to watch the game, which predictably led to another argument with Matt. When Matt heard that Jimmy had been dropped from the game, even though he'd been critical of Jimmy's tackling, or lack of it, he did feel sorry for him. But when he went to speak to Jimmy to tell him to keep his chin up and Jimmy had mentioned that he wouldn't be travelling to Woodview Primary to watch the game, but instead would be on The Rec with Oscar, practising his place-kicking, Matt got angry.

'What is it about you and that boy? I can't believe you're not coming to the game. Fine captain you are,' snarled Matt.

'That boy is called Oscar, and he's got nothing to do with my decision,' replied Jimmy with a calmness that masked his rising anger.

'Yeah, right,' replied Matt with a sneer.

Again, trying to remain calm, Jimmy replied. 'What is it about Oscar that you don't like, Matt? You're the only person I've met in the whole school that doesn't like him. What's your problem?'

'I just can't believe you've abandoned us for that freak, that's all.'

'Careful, Matt,' said Jimmy, holding Matt's gaze with an angry stare, 'he's not a freak.'

'You'll be rocking back and forward and flapping your hands about soon, too! What's all that about anyway?'

Jimmy refused to rise to Matt's bait. Instead, calmly, he thought the best approach would be to try to educate his clearly ignorant friend.

'It's called stimming, but I wouldn't expect you to understand what that means as you've taken no interest at all in trying to understand him.'

'Stimming,' brayed Matt. 'Pathetic!'

Jimmy carried on, ignoring the insult.

'Stimming is a way that he shows his emotions and it's not stupid or pathetic, it's just what he does. But if you want to look at it negatively, then let's look at you. I'm guessing when you scored that try on The Rec last Saturday, and ran off screaming, waving your arms around your head before sliding on your knees, maybe Oscar thought the way you showed your emotions was a bit pathetic too . . . yet to you, it's just what you do.'

Matt started to speak, but got all tongue tied as if he wanted to say something, but couldn't quite get it out. In the end, he just managed to blurt out, 'You should be there at the match, that's all I'm saying.'

'Maybe. But you need to be more understanding of people who are different to you and stop being so unkind, blowing out someone else's candle won't make yours shine brighter . . . that's all *I'm* saying.'

Matt glared at Jimmy, then turned and silently walked away. That was the last time these two great friends had spoken in over a week. Jimmy was quite sad about that, but didn't feel as if he'd done anything wrong. Because of that, he didn't change his mind about not going to the game. Instead he had a great time on the Thursday after school, practising his place-kicking with Oscar. As usual, Oscar kept all the stats of Jimmy's kicks and helped him collect the balls once Jimmy had kicked them all. Jimmy was so grateful to have Oscar's company, and enjoyed their time on The Rec together so much, he hardly gave a thought to the quarter-final being played at Woodview.

He didn't miss a great deal.

Central ran out 10–5 winners in what, as predicted by Mrs John, was a very tough encounter. Apparently, the two heroes were Manu and Kitty. Manu basically tackled himself to a standstill, not missing a single player from Woodview who dared run in his direction. When telling Jimmy all about it, Kitty said that even the parents at Woodview went up to Manu at the end to tell him how well he'd done. Jimmy was delighted to hear that he'd had such a fantastic game. Kitty had been too modest to talk about her own contribution, but Jimmy had heard from other members of the team that she scored two sensational tries, both from interceptions where she ran almost the length of the field. By all accounts, she ran both tries in exactly like her idol, Jaz Joyce.

Again, Jimmy was so chuffed for his friend, he loved it when she had success. He always remembered something his grandfather had told him when they were chatting about sport one day. 'Never get envious or jealous of a teammate of yours doing well, son,' Will had told him. 'Instead, use it to inspire *you* to do even better. Enjoy their success.'

Enjoy their success. Jimmy had always liked that phrase and always tried to live by it. Even when he'd been struggling so much with his tackling, he took comfort from how well Manu, Kitty and even Matt were doing, it made him happy. And Jimmy used that happiness as a positive thought to push himself to be successful too.

Even though he wasn't a part of it, he enjoyed the fact that Central had won the quarter-final. No school had ever retained the Cluster Cup in its ninety-six-year history. Central were certainly giving themselves a chance to do it this season, with or without Jimmy. That made him happy.

OPTING OUT

On the Tuesday before the cup semi-final that would be held on the following Saturday morning, Jimmy made a decision. Kevin was the first person he told.

He was around at Kevin's again for what Kevin had thought would be their last tackling session before Jimmy's imminent return to action.

'I'm not going to play,' said Jimmy. 'There's too much at stake for me to play and then find out that I'll pull out of a key tackle. I'll just be letting everyone down. I can't bear the thought of it. Maybe if I can have another week's practice with you, I might be ready if we get to the final.'

Kevin looked at him.

'I understand what you're saying, Jimmy, and I'm not going to push you either way. You have to be happy and you must make the final decision, nobody else. I want you to know that if you need more help, I'll put in as much time as you need. But for what it's worth, I think you're ready to give it a go, I really do. But as I said, the decision must be yours.'

'Thanks Kevin,' said Jimmy rather solemnly.

'I just want you to know another thing too. It's quite important and you should take it into account when you make your decision.'

'What's that?'

'Well, if your team does make it to the final, then it would suggest that your team would have played well, including the person who would have taken your position. And you must know something about my wife is that she's incredibly loyal. She thinks the world of you, Jimmy, and like me knows how talented you are and has seen how much work you've been putting in with me.'

Kevin stopped, as if trying to find the right words.

'The fact is, Jimmy, she won't change a winning team if they made it to the final. No way. The best you can hope for is a spot on the bench and then injury to someone. And nobody ever wants to see that.'

Jimmy nodded thoughtfully in response then carried on the session with Kevin, without talking about it again. They started on the tackle bags, which Kevin was now hitting at three quarter pace, and really giving Jimmy a jolt. Then, without the tackle bag, Kevin would run at Jimmy at a much slower pace, and get him to try to tackle Kevin hard. It was here that Jimmy still struggled. Kevin could instantly tell that Jimmy's heart wasn't in it.

After about six lacklustre tackles, Mrs John appeared.

'How are you getting on, you two?' she asked with a smile.

The silent reply from both of them spoke volumes.

'Miss, I'm really sorry,' said Jimmy eventually. 'But I just don't think I'm ready to play. I'm really worried that if I miss a tackle, it'll cost us a chance of getting to the final. I would hate for that to happen.'

'That's very honest of you, Jimmy,' said Mrs John, 'and it shows just how unselfish you are and I love your attitude to the team. Now, you might not feel it, but I've seen a definite improvement in you. I know Kev's not running at you quickly, but your body position is excellent and the mechanics of your tackle are spot on.'

'I know, Miss. But I know in here,' said Jimmy tapping his heart, 'that I still haven't got it yet. I just shut my eyes and try to get it over with. I know Kevin's not going to hurt me, but still I'm uncertain at the point of contact. I know I'll feel 100 times worse on a match day, especially in a match as big as the semi-final.'

Jimmy stopped, but neither Kevin nor Mrs John spoke.

The silence forced Jimmy to begin again.

'I know it's a risk, Miss, but I'm not going to play. I've decided. I'd rather work with Kevin for another week or so and by then, I know I'll be feeling much more confident. I may never be a tackler like Owen Farrell, but I know I can improve in time.'

'What do you mean by risk, Jimmy?' his teacher asked.

'Well, the risk is, if I don't play in the semi-final, and we get to the final, that you may not pick me for the final.'

Mrs John looked at Jimmy carefully.

'Jimmy, I hate to tell you, but that's not a risk. That's a certainty. If we get to the final, it means we'll have been successful. That means the players would have earned their chance for the final. You'll make my squad Jimmy, but you won't start. That's just the way it has always been for me. I must reward those who turn up and put themselves on the line. I fully understand why you are making this decision and while I'm disappointed, and think you're wrong, I do respect it. I hope you can respect mine.'

'Yes, I do, Miss,' said a solemn-looking Jimmy.

But he couldn't shake the feeling that he'd just made the worst decision of his life.

44

JIMMY'S SECRET GARDEN

That following Saturday morning, Central did go on and win the semi-final, and once again, Jimmy couldn't bring himself to watch.

Instead, he asked permission from Kevin to bring someone else to his garden to take part in tackling practice, away from prying eyes of people on The Rec. Kevin agreed. He wouldn't be there because he'd be supporting his wife at the semi-final, but said he'd leave the side gate unlocked and a bag of balls inside the old coal house for Jimmy and his friend to use.

'Which friend will you be bringing, Jimmy? Most of your gang will be involved in the semi-final.'

'Well, it's not a friend as such,' said Jimmy laughing. 'It's my brother.'

*

'Wow! What a place this is!' shouted Jonny, his voice crackling with excitement. 'Imagine living here! I'd never leave again!'

'Yeah, not bad, is it?'

'Not bad? It's fantastic, no wonder you spend so much time here.'

'I know,' replied Jimmy, 'I've been very lucky. Kevin and Mrs John have been really good to me.'

His brother nodded.

'So, what do you want to do then, Jim? Tackling is it?'

'Yes.'

Despite initially feeling embarrassed, Jimmy had eventually shared his tackling problems with his brother. Jonny had been so supportive and helpful, that Jimmy felt a little bit stupid that he'd doubted that his brother would have been anything but supportive.

'Kevin has given me some drills to do, it's on this bit of paper in the net of balls.'

Jimmy read out the instructions to Jonny who listened and nodded.

'Okay, very straightforward. Basically, I'll be tackling you, and you'll be tackling me. Come on, let's go. I'll turn you into Brian O'Driscoll before you know it!'

With that, Jonny walked over to the patio table and chairs and pulled his fleece off over his head, to reveal a tight-fitting Under Armour t-shirt. As usual, Jonny looked so cool to Jimmy, and looked even cooler when he saw his wrists.

'What have you done there?' said Jimmy pointing to his brother's wrists, which were wound and bound with what looked like white bandage.

'Oh, these? Yeah, cool aren't they? Just some bandage from Mum's first aid kit. I saw Richie Mo'unga on TV the other day, and he had his wrists strapped, thought he looked mint, so, decided I'd do it. If I say so myself, I look well good!'

Jimmy laughed. 'Idiot. Let's get on with this session, you big wannabe.'

'Watch your step, bro, or I'll splat you in the first tackle.'

Jimmy laughed again. His brother might be nuts, but Jimmy had to admit he did look pretty cool with his wrists strapped. He'd bear that in mind if he was lucky enough to make the final.

Unknown to Jimmy, at the very moment that he tackled his brother for the first time in that wonderful garden, albeit off balance and with both eyes still shut, Kitty ran in and touched down for her first try of the semi-final. It was made for her thanks to an excellent break by Jimmy's replacement at fly-half, Jordan Marshall. Kitty would go on and score another try in the second half. Jordan would score two himself.

As Jimmy tried – and failed – to prove to his brother that his tackling demons were behind him, Central cruised to the final. Jimmy's gamble had failed. His tackling was improving slightly, but there was no way he was going to start the final. There was only going to be one person Mrs John would pick for the fly-half position, and that would be Jordan Marshall.

And a very well-deserved selection it was.

THE FINAL COUNTDOWN

The week leading up to the final was a difficult one for Jimmy.

He couldn't help but think back to last year. He had been the centre of everything with Peter Clement in those final training sessions. Also, the thought of running out on the Wolves' ground for the first time, in front of a stadium full of fans, had been the icing on the cake. But this year, it was so different.

In fairness, the training was just as much fun. Mrs John was an excellent coach and so creative with her drills. She kept telling all the players, every day, 'Enjoyment and hard work is key to all training and practice in sport. Enjoy your training and work hard at it and that smile will show itself in every competitive game you play.' Jimmy believed in that point of view entirely.

What was also refreshing was that Mrs John put a training session on every single evening of the week, and the one thing she banned was tackling.

'I don't want any contact at all this week, I will not risk any single one of you missing this final through injury. This is the last game of your season, so your fitness levels are fine. This week is all about skills and enjoyment.'

For Jimmy, it was music to his ears. On the Sunday of that final week, he'd had his last session with Kevin. And while everything Jimmy did was technically perfect, he still struggled to really commit at the moment of impact. Kevin told him that his tackling had improved by 500%, but unless he really committed himself at the point of impact, he would always run the risk of injury.

'I honestly can't teach you any more, Jimmy,' Kevin had told him over a glass of orange squash that Sunday morning. 'Technically, you know it all, and when we slow it all down, you're perfect. It's all going to come down to your mindset now and that moment out on the pitch. And in many ways, it will suit you coming off the bench.'

'Why's that?' inquired Jimmy.

'Well. The game will be in motion, everybody will be up to speed. It's almost certain you'll be faced with a tackle straight away, because both teams will be flying.'

Jimmy gulped. He hadn't thought of that.

Kevin noticed his trepidation.

'It'll be fine, Jim. It's the best way. I welcome seeing you faced with that first tackle, because I know you now have all the tools to overcome it. And if you don't get presented with a tackle in front of you, go and find one. And then you'll know I'm right.'

'How can I go and *find* a tackle?'

'You'll find a way. You'll figure it out . . . believe me.'

The other thing that was different about this year's final was the venue. The Wolves were away on the day of the final so there would be no warm up curtain raiser game in front of the loyal home fans. Instead, the big, black iron gates of the lovely old ground would be locked and chained. In its place, the final venue had been announced as the Eagles training ground at Underhill and would be played on their main pitch. That news was enough to produce another gulp from Jimmy as it didn't hold many happy memories for him. But he'd have to deal with it – if he was lucky enough to get on, of course. And he'd also have to deal with seeing Mark Kane, who was bound to be there, casting his eye over the leading talent in the region, deciding who he would be choosing to attend that summer's two-week camp in August – and if Jimmy didn't get on at some point in the match, it certainly wasn't going to be him.

The last thing that was different compared to the previous year was Jimmy's relationship with Matt. It had really gone downhill since he'd failed to be supportive of Jimmy's tackling issues and had fallen off a cliff when they had clashed over Oscar. It was a situation that Jimmy just couldn't understand. And when he'd decided not to support the team in the quarter and semi-finals, Matt hadn't wanted anything to do with him. Even Manu and Kitty working hard behind the scenes to bring Matt round had failed. In that whole week of after-school practices, Matt hadn't said a single word to him. Jimmy found it tough, and he knew deep down that he should have gone and supported the team, but, to pinch Jimmy's grandfather's favourite saying when describing a situation that was far less than perfect, 'It is what it is.'

Jimmy didn't lose any sleep over it.

But he was still losing some over the thought of that first tackle. If he was lucky enough to get on.

FINDING FEKITOA

On the morning of the final that Saturday, Jimmy woke early. As usual, he connected his headphones to his mum's iPad, put them in his ears and tapped on YouTube to watch some rugby clips. He decided to watch a video of Dan Carter's greatest moments. He really loved the way the great All Black had played rugby, and even though he was now retired he was still one of Jimmy's favourite players. He also noticed the strappings on Dan's wrists, similar to the ones his brother had copied from Richie Mo'unga. A few players had them and he wondered why he'd never noticed them before. The more he looked at them, the cooler he thought they looked.

After watching YouTube for about forty minutes, he decided it was time to get up. Down at breakfast his sister had prepared a special cup final meal. It was like a mini version of the buffet Jimmy had experienced at the Eagles Academy. There were four different fruit options, yoghurts, oats, cheeses and cooked meats.

'Aw, Julie, did you do this all on your own?'

Julie smiled. 'I did. I went shopping with Mum last night and picked it all out. I got the stuff you said you'd had at your training camp. It's important you have a good breakfast on cup final day.'

'That's really thoughtful, Julie. Thanks.'

'Yeah, thanks Julie, really thoughtful,' said Jonny, filling his breakfast bowl with oats, yoghurt and a fruit compote. 'I wish Jim had a cup final every Saturday!'

After a great breakfast, Jimmy did what he always did on a match day and called in to see his grandparents.

As usual, his grandmother had the kettle on as soon as she saw Jimmy's head pop around the door and Jimmy went in and sat with his grandfather.

'So how do you feel about not playing then, son?' he asked.

'It just feels a bit odd, Gramp, to be honest. I mean last year, I was in the middle of everything, but this year, I feel a bit left out. But I've got nobody to blame but myself. I sort of wish I'd played in the quarter- and semi-final now. Maybe that was a mistake, but I just didn't feel ready. Perhaps I should have just gone for it.'

'Mmmmm. Maybe,' was the thoughtful reply. 'But I'm a big believer in gut instinct, Jimmy, and if you didn't feel it was right, well then it probably wasn't. There's nothing you can do about it now anyway. It is what it is.'

Jimmy smiled at his grandfather's well-used catchphrase, he seemed to say it to sum up any tricky situation.

'So, has your teacher given you any clue if she'll definitely bring you on at some point?'

'Not really. She said she'll try to give us all a game, but Mrs John is really competitive and I know she'll want to make sure we're winning before she makes any changes. In fairness, Jordan – the boy who has taken my place – has been playing well all week. He's normally a centre, but I've been really impressed by him in training. So good luck to him, I don't really want to see him having a bad game, so we'll just have to see what happens.'

'You're a good lad, Jimmy, I have to say that. And you know what I always say, 'Good things happen to good people,' so I expect it all to turn out well for you somehow.'

'I hope so. Thanks, Gramp.'

'Do you think Mark Kane will be there?'

'Probably. He'll no doubt be pleased that I'm not playing. But I'm past caring about him, to be honest, Gramp. He's never going to rate me so it's no use worrying about whether he's going to pick me for the Eagles again or not.'

Then, glancing up at his grandfather, he said, 'It is what it is.'

Will laughed, 'Ha! You're right about that, son.'

Jimmy spent the next hour or so with his grandparents, chatting about nothing in particular. He loved spending time with them, especially on a match day. He found it calmed him down. Although, today, because he was starting on the bench, Jimmy felt less on edge than normal, so he was able to relax and enjoy the morning with them.

As he was leaving to get all his kit prepared, his grandfather called him over.

'Here we are, Jim,' he said, reaching into a carrier bag he had at the side of his chair, and pulling out his usual pre-match treat for Jimmy: a trusty Mars Bar. 'Just to keep you going.'

Jimmy smiled again, 'Ta Gramp, I'll eat it on the bus.'

'Good lad, see you later. And remember: like my rope ladder

training, you've done all you need to do regarding your tackling. When the opportunity comes, just make the most of it and give it your best. It'll all work out for you.'

For the first time that morning, with the mention of tackling, Jimmy stiffened up a little bit. Maybe it was a good thing he was on the bench after all. As he walked back to his house, he tried to banish the negative thoughts from his mind, yet they still remained. But he resolved to do the best he could if and when the moment arrived and take it from there.

As he reached the front door, his iPhone buzzed. He looked at the screen – it was a message from Kevin.

'Good luck today, Jimmy, you'll be fine. You're ready for this and you have the ability to deal with any tackle you may face. I'm certain of it. Don't worry about anything, and if you get the chance, be like Fekitoa!'

Beneath the message was a YouTube link titled 'Fekitoa's big hit on Conrad Smith'. Jimmy tapped on it and a short, forty-four second film opened.

Jimmy knew who Malakai Fekitoa was, he'd read about him in *Rugby World* magazine, which he'd read every month in the local public library. He was a Tongan born former All Black centre who had given up playing for the All Blacks to play in Europe, because he wanted to earn enough money to provide for his family in New Zealand and Tonga. He'd read that Fekitoa's dad had died when he was young and since then, he'd taken it upon himself to always support his mum and brothers and sisters. With the money he earned from rugby, he helped support his nieces and nephews too and in all, helped over thirty members of his family. Jimmy loved Fekitoa for that, he thought it was a brilliant thing to do. He'd seen plenty of Fekitoa on YouTube, playing for the Highlanders, Toulon and Wasps and scoring some incredible tries. He was a brilliantly powerful runner. Jimmy dreamed of having the power that Fekitoa had.

Jimmy watched as the video loaded. It was a game from Super Rugby – the Highlanders versus the Hurricanes.

The clip started as one of Fekitoa's Highlander teammates kicked the ball deep down field. The ball went over the heads of the Hurricane defence, who had to turn, and their right winger collected the ball near his right touchline. He passed inside to Beauden Barrett who jogged forward, looking at the options in front of him. He didn't have much on, so he just moved the ball along to his captain in the centre, Conrad Smith. Just as Smith caught the ball, he was absolutely smashed in the tackle by Fekitoa. The commentator screamed, 'Oooooh, what a shot! Malakai Fekitoa just sat Conrad Smith right down!'

Jimmy was mesmerised. He watched the slow-motion replay and saw how far out Fekitoa had been when he made the decision to hit Smith. Barrett hadn't seen him coming when he made the pass and Fekitoa hit Smith with just about the perfect rugby tackle, taking man and ball and winning the penalty straight after from the referee. Jimmy watched it again and again until the picture of the tackle was burnt into his mind. Then he read Kevin's text again.

'Be like Fekitoa.'

Well, Jimmy wasn't from Tonga, he hadn't played for the All Blacks and certainly didn't possess thighs as big as tree trunks, but if he got on today, he vowed he would be like Fekitoa!

THE ROAD TO THE FINAL

Jimmy arrived at school to board the minibus that would take the squad to Underhill.

The first to greet him was Manu.

'All right Jimmy boooooooyyy?' he shouted at him and, as usual, tried to wrap him up in a smother tackle.

'Get off me you maniac, save your tackles for the game!'

Manu laughed, 'Don't worry about that, I'm going to munch a few of them today. They'll be sorry they ever took the field against Massive Manu from Central Primary,' and with that, he dropped his back pack to the floor and flexed his biceps.

'Not again!' cried Kitty rolling her eyes. 'You're hardly the Rock.'

'Yeah, more like the Pebble,' said Ryan, who always managed to find the right quip to bring someone back down to earth.

Everybody burst out laughing, even Manu.

'That's what I like to see, laughing and smiling. A happy squad is a successful squad,' said Mrs John as she walked past to open up the minibus.

'Peter Clement said the very same to us before the final last year,' said Kitty, rushing forward to be near her favourite teacher.

'Well, great minds clearly think alike, don't they? Come on, get on the bus you lot, it's time to get this show on the road!'

They all got on the minibus, a picture of smiles and joy. The only one not smiling, Jimmy noticed, was Matt. He looked as if he had the world on his shoulders. As usual, he hadn't said a single word to Jimmy and boarded the minibus without really speaking to anyone.

They arrived at the Underhill complex and those that hadn't been there before were hugely impressed. Jimmy had forgotten just what a brilliant place it was. Because he'd been so unhappy there in the summer, he hadn't really taken in what a great facility it was. As they walked from the car park to the main entrance, a man walked out from the building and turned left towards the entrance to the main playing area. It was Mark Kane.

He obviously heard all the voices from the Central players, who were chattering nineteen to the dozen with excitement, but blanked everyone completely and just carried on walking.

I hope that's the last time I see him today, thought Jimmy.

Inside the changing room, the Central players were in seventh heaven. It was superb.

Unknown to them, Mrs John had sent Kevin ahead with the kit that morning and he'd laid it all out on the individual seats in number order, starting with one on the left, all the way up to include the replacements' numbers. The kit looked so professional, laid out as it was, folded with the white number standing proud on the red and black colours of the brand new jerseys.

Despite the kit being brand new, when Mrs John had checked

it the day before, she found that one of the replacement's shirts was missing. She asked Jimmy if he wouldn't mind wearing one of the old ones. 'Can it be number 10, Miss?' he asked hopefully. 'I don't see why not,' she said, smiling.

In the middle of the room, on the treatment table, he'd laid out bottles of water for everyone and a selection of energy bars. As soon as he walked in there, Ryan bolted to the table and picked up about six energy bars. 'I'm having these,' he said stuffing them into his backpack.

'Ryan, really?' said Mrs John laughing.

'Haven't had breakfast, Miss. I need fuel. Like a Rolls-Royce I am, give me the right fuel and I run like a dream!'

Everyone just laughed . . . people usually did around Ryan.

Jimmy felt relaxed and happy. He'd come to terms with the fact that he wasn't playing and had resolved to just enjoy the day and deal with whatever fate threw his way.

When everyone started to get changed, Jimmy strapped his wrists with the white surgical tape he'd asked his mother to get him from Boots. He wound it tightly around his wrist, starting at the base of his hand and going up to just about where his forearm began. When he had done both wrists, he looked down at his handiwork. He couldn't explain it, but the strapping just made him feel good. Little did he know it then, but he'd never play another game in his life without strapping his wrists up. It became his own personal match-day tradition.

Just before they walked out onto the field, Mrs John called them all together.

'No big speech from me today,' she said. 'Just get out there and enjoy the game. It's been a joy getting to know you all this year, and to see the effort and total commitment that you've all given has been a genuine highlight of both my rugby and teaching career. Thank you.'

As Mrs John paused to emphasise the sincerity of the moment, Ryan punctured the silence and said, 'That's all right, Miss, you're very welcome.'

Everyone stifled a laugh, not wishing to spoil Mrs John's moment, until she burst out laughing herself, which opened the laughter floodgates for everyone else.

As the laughter died down, Mrs John continued. 'That sums up this whole experience: fun, joy and laughter. Take that enjoyment out onto the pitch and express yourselves, enjoy every single minute. You are a very talented squad, and if you can link the enjoyment with your ability, you'll be bringing that cup back here later on. Good luck.'

At that point, Matt, who had been handed the captaincy by Mrs John in Jimmy's absence screamed, 'Come on Centraaaaaaaaaallll!' at the top of his voice and rushed towards the door. His team followed him through the exit at a jog, studs clacking on the tiled floor as they went.

Jimmy grabbed his training top and orange bib. He waited for everyone to leave and was last out. Just before he left, he took his glasses off, put them in his bag and grabbed his inhaler and took two big puffs before grabbing his gumshield and tucking it in his sock.

'Right then. Let's go and see how this all develops,' he said, and walked out of the room, closing the door quietly behind him.

48

CRASH, BANG, WALLOP

Jimmy joined the other replacements on the sideline.

In front of the small, purpose-built stand on Underhill's main pitch, which was packed full of parents, friends and family, were two small enclosed seating areas. The dugouts. One was marked 'Home'. The other was marked 'Away'.

Jimmy and the replacements took their places in the 'Home' dugout. Just as Jimmy did, he heard a distinctive whistle. He recognised it instantly. It was his grandfather. He looked up into the stand and scanned the faces that greeted him. He quickly saw his family, made up of both his grandparents, his mother and his brother and sister. Sitting next to Julie was Jimmy's dad. Jimmy gave a quick wave and thumbs up to them and they all waved back. He loved that they were all sitting together. This time last year, his parents weren't even sitting in the same stand, let alone just a couple of seats away from each other. Jimmy thought it was great that his parents had somehow found a way to be friendly to each other and focus on making the best they could out of life for the benefit of their three children. It gave Jimmy a satisfied, warm feeling.

Jimmy loved that his whole family – not just his mum and dad – took an interest in his rugby career and offered him such support. He knew not everybody was that lucky. His mind went straight back to the way Mike Green's father had behaved in the last final. He hoped no player would have to experience anything like that today.

Mrs John was nervously walking in front of the players' dugout, and was soon joined by Kevin. Kevin glanced round and saw Jimmy and winked at him. Jimmy waved back. He felt good that Kevin was there. It reassured Jimmy and made him feel that everything was going to be all right, whatever happened.

Then, a few moments later, the referee blew his whistle to start the game. Jimmy's replacement, Jordan, took an immaculate drop kick from the centre line to begin the contest. He judged it perfectly and Jimmy watched it hang in the air as both sets of forwards charged after it to try to gain possession. Jimmy watched the arc of the ball and said out loud to nobody in particular, 'Good kick, Jordan, great start.'

A forward from Central's opponents, Brookdale Primary School, got there first. He was instantly snagged by Andrew Beasley and Ryan who hit him with a twin tackle. Both sides fought for the ball, but it wasn't coming out, so the referee blew for a scrum. He gave the put-in to Brookdale.

This was to be the pattern of the first five minutes or so of the half. Lots of commitment and endeavour, but all of it happening amongst the forwards, with the referee often stopping things and restarting with a scrum. It wasn't the most entertaining of starts.

In fact, the only rugby highlight of note was watching Manu's crisp, accurate passing. Jimmy hadn't seen him play for a while and he'd obviously benefited from practising since the day they'd all found that training equipment at the Memorial Ground the previous summer. Manu looked as sharp as Jimmy had ever seen him . . . practice clearly made perfect.

But then it happened.

From the base of yet another scrum, the Brookdale scrum-half won the ball and quickly passed to his fly-half. Just as quickly, the fly-half moved the ball on to the inside centre, a very big lad who had run an excellent line at pace. It was like watching Manu Tuilagi at his best. Until, of course, he met Central's own Manu.

Manu had predicted what was going to happen when he saw his opposing centre lying deep, even before the scrum-half had passed the ball. When it made its way to the centre, Manu was ready and absolutely smashed his opponent.

But something went horribly wrong.

It was obviously a complete accident, but a combination of Manu not placing his head safely and the Brookdale player raising his knee as he sprinted at his tackler, saw Manu take the impact of the rising knee straight in his face.

Manu didn't even have a chance to wrap his arms around his opponent. He fell to the ground instantly, like an old oak being chopped down in a forest. It was terrible.

The noise from the clash was sickening and drew a collective gasp from the crowd.

The first person to tend to Manu was Matt, and he was upset by what he saw. There was blood flowing out of Manu's nose and above his right eye a bump had swelled up like a small pumpkin.

A moment later, Matt was joined by the medical staff from the Eagles Academy who, luckily, were attending the game, and they quickly moved Matt to the side and began treating Manu. They immobilised his neck and began talking to him, assessing straight away if he'd lost consciousness. Thankfully, he hadn't. When all the other players had moved away to form a huddle, Matt stood by, until Mrs John reached him and brought him away from the scene. He was visibly shaken.

After about five minutes of treatment, the medical staff focused on checking Manu's awareness and were satisfied that he wasn't suffering from serious injury. However, they still had to check for concussion, so they turned to Mrs John, and told her that they were going to take Manu to the changing rooms to carry out a full HIA. Manu was now standing up and talking very freely to the medical staff. Matt went to talk to him and was so relieved to see his great friend being able to talk and seemingly well recovered from such a big bang.

Mrs John looked across at Manu and walked towards him.

'I'm really sorry, Manu, but even if you pass the HIA, I just can't risk you taking another knock to the head, so soon after this one. I have to be very careful not to risk you getting a further injury. I have some doubt, so I've no option but to sit you out. Please understand.'

Manu tried to protest, but it was no good. Mrs John would not be swayed, and she watched sadly as Kevin came over and helped lead Manu off the field.

Mrs John jogged quickly over to Jimmy.

'Well, it's not the way we would have wanted, Jimmy, but that's rugby. Come on then, get changed, you're on. I want you to go straight to fly-half and Jordan will move over to centre. I'll tell him now.'

'Yes, Miss,' replied Jimmy as he pulled his gumshield from his sock and took his bib and training top off.

As he passed Mrs John, she stopped him and said, 'Good luck, Jimmy . . . you can do this. I believe in you.'

Jimmy just nodded. He hardly heard her.

The first thing that Jimmy did was to jog over to see Manu, who was now putting a tracksuit top on over his bloodied rugby shirt. Jimmy was relieved to see that the blood had stopped. Manu gave him the thumbs up and said, 'Good luck, Jim . . . go and win this for us. You've got this.'

Jimmy looked for Kitty and was about to jog over to her, but somebody put their hand on his shoulder to stop him.

It was Matt.

DUTY CALLS

Matt looked at Jimmy, deep into his eyes.

'Jimmy, I've got something I need to say.'

Jimmy guessed what was coming.

'It's okay, Matt, you don't have to say anything.'

'No, I do,' replied his friend. 'I'm just really sorry about the way I've behaved,' he began. 'Seeing Manu getting injured like that frightened the life out of me and for a split second I was terrified that something was really badly wrong with him. When they were treating him, I realised what a great friend he's been to me and I started remembering some of the great things we've all done together. It was then I realised that most of those memories included you, too. I'm so sorry, Jim, I've been such a fool.'

'Don't worry, Matt, it's not a problem. Honestly, don't worry.'

They both heard a noise from behind them and saw the medical team taking Manu to the changing room. The crowd started to clap and cheer. Everyone was relieved to see Manu smiling and waving to his family as he walked away for his assessment.

The referee was in discussion with his assistants as he'd apparently forgotten to stop his watch when the incident with Manu had happened, and needed to know exactly how much time was left in the half. It gave Matt enough time to get his feelings off his chest.

'I'm so sorry that I've been jealous of your friendship with Oscar,' he continued. 'Really I am. I always thought that along with Manu, you'd be my best friend for good. I just couldn't deal with you and Oscar being so close and spending so much time together. I was scared that he would split our friendship up. I was stupid. And not just that, I was so horrible about his condition.'

Jimmy stopped his friend quickly. 'It's not a condition, Matt, it's just him.'

'I know, I know, I'm sorry. I've been reading about autism, and I want to know more. I promise, I'll do better.'

Jimmy smiled. 'Well, that's great to hear. It really is . . . nice one.'

'But I'm even more sorry that I didn't help with your tackling problems. I should have supported you more, but that changes from today. Don't worry about the tackling at all, I'll cover you for that. You just get out here and play and show everyone what you're able to do. You're the best player we've got by a mile, just go and prove it.'

Matt held out his hand for Jimmy to shake. Jimmy took it and smiled.

'Come on then, mate,' he said. 'Let's see what we can do.'

When the game eventually restarted after one of the parents had to help with the timing issues as both the assistants had forgotten to stop their watches too, the referee chose to restart the game with a scrum. It was Central's put-in, right in the centre of the pitch.

Matt held the ball tightly to his chest and looked at Jimmy, darting his eyes over to the opposition full back. Jimmy looked over to where Matt was urging him to look. The full back was way out of position, leaving a huge amount of space behind him. It was the perfect opportunity for Jimmy to put in a long raking kick for Kitty to chase. If he judged it right, it would be a certain try for his friend to give Central the lead. Jimmy felt supremely confident, he knew exactly what he had to do.

As Matt fed the ball into the scrum, Jimmy remembered Peter Clement's words of last year, 'always play what's in front of you and make a statement.'

Jimmy made a statement all right.

He dropped the ball.

He couldn't believe what had happened. Matt had fed the ball in, picked it up from the rear of the scrum and delivered the most perfect spin pass to Jimmy – chest height, just in front of him for Jimmy to move on to. Incredibly, Jimmy just spilled it and knocked it on.

He looked down at his hands, completely mystified at what had just happened.

'Knock on by red. Scrum down, blue ball.'

Matt ran up to Jimmy, 'Don't worry about that, Jim, bit rusty, that's all.'

Jimmy clapped his hands and rubbed them together, hoping to get the blood moving in them to warm them up. He didn't really know why, it was a beautiful spring day, but he felt he had to do something to help explain to everyone why he dropped the ball.

Brookdale Primary's scrum-half popped the ball into the scrum on the referee's instruction and shot round to the back of it to pick the ball up. In one swift movement he swept the ball up from the floor and delivered a perfect pass to his fly-half. The fly-half had been lying slightly deep so that he could run onto the ball and timed his run to perfection. He took the pass without breaking a stride and headed for his target.

Jimmy.

Well, this was it. The moment everybody was waiting for. Kevin was right, it would happen straight away.

On the sidelines, Mrs John took a deep breath and bit her lip. Kevin had his hands over his mouth and nose and stared in silence. Will stood motionless, fingers crossed. Mark Kane, stood alone on the far corner of the pitch with a smirk across his face.

The fly-half, unaware of the full significance of this moment, bombed towards Jimmy.

But Jimmy was ready. He steadied himself, rose up on his toes and looked for the imaginary metre circle around the feet of his onrushing opponent. This was it. Moving forward to meet his prey, Jimmy caught sight of something from the corner of his left eye. It was Matt.

Guessing that his opposite number would make the pass to his fly-half, Matt had made his move, completely unseen by Jimmy. Just as Jimmy was getting ready to have his moment with tackling destiny, Matt flew in like Superman and smashed the speedy fly-half before Jimmy had a chance to test out his new-found tackle technique.

The fly-half was so surprised at the speed, quality and unusual angle that Matt had made his tackle from, that he was unable to hold on to the ball, which flew from his grasp, straight into the path of Jimmy's run.

Instinct took over. Jimmy scooped the ball up and looked up the field, again the opposition full back was out of position, so again Jimmy opted to kick for Kitty. And again Jimmy made a mistake. He couldn't believe it.

This time, he just kicked the ball way out of play, directly into touch. He *never* did that.

There was no rubbing of hands this time. Instead he just looked down at his beautiful Adidas Predators as if demanding an explanation from them.

Jimmy heard the shrill sound of the referee's whistle again. 'I'd already called advantage over on the kick,' explained the ref. 'Ball kicked straight in from outside red's twenty-two. Blue lineout, in line with where the kick was made.' Jimmy's head dropped as he realised the significance of his error.

There was no doubt that it was a dangerous moment for Central. There was less than ten minutes played and it was still nil-nil, but the attacking lineout gave Brookdale plenty of options to get that crucial first score on the board.

The option that the Brookdale fly-half took was an up and under. His plan must have been to put pressure on the Central full back, but if so, he was off target. Instead he got under it too much and the ball was heading high and straight at Jimmy.

As he stood under it, waiting to make a safe catch, Jimmy blocked everything out. His concentration was 100% on the ball, nothing else. As a result, he didn't see half the Brookdale pack charging down on him, all of whom were offside as they had been in front of their kicker when he made his kick.

None of that mattered to Jimmy.

He watched the ball swirling above him and didn't even blink as it fell to earth. At the split second that Jimmy gathered the ball perfectly into his arms, he was flattened by two of the Brookdale forwards.

It was a heck of a hit.

The crowd gasped as Jimmy crumpled under their weight. The sound of the hit meant they all feared it would be another injury to rival Manu's in its seriousness. Jimmy's mother turned to Will and said, 'Oh no, Dad, he's injured again isn't he? I can't look.'

Will shouted from the sidelines, 'Referee!! That was offside by miles!'

But the referee didn't need Will's advice. He'd already blown for the penalty to Central.

Jimmy rolled away from his tacklers but stayed on the ground. One of them had smashed his shoulder straight into Jimmy's collarbone. Jimmy put his arms straight to his collarbone, fearing the worst. But there was nothing. No pain whatsoever. He moved his arm around slowly, it rotated perfectly. He was absolutely fine.

Jimmy got to his feet and brushed some of the loose dirt off his jersey. Then he gathered up the ball and jogged over to where the referee was standing to show where the penalty was to be taken from. When he got there, the referee spoke to him.

'You okay, son? That was a hell of a bang you took. But fair do's, you didn't drop that ball. Brave that.'

Jimmy just looked at the referee, his words of praise ringing in Jimmy's ears. Brave that.

It was as if a light bulb had gone on in Jimmy's brain. Yes, it *was* brave. Those forwards from Brookdale had deliberately run from an offside position to shake him up. Jimmy knew everyone thought he was scared on the field because of his tackling problems, but it was never about that for Jimmy. It was just a mental block that he'd developed about one thing in particular: tackling somebody head-on. He'd just demonstrated his bravery – which Jimmy thought had never been in doubt – now he just wanted an opportunity to demonstrate his tackling skill. It was time to find a tackle.

But first, he had to deal with the medical team who had rushed on to treat him. Jimmy looked bemused.

'There's nothing wrong with me, and they never went near my head, look, here's the mud, on my collarbone.'

Then, before they could say another word, Jimmy started counting. And he started counting backwards from 17 to 12. The medics just stared at him. Then he said, 'We're playing at the Underhill show pitch, it's nil-all, Central won their last game, but I didn't play because I've been out of the team for a while.' Then, he stood up on one leg, hopping about, showing perfect balance before saying, 'My mate Manu is the player who's gone off . . . oh, and also, boomerang, Venus and waterfall.'

At this, Kevin John, who heard every word of Jimmy's speech to the medics burst out laughing, and jogged over to them.

'He's fine, lads . . . believe me.'

The medics laughed, looked at Jimmy and said, 'That was a pretty thorough HIA you just gave yourself, son, but we know you didn't hit your head, we were only going to check your shoulder!'

'It's fine, honestly,' said Jimmy, rotating it like an aeroplane propeller.

'Seems it is,' said the medic, turning around and walking off the pitch.

Kevin walked over and looked at Jimmy, amazed. 'You really don't miss a single trick, do you?'

'Not if I can help it, Kev. And it *was* Venus for the HIA, wasn't it? I wasn't sure if it might have been Mars for a minute?'

Kevin just shook his head and laughed. 'Yes, it was Venus . . . now go and win this match, will you?'

But Jimmy didn't hear him, he was already focused totally on the restart.

He stood calmly over the mark that the referee had made. Everybody on the pitch expected him to kick to touch to set up a lineout deep in the Brookdale half so that Central could launch an attack.

But Jimmy had other plans. For the first time in his short rugby career, Jimmy was going to do something for himself. It was time that he showed everyone just how brave he really was.

He glanced up field and saw that the full back, for once, was in the correct position. Jimmy knew what he had to do.

The referee's whistle went and instead of drilling the ball towards touch, Jimmy swung his body away from the touchline, towards the middle of the field. Then, with all his power and timing, he punted the ball straight towards the Brookdale full back. From the second that the ball left his boot, Jimmy was off.

On the touchline, Mrs John turned to her husband.

'What on earth is he doing that for, Kev? He should have

gone for touch. Perhaps he *did* have a bang on the head, I've got no idea what he's thinking.'

'Oh, I do,' smiled Kevin. 'He's gone to find himself a tackle.'

THE MOMENT OF TRUTH

The whole Brookdale back line were taken by surprise by Jimmy's kick. They were all looking over to the touchline when Jimmy changed the direction of his kick and fired it towards their full back.

In fact, the first time they really noticed it was when they saw a flash of red and black sprinting towards them as though his life depended on it. In Jimmy's mind, his rugby life *did* depend on it.

The Brookdale full back was probably the only player who had seen what Jimmy had done. He never took his eyes off Jimmy's kick and steadied himself under the high ball, focused on catching it. There was only one thought on his mind. Catch it safely and run it straight back.

Within seconds, the ball was nestled into his hands. He looked up and saw chaos. Some of his teammates were still confused as to what had happened and as a result were not switched on to his run. In fact, the only person who seemed to know what was happening was Jimmy.

Jimmy had kicked the ball so far, the full back had lots of time to consider his options, but once he saw the onrushing Jimmy, the full back remembered the words of his teacher in the dressing room before the game.

'They've got one really talented player. He's the fly-half and his name is Jimmy Joseph. Apparently, he may not start the game, but if he comes on, he's capable of cutting us to ribbons. But he can't tackle, that's why he might not start. If you get the chance, just run at him. He'll let you pass by like a draught through the crack in a broken window.'

The words made up the mind of the full back. Even though Jimmy was the only Central player chasing his kick, and there was loads of space to run into where he wouldn't be challenged, he was going to run straight at him. Just like his coach had said.

Jimmy saw the full back gather the ball. It was a good catch. Jimmy was running at full speed, desperate to get to the player as quickly as he could. But he'd kicked the ball too long. The full back had loads of time and loads of space to do anything he wanted. Jimmy was worried his plan wouldn't work and that maybe the full back would kick it.

'Come on, run it, run it to me,' Jimmy said under his breath as he continued his chase. 'I want this tackle.'

It appeared that Jimmy would get his wish.

The full back looked up at Jimmy and ran straight at him, as fast as he could.

'Oh my God,' said Mrs John to her husband, when she saw the impending collision. 'This isn't going to end well.'

'Don't be too sure,' replied Kevin, 'the big difference is, he wants this now.' Then Kevin quietly whispered to himself, 'Get

260

that head to the side, Jimmy, drive those legs . . . ring of steel, mate, ring of steel. Be like Fekitoa.'

'What did you say?' asked his wife, but she got no reply, Kevin was completely focused on what Jimmy was about to do.

So was Jimmy.

The troubles of the last year swirled around his mind like a whirlwind. With every stride he took it seemed like a different image popped into his thoughts: the troubles at the Academy, Mr Kane, giving up his Eagles kit and boots, missing those tackles, falling out with Matt, breaking his collarbone, Oscar, working with Kevin . . . it all came down to this moment.

And what a moment it was.

Jimmy pulled off the most perfect, textbook tackle any of the spectators had ever seen. The speed that both players were moving at suggested to those watching that it was going to be a classic rugby hit of the type that a tackling genius like Hamish Watson would deliver. They weren't wrong.

Jimmy slowed down slightly as he approached the speeding full back. The crowd noticed how he seemed to be setting his feet before driving in with the tackle. Jimmy got right in front of his opponent before planting his right foot down. As he did, he ducked his body and hit the full back around the waist with his right shoulder, expertly moving his head to his left, so that it ran smoothly underneath the full back's hip and along to his butt cheek. Then, instantly locking his arms around the back of the full back's legs at the exact same moment as his shoulder made contact, Jimmy drove through with as much power as his legs possessed. Added to the speed that Jimmy brought into the tackle, the impact was significant.

The crowd gave a collective, 'Ooooooooh!' when they saw the ferocity of Jimmy's tackle, but that quickly broke into admiring applause when they saw the perfection of the tackle. Make no mistake, this wasn't just a hit or a collision, this was a perfectly timed, perfectly carried out rugby tackle. It was a textbook move from Jimmy . . . and it sat the full back right down on his backside.

'Fekitoa,' said Kevin with immense satisfaction, clenching his fists in celebration.

Up in the small grandstand, Jimmy's mother put her hands over her eyes.

'Oh no, what's he doing? That's bound to injure him!'

Will laughed. 'Not at all, love. He's as safe as houses. He's just climbed his own personal rope ladder.'

'Climbed his what? Dad? Are you alright?'

But Will was alright. He was as happy as he had been since his illness scare earlier in the year.

His grandson had just managed to scale his own Second World War cliff face, and he'd done it with ease. Will couldn't have been prouder.

HANDS DOWN!

On the field, Jimmy had no thoughts for anything but the ball.

His tackle had indeed been textbook, and so was what happened next.

His momentum had not just stopped the Brookdale full back, it had driven him back and dumped him on his backside. Fair play to the full back, he hadn't spilled the ball, he had somehow managed to hold on to it, despite the force of Jimmy's tackle. How he did was a mystery, because the impact of the hit was enough to shake a ball loose from the strongest of grips, but as he landed on the floor, he now had no option. He had to let go of the ball.

'Release, release!' came the call from the referee, instructing both Jimmy and the full back to let go of the player and ball respectively.

Jimmy's senses were so alert now, he was the first to react. He didn't wallow in the glory of his tackle, no matter how satisfying it was to him. Instead, he sprung instantly to his feet. Then, he quickly stepped over his stricken opponent, and reached down for the unguarded ball. In a flash, Jimmy gathered it and sprinted towards the posts. From his left-hand side, Jimmy could see the Brookdale Primary right wing hurtling towards him, covering like all good wingers should.

Jimmy looked at the distance between him and the goal line. It was going to be close. As he lengthened his stride for the line, he just sensed that the exertions of the last fifteen or so seconds were catching up with him. He drove and pumped his legs as quickly as he could, but with ten metres to go, he sensed his legs tightening up. He glanced across to the winger who was now moving much quicker than Jimmy. Jimmy knew that the smart option was to run towards his right-hand corner, to lengthen the distance that the winger would have to run. But that would lengthen it for Jimmy too. He wasn't sure he was going to make it. So he did what nobody would have expected him to do. He veered left, straight into the path of the covering winger. Just as the winger was about to make his tackle, five metres short of the line, which would have no doubt prevented the try, Jimmy switched the ball from being cradled under his left arm, to his right.

At the very moment that the winger threw his body towards Jimmy for the tackle, Jimmy thrust out his left hand and arm like a steel pole. He pushed his arm into the throat area of the winger with all his power and delivered the most amazing hand off which stopped the winger in his tracks. Stumbling slightly after the effort of the sprint and hand-off, Jimmy just managed to fall over the line for the try.

The crowd went wild.

They had seen the most amazing example of rugby bravery anyone could ever wish to see from a player so young. To actually create a tackle situation like Jimmy had done, and to then put in such an incredibly powerful hit, collect the ball then deliver the most robust of hand-offs was simply immense. Everyone was clapping.

The referee's whistle rang out.

But not to award the try.

'No try, no try. Hand-offs not allowed in Under 11 rugby. Penalty to Brookdale.'

'What?' shouted Will from the touchline. 'No hand-offs? This is supposed to be rugby, isn't it?'

Mr Davies the Headmaster was sitting behind his old friend.

'They're not allowed, Will. You can only do them in Under 12 rugby, and then chest only. The referee is correct.'

Will sighed. 'Rules. Pah! They've stopped a perfectly good try.'

'I don't think Jimmy is worried by that, Will, look at him.'

Jimmy ran back to his position with a smile as wide as Ellis Genge after winning one against the head, punching the air in celebration. Anyone would swear that he had scored a try, but he was celebrating something far more important to him.

He would never worry about making a tackle in his rugby career ever again. The impact of the tackle – both physically and mentally – ensured that ghost had been laid to rest for good.

52

ARM WRESTLING

The rest of the half was played out with no scores. Both teams were very strong, but it was a game of defences and there was no better defender on show than Jimmy. He literally tackled anything that moved.

He tackled forwards, he tackled backs, he tackled on the wing, he tackled in midfield. In fact, due to one mix up in the positioning of the referee at a ruck, Jimmy even tackled him, much to the amusement of the crowd, and his own players.

'Flipping 'eck, Jimmy boy,' said Ryan, 'you couldn't tackle a hot dinner three weeks ago, now you're splattering the officials.'

Everyone was still laughing at that one at half time.

One person not laughing was Mrs John. She was concerned.

'Right. You're allowing them to drag you into an arm wrestle. That's what they want. But you are so much better than them with ball in hand. Look for space, don't always take the contact. This game is going to be settled by just one try I think, it's that close. Let's make sure we're the team that gets that try.'

She turned to Jimmy.

'Well, aren't you the one full of surprises?'

Jimmy laughed.

She moved closer so that only he could hear what she had to say.

'Jimmy, I think it's fantastic that you've proved everyone wrong about your tackling. It's been inspirational to watch. You've put in more tackles than Courtney Lawes!'

Jimmy smiled. That's not an accolade he ever expected to hear when he was running around her garden thinking of ways to avoid contact with her husband just a few short weeks ago.

'But you're taking on too much contact now. I know you probably feel like you want to hit everyone in both defence and attack, but don't forget what brought you to the attention of the Eagles last year. I had a long chat with Kevin and Peter Clement a couple of weeks ago, and Peter said how much he hoped you could sort out your tackling problems, because going forward, you're untouchable.'

Jimmy blushed at such praise.

'But in that half, you were anything but untouchable. You took contact every single time you carried the ball. Remember that touch rugby tournament you played? Remember the way you play with your friends on The Rec? I've seen you. They call you "The Ghost" don't they?'

Jimmy laughed. 'Some do, yes, Miss.'

'Well, let's see The Ghost this half. You've been like a hammer up to now, not a ghost! Tackle when you have to, but find space when you can. And run, Jimmy. Nobody can run like you.'

The referee's whistle blew to call the teams together for the second half. The last words from Mrs John were ringing in everyone's ears. 'Don't forget. Nobody has ever retained the Cluster Cup. Ever. Go out and take your chance to make history.'

As Central jogged back onto the field, Matt joined Jimmy and Kitty as they talked about ways to bring Kitty into the game because she'd hardly seen the ball. Matt interrupted them.

'I've just seen Manu. He's okay, but has a massive headache. I think we need to win this for him. What do you think?'

Jimmy looked at his two oldest friends. None of them said a word. The steely look in their eyes was enough.

The first ten minutes of the second half were a carbon copy of the first. Pure attritional rugby. Brookdale Primary had a distinct way of playing, and that was keeping it tight. The ball was hardly ever thrown out to their back line, it was just driven on and on until, at some point, their discipline failed them and they lost the ball. In the few times Jimmy had possession, he had no space in which to operate, so instead of taking the contact, as Mrs John had urged him not to do, he kicked.

The trouble was, Brookdale then regained possession and simply drove the ball back and the grind would begin again.

The crowd all knew that no team had ever retained the cup. They also knew there had never been a nil-nil draw.

With five minutes to go, it seemed that a nil-nil draw was going to be the only outcome. Every time Central tried something creative, it was smothered and Jimmy's kicks, as good as they were, led to nothing. The Brookdale approach didn't alter, but Central's defence was heroic.

Despite the clock running down fast, Jimmy hadn't given up hope. He just wanted that one chance, that one moment to show what he could do with the ball in his hands. The question was, would the opportunity come?

With just two minutes left, Jimmy got his answer.

Matt had secured a ball from the base of a Central scrum. Jimmy called for the ball. Even though they were deep in their own half, Jimmy sensed that there was a gap between his opposite fly-half and the inside centre. A pass now and Jimmy would be off. But probably because he'd been dragged into the kicking game that Brookdale had adopted, Matt decided to box kick.

It wasn't the option that Jimmy would have chosen, but it was a good kick – long, high and deep into the Brookdale half.

There was no surprise at what happened next. The Brookdale full back gathered the kick, steadied himself, then drilled the ball back into the Central half. He had hoped to kick it long, but he didn't connect with his kick perfectly and, instead, the ball screwed in-field to where the Central forwards were gathered.

Running slightly sideways and backwards, Central's giant lock, Andrew Beasley, took the ball cleanly. Jimmy hoped Andrew would pass the ball out to him quickly. However, again, the big lock forward was drawn into thinking defensively, so inexplicably, went to ground, followed by his forwards. This gave time for a few of the Brookdale players to arrive, forming a ruck.

Jimmy had seen enough.

As the ball emerged on the Central side, Jimmy screamed as loudly as he had ever screamed to Matt, 'Pass, pass!'

Almost without looking up, Matt fired a pass, instinctively knowing where Jimmy would be. The speed of that pass made all the difference.

Jimmy was onto it like a flash.

His angle of running took him straight towards the on-rushing defensive line. Immediately, Jimmy passed to his left, to his inside centre. The whole Brookdale defensive line moved to follow the ball. But the ball had never left Jimmy's hands, it was the most outrageous dummy of all time.

The dummy had bought Jimmy the one thing he needed. Space. He glided through the gap he had created between the opposition fly-half and centre, just like the ghost that Mike had rapped about back in the summer. Jimmy was finally living up to his nickname. And then he was off, like Usain Bolt on the sound of the starter's gun. Jimmy's legs ate up the ground as he ran into space, crossing the halfway line, into the Brookdale half of the field.

Jimmy made seven huge strides at great speed, but then, to his right, the Brookdale scrum-half came for him. Incredibly quick over the first ten metres, it seemed that Jimmy's burst for freedom would be over before it had begun, but Jimmy had seen him. Switching the ball to his left hand, Jimmy swerved his hips, just as the scrum-half scragged the corner of his shorts. Jimmy swung his free right arm down, brushing away the desperate challenge. For a split second, Jimmy was worried that the referee might have seen his action as a hand-off, but the call of, 'Play on, play on!' from the official was music to Jimmy's ears.

And play on Jimmy did.

Free from the clutches of the scrum-half, Jimmy changed his angle of running again and also swapped the ball back to his right hand. Now he was heading from the middle to the right side of the field and into more space.

He looked up and saw the full back. The player who had

played his part in helping Jimmy come back from the rugby dead was the next obstacle to overcome.

Six, eight, ten strides, Jimmy was gathering pace, as was the full back who was lining Jimmy up.

Jimmy knew what the full back was doing. He was watching Jimmy's feet like a hawk, he wanted to get close to Jimmy, into his one metre circle to bring him down. At full speed, Jimmy waited for the full back to commit to the tackle. He watched as the full back lowered his body angle to begin the tackle, and at that precise moment, Jimmy threw all his weight onto his right leg, which had the effect of almost standing Jimmy's body up and slowing him down just enough so that the full back was not close enough to make an effective tackle. Jimmy brushed off the, now, weak attempt from the full back and hurtled again towards the right corner of the field.

However, that slight step had slowed Jimmy's momentum just enough to allow one of the Brookdale forwards the time to desperately dive at Jimmy's feet, to try and pull off a last ditch tap tackle. But Jimmy's awareness was second to none and as the forward made the despairing dive, he managed to pull off a little hop into the air, which meant that the tap attempt from the forward went clean beneath Jimmy's right boot.

All that was left now was the wingers. Jimmy could see their left winger was coming like a bullet from his right, but could also hear Brookdale's right winger coming from his blind side. Jimmy's instinct was that the winger coming from his left side was closer, so he had no option. He gambled that his pace in a straight line would take him to the whitewash, quicker than the left wing would get there.

Jimmy gave everything in those last five strides and sprinted faster and more effectively than he had ever done – he was in full Beauden Barrett mode. When he was a yard short of the line, Jimmy felt the arms of the desperate winger finally catch him from behind, just as the winger from his right arrived on the scene, but using every ounce of strength he possessed and straining every sinew, Jimmy threw himself forward to the line. As he did, the momentum of the right winger's tackle spun Jimmy around and his body took the legs from under the left winger. All three of the players slid over the line together. Jimmy was enveloped by the right winger who in turn had the left winger lying over the top of him, desperately trying to get his hands under the ball to prevent Jimmy grounding it.

Nobody in the crowd could tell what had happened.

But the referee knew. Perfectly positioned, he blew his whistle, loudly, pointing to the ground under Jimmy's body.

'Ball clearly grounded, while under the full control of the attacking player. Try for red.'

The crowd went wild.

So did the Central players . . . Jimmy was mobbed.

The first one there was Kitty, obviously, who quickly pulled the two distraught Brookdale players off her friend, to reveal Jimmy, face down, clasping the ball tight to his chest, almost up around his throat. Before Kitty could even say a word, she was knocked over on top of Jimmy by Matt who was screaming like a banshee. He was quickly followed by big Andrew Beasley and several of the other Central players. It was a classic pile on.

The only one who didn't join in was Ryan. On seeing the referee awarding the try, he ran straight to Mrs John, screaming and shouting, 'He did it, Jimmy blinking well did it!' When he arrived he jumped straight into Mrs John's arms. Kevin said later that it was one of the biggest hits his wife had ever taken in her whole rugby career.

The referee stepped in to usher the Central players back to their own half. Jimmy picked up the ball and was hauled to his feet by Matt.

'Fantastic Jimmy, that was just fantastic!'

Jimmy smiled. He was so glad to be back on good terms with his friend.

Then Matt moved his head in very close to Jimmy's as they walked with the referee to where Jimmy would attempt the conversion.

'Take your time with the kick, Jim,' Matt whispered, 'we don't want the game restarted to give them a chance to score and draw level. Take your time.'

Jimmy nodded.

As Jimmy reached his mark for the conversion, he asked the referee how long was left.

'Long enough for you to kick this and me to restart the game.'

Jimmy smiled to himself, the referee had seen through Matt's plan.

Oscar ran onto the pitch carrying Jimmy's kicking tee. Jimmy had asked him before the game if he'd look after it for him and bring it on to him if he needed it.

'Just wait behind me, Oscar. Once I've kicked this, you can take the tee back off again.'

'I will,' said Oscar. 'My mum's going to take a photo to put in our book . . . so make sure you get this.'

'With my stat man here, I'm sure I will,' said Jimmy with a wink.

Now that there was no need to draw the kick out, Jimmy took the kick quickly. He couldn't really miss, he was right in front of the posts. But in Jimmy's haste, he didn't notice the piece of loose turf at the left side of his kicking tee, just where he would plant his standing leg.

He lined the ball up with the posts as normal, then in his best Owen Farrell way, approached the ball and struck it. But as his right foot connected with the ball, his left one gave way on the loose turf and Jimmy slipped. The result? The ball dived to the left and smashed straight into the upright. Jimmy had missed the extra two points.

'Oh, no!' shouted Jimmy.

'That's a miss,' said Oscar. 'That won't look good in the book.'

But Jimmy was already sprinting away from his friend to take his position. There was one final play to defend.

53

THE END GAME

According to the rules of Under 11 rugby, Jimmy had to take a drop-kick to restart the game, giving possession straight back to Brookdale. He knew that the next time the ball went dead the game would be over. He had to just make sure that the ball didn't go dead with Brookdale having scored a try. Because if that happened and Brookdale got the conversion from in front of the posts, Central would have lost 7–5. There would be no time for a restart. This was the final play.

Jimmy didn't know whether it was best to try and put his kick as deep as possible, or at an angle, to try and bring the touchline into play which would act as an extra defender. He knew that option was risky as it might mean the ball being kicked straight out, which would give Brookdale a restart in the centre of the field. He also knew though, that the Brookdale full back was seriously good under the high ball, and would run it straight back, so maybe that was an even riskier option.

The referee blew and Jimmy went for broke. He put his drop

kick as high and as deep as he dared to the left-hand touch line. As it was in the air, Jimmy's grandfather said, 'He's struck that well, this is going to be close.'

And close it was.

The ball came down just a yard in-field, right into the arms of the Brookdale right winger. On another day, the winger would have tried to move his foot into touch as he caught it which would technically mean Jimmy's kick would have gone straight out, but today, he was more concerned with not knocking it on. So he took the straightforward catch. Then he was off.

Like Kitty, as a winger in a tight game such as this, he had hardly touched the ball. It might have been twenty minutes since he had touched it last, and he was determined to make the most of it.

He ran like the wind.

The winger chose to run in-field, and in doing so, he completely bypassed the Central forwards. They were effectively now out of the game. With his back line in full support, the winger straightened up his run and headed for Matt. Central were in trouble.

A combination of thinking they'd already won the game and confusion at how quickly the winger had turned defence into attack, meant the Central back line was all over the place. As the winger was tackled by Matt, he popped the ball inside to his fly-half.

To Jimmy's horror, Central's full back had completely lost the plot and sprinted up beyond Jimmy to try to make the tackle.

Jimmy glanced behind him to see acres of space. He screamed across to Kitty, 'Kitty, full back, cover full back.'

Kitty had already seen the danger, and sprinted in off her wing to cover the full back who was now way out of position. The fly-half easily avoided Central's full back's impetuous tackle attempt and instantly saw what Jimmy had already seen. The huge space on Central's right wing, created by Kitty running over to cover her absent full back. The fly-half did exactly what Jimmy would have done and he threw a long pass, missing out the inside centre and giving the ball straight to the outside centre. Jimmy was out of the game.

He turned and watched as the outside centre drew his opposite number. Before the inevitable pass was made to the Brookdale left winger, Jimmy was off. He turned and sprinted as fast as he could towards the right wing. He had to try to stop the winger going one-on-one with Kitty.

Jimmy's long strides ate up the ground. Just as the Brookdale winger received his pass, Jimmy felt he had the right angle to catch him. The winger must have felt the same too, because after six quick strides, he didn't trust his speed to beat Jimmy to the corner either, so he turned in-field, opting to take the contact with Jimmy and keep the ball alive. The collision was immense. Once again, Jimmy had pulled off a textbook tackle. It was a thing of defensive beauty. But this time, the winger had expected the force of Jimmy's tackle and wasn't surprised by it, instead, he just lobbed the ball over his head at the point of impact.

As Jimmy hit the floor, pinned to the winger with his perfect ring of steel, he watched helplessly as the ball hung in the air, seemingly on a string. As it fell to the ground, just a yard from Jimmy, the ball bounced backwards, and straight into the arms of the onrushing inside centre who had been missed out in the earlier passing move. He had the try line gaping in front of him, surely he would score.

The centre collected the ball at pace and sprinted for the corner and the certain try that would seal the win for Brookdale. There was no way that their kicker would slip and miss the conversation like Jimmy had. It was all over.

But then an incredible thing happened.

Just as the Brookdale centre was approaching the try line, Kitty appeared, moving so fast it seemed as if she was just a blur of red and black. As the centre reached forward to ground the ball, just inches in from the touchline, Kitty threw herself at him. Her arms connected with his outstretched arms and chest and her momentum flipped him over as if in a judo move, and both players flew into touch.

The referee was right on the spot, as usual.

'Ball not grounded by blue, tackled into touch by red. No try.'

And with that, he blew the whistle for the end of the match. Central had won the Cluster Cup for the second successive year, the first team to ever achieve that feat.

Jimmy was the closest player to Kitty and ran towards her shouting, 'Wow, Kitty, wow! You did it! What a tackle!'

The Central players, for the second time in three minutes, went berserk. The calmest though was Kitty. When Jimmy reached her and hugged her, she just looked at him and said, 'And that's how I cope with tackling.'

Jimmy just burst out laughing, then quietly he said, 'True, but your head was in completely the wrong position . . . so don't get too big for your boots!'

The dig in the ribs that Kitty gave Jimmy was the fiercest she'd ever given him, but Jimmy laughed like a drain.

Rugby just didn't get any better than this.

EPILOGUE

Dear Mrs Joseph,

I write on behalf of the Eagles Professional Rugby Club Limited, with regard to your son, Jonny.

Following another excellent season of continued improvement, Jonny has consistently demonstrated that he possesses the required skills, abilities and attributes to become a potential Eagles player of the future.

Therefore, it is with great delight that I offer your son a place in the two-week summer residential training camp that will take place at the Eagles' Training Academy later this year. The course will run from Sunday 5th August to Saturday 18th August. All board and lodging will be provided. Transport there and back is also available and we will provide all towels and toiletries, however, your son should bring his Eagles kit from his previous camp. If any replacement kit is required, please see the enclosed voucher that will entitle you to claim a 50% discount on the price. He will also need to provide his own gum shields and boots.

I hope this covers everything you require in terms of organisation for the training camp, however, should you require any further information, please do not hesitate to get in touch.

It is not normal practice for me to comment on other players, but it would be remiss of me not to mention your other son, Jimmy. There is no question that Jimmy is a talented rugby player, but unfortunately, a bit-part performance in a cup final victory is not enough for him to be considered as a future elite player. As such, he will not be invited to the summer camp. I am aware however that Wolves RFC do run daily summer *fun* rugby camps and perhaps your son will be more suited to that, more relaxed, environment.

Finally, I should point out that Stuart Withey, our former Academy Director has decided to embark on a well-earned retirement. It's with great pleasure, therefore, that I can announce that I've been appointed as his replacement and, as such, will have full responsibility for the selection of all future players to the Eagles' Academy over the coming years.

I trust this makes the situation clear for you and the new, competitive direction that our elite Academy will now be taking. I look forward to welcoming Jonny and trust that Jimmy enjoys his time at the fun camp.

With the kindest of regards,

Mark Kane

Mark Kane
Eagles Academy Director

CHASING A RUGBY DREAM

YOUTUBE SKILLS

Are you chasing a rugby dream like Jimmy and his friends? If you would like to learn new skills and take part in challenges to improve your game, check out my YouTube page: *Chasing a Rugby Dream with James Hook*

If you enjoy the videos, please like and share and leave any feedback or requests in the comments section.

And just remember Peter Clement's mantra: have fun!

POLARIS
PUBLISHING